Conspiracy of Ravens

"Raven is my kind of people. Half hot-mess, half bad-ass, all awesome... the story was had plenty of humor, action and mystery rolled up in a nice paced story."   –Urban Fantasy Investigations

Nevermore

"The dramas, dangers, intrigue, and tension of NEVERMORE will have you glued to the pages, and when it is finished, Ms. McKenzie will have left you satisfied yet wanting more." –*Fresh Fiction*

The Night House

"From the very first page till the very end I was hooked on this book and read it in less than one day...it had everything you could want from a story romance, secrets, lies, suspense, surprises and more."   –Linda Tonis, Paranormal Romance Guild

Dangerous Dreams

"This new world promises to be an adventurous one full of snark, passion, thrills, romance, danger and wonderful characters and I can't wait to read the next one."   –*Stormy Vixen Reviews*

Dangerous Liaisons

"Loved this story and loved Raf and strong, stubborn Lara and I can't overlook Lara's dragon who brought humor to this story." – *Paranormal Romance Guild*

The Good Griffin

"THE GOOD GRIFFIN is as addictive as a double shot of espresso, only without any of the withdrawal symptoms." –*N. N. Light*

Books by J. C. McKenzie

Conspiracy of Ravens
Nevermore
Queen of Corvids
The Call of Corvids

The Night House

Shift Happens
Beast Coast
Carpe Demon
Shift Work
Beast of All

Dangerous Dreams
Dangerous Liaisons
Dangerous Decisions

The Good Griffin

The Shucker's Booktique

Be My Love

A large burly humanoid male stepped out of a swirling black cloud of sparkling mist and huffed at the cold air. The rain instantly doused his curly brown hair to his face, revealing short horns that protruded from his skull. Wearing a black shirt tucked into black leather pants, his outfit gave him away as an Other almost as quickly as the horns did. He scanned the parking lot and his black eyes blazed red when his gaze found Raven and Cole.

Cole leaned over. "Do you want to flex your queen muscle, or can I handle this for you?"

"Maybe he wants to talk?" Raven didn't get into physical fights to resolve her disagreements. She had next to nothing in combat training, unless kicking her brother in the nads to get out of a headlock counted.

Cole snorted and turned to the horned man. "Is she right? Are you here to talk, Frey?"

Frey snarled and unsheathed a sword strapped to his waist. "I'm gonna squash you and then rid the shadow realms of that abomination."

Raven pointed at her chest.

"Frey is one of Freyr's many bastard children," Cole said, very matter of fact. "His mom has a little corvid essence."

Frey roared and ran at her.

"Me or you, Einin."

"Me." She gripped her scythe and let its power flood through her veins. Banshee's tit. Why had she said that? Why did she choose now to strive for independence?

Praise for novels of J. C. McKenzie

Shift Happens

"SHIFT HAPPENS has excitement, intrigue and lots of danger. I love the whole cast of characters and how they played a part in the story" —*Fresh Fiction*

Beast Coast

"I loved this book as much as the first. There are secrets, surprises, and all manner of supernaturals." —*Paranormal Romance Guild*

Carpe Demon

"The story keeps the adrenaline pumping and spine tingling tension building throughout the story with well written scenes full of vivid details that capture the imagination and make it easy for the reader to become engrossed..." —*Literary Addicts Book Community*

Shift Work

"It's a terrific series and if you like supernatural reads, with a side of romance, the sort with solid and intense plots, gripping and very real dangers, hard choices, supernatural people some of whom can be selfish, cruel and bloodthirsty...You'll be hooked." —*Jeannie Zelos Book Reviews*

Beast of All

"This time out, J. C. McKenzie has outdone herself with high-velocity action, soul deep emotions and one of those finishes that you want to replay over and over!" —*Tome Tender*

QUEEN OF CORVIDS

A RAVEN CRAWFORD NOVEL, BOOK THREE

J. C. McKENZIE

COPYRIGHT INFORMATION

Contact Information: jcmckenzie@jcmckenzie.ca

Cover Art: Eerilyfair Design
Raven vector artwork: Yauheniya Piatrouskaya
Raven in nest artwork: Chad Keith
Raven on gravestone artwork: Jelena Jovanovic

Publishing History:
First JCM Publications Edition, 2020

ISBN: 978-1-9992394-4-2 (print)
ISBN: 978-1-9992394-5-9 (ebook)

To our sweet, sweet Roxy Bear,
Who left us for a trip across the rainbow bridge.
You will be forever in our hearts.

Author's Note

Well, we're three books deep into Raven Crawford's world now, so I'm not sure the Canadian Disclaimer is needed anymore. But, for the readers in the back, or for those just joining us now, please note, both Raven and I are Canadian. Don't worry, it's not as bad as it sounds. It's not even contagious. It just means I'm going to use Canadian spelling.

For those unfamiliar with the True North, we love the letters U and Z, while fostering a fondness for the double L. For example, it's "colour" not "color," "organization" not "organisation" and "traveller" not "traveler."

Also of note: Although we are technically a metric nation, our proximity to our American neighbours (see how I spelled that?) means we are well versed in the imperial system. Many of us still use feet and inches to describe our height and pounds for our weight.

Canadians. We spell like the British, swear like Americans and use just enough French to freak everybody out.

You may write me down in history
With your bitter, twisted lies,
You may trod me in the very dirt,
But still, like dust, I'll rise

~Excerpt from *Still I Rise* (stanza 1),
Maya Angelou

Chapter One

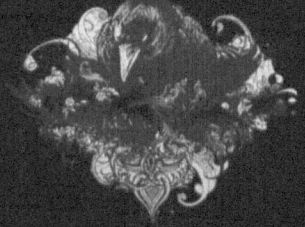

"The most terrible thing about life is finding it gone."
~ Charles Bukowski

aven skipped down the front stairs of the house, ignored the cold air slicing at her face, and halted on the landing. Her stepfather, who'd been more of a dad to her than the sperm donor who sired her and her twin brother, stood in the corner of the frost-encrusted winter lawn gripping a wide collar. As a fox shifter, he maintained a lean figure, but lately, he'd started to soften around the middle.

"Dad?"

Terry Crawford turned to her with red-lined, tear-brimmed eyes and sniffed. "He's gone."

"Who's gone?"

"Pepe," he growled and shook the collar. "Someone stole him."

A few months ago, after a long string of provocations from their bigoted, hate-filled neighbour, Dad acquired a goat from a friend to rehome in the front yard to piss off Mrs. Humphreys. Why? Because nothing in the city code prevented him from doing so and the Underworld hath no fury like a middle-aged man sporting a dadbod and an uncanny ability to dissect by-laws.

"Someone stole your spite goat?" She pried the worn collar from his shaking hands. That didn't make any sense. Sure, she noticed Pepe's absence in the yard—everyone did—but after successfully making his point, Dad had relented to Mom's nagging and agreed to let Pepe return to the farm. Surely, Dad was mistaken.

"Not someone. Mrs. Humphreys." He snatched her wrist. "And you're going to help me get Pepe back."

Oh, Banshee's left tit. These things never worked out well. "I thought your friend from Mission came back and took him home."

"So did I, but when I called to check on Pepe, Ethan had no idea what I was talking about. Apparently, when he came by the house to pick up Pepe and found the yard empty, he assumed I had a change of heart. He planned to call me in a few months to revisit the subject."

"You called to check on a goat?"

Dad glared.

She took a step back. Pepe's collar and tags jingled. The weak afternoon sun did little to melt the frost or soothe the chill running up her spine.

"Good thing I called." Some of the anger in Dad's voice faded. "We wouldn't have found his collar and learned the truth until everything thawed. I don't mow the lawns in winter."

"False spring." She nodded.

In the area formerly known as the Lower Mainland or Greater Vancouver Regional District, they always got a week or three of superb weather at the tail end of winter—just long enough for the inexperienced to rejoice and herald the arrival of spring—but surprise! Snow, frost, freezing rain and slush determined to destroy the proclamation of spring rained down on the optimistic every time.

"So now Pepe is missing, and your friend is upset you lost his goat," she said.

"That sums it up. Yeah."

"What makes you think the old crone took him?"

"She's been making a big production all week about barbequing. In winter. I thought it odd at the time, but now I know why."

Raven recoiled, her stomach churned. "She...she barbequed Pepe?" Anger rose fast and furious within her and her dark fae magic surged, demanding action. That crazy bat had taken her hatred too far this time.

Pepe was a family pet. Raven would make sure Mrs. Humphreys paid.

Dad rested his hand on her shoulder and shook his head. "No. It was beef." He dropped his hand to tap his nose. Fox shifters had a phenomenal sense of smell. "I think she's taunting me. Us."

Raven folded her arms over her chest and let some of the anger drain from her limbs. Pepe's collar bumped against her sweater.

"I tried following his scent," Dad continued. "Someone used a blocker. The traces of magic run this entire side of the block."

"What about the wards?" Her twin's bestie from childhood, Marcus, had set up wards around the house after Queen Lloth sent dark fae soldiers to cart Raven off to the Realm of Shadows. He said no one with ill intent could trespass on their property. Honestly, they should have had him set something up a lot sooner, but they'd grown complacent with having the Lord of Shadows' personal assassins guarding the property.

"She must've got around it as well. Wards can be broken, Rayray."

Raven's eyebrows shot up. "I'm surprised Mrs. H would resort to cavorting with witches. She hates them almost as much as shifters." And she despised the fae, though as far as they knew, their neighbour didn't know Raven and her twin were half fae.

Dad nodded.

"But if the scent-blocking spell extends for this block, it means either someone else smuggled him into

a vehicle and took off, Mrs. Humphreys took him, or..."
Raven and Dad turned to the other neighbour's house in unison.

"Tarzan," Dad finished, naming their other neighbour by the nickname they gave him.

"Why in the Mortal Realm would a nudist need a goat?"

They recoiled in unison. It was a bit of an unfair reaction, really. Nudists were pretty harmless. Nothing connected them with any of the sexually deviant communities besides deviating from "the norm," but something about Pepe having to potentially coexist with the free willy of their neighbour upset her.

She frowned. Why would their chest-thumping neighbour take Pepe? Goats ate everything and were a general pain to keep indoors and out of sight. The other two scenarios were more likely, but they couldn't rule anyone out yet.

"Will you help me?" Dad asked.

Raven had financial and fae debts to pay, worked days at the family PI business, busted her ass at night at a sketchy twenty-four hour diner, needed to learn her role as the new Queen of Corvids, and had a shiny new relationship to enjoy and explore. But all those things took a back seat to the sadness in Dad's eyes. Nothing mattered to Raven more than her family and their well-being. If she could, she'd move mountains for them. "Of course."

Chapter Two

"I have never faked sarcasm in my life."
    ~ Unknown, but also Raven Crawford

Well over six feet, with broad shoulders and a commanding presence, the Lord of Shadows loomed over Raven holding a large package. No, not that kind of package. Unfortunately.

Cole, also known in the Underworld among his dark fae brethren as *Beul na h-Oidhche gu Camhanaich*, Patron Fae of Assassins and Lord of Shadows, Son of Erebus born of Chaos, had skin that shone like smooth porcelain, contrasting sharply with his dark features and ink-black hair. But it was his gaze that enthralled her—piercing pools of black, as if the pupil bled into the iris, leaving only a sliver of silver along the edges. She often thought about how she could lose herself in the depths and not care if she drowned.

Roughly translated from dark fae to English, Cole's name meant "From the Mouth of the Night to First Light" and was pronounced something like "Bee-al nuh huhee-khye guh Ca-van-eekh." Raven had practiced saying his name over and over again until the sounds felt as natural on her tongue as he did.

Raven sat in one of the old armchairs in her basement bedroom while Cole's Otherness rolled over her in dangerously sweet waves. The material creaked as she straightened and scooted to the edge of the cushion. Her Raven's Eye necklace bumped against her breastbone. Normally, she forgot about the presence of the multi-faceted black diamond, but sometimes gravity reminded her she wore an enormous jewel that had magically protective attributes.

Cole had given her the Raven's Eye through an elaborate ruse. He feared she would refuse the gem if he tried to give it to her directly, and also worried she'd sell the Raven's Eye to pay off her bank loan if she knew what it was and what it was worth. Though he had her safety at heart, he essentially manipulated her into keeping a necklace. He could've just had a conversation with her. But what pissed Raven off more, was learning her own twin brother, Bear, knew who the necklace was from the entire time but didn't say anything because "she never asked him." Grrr.

Lesson learned, she now asked as many questions as possible.

"What is it?" she asked, pointing to the package in Cole's hands.

He handed her the pale teal box with a white ribbon and dragged a hand through his hair. "It's your underworld court attire."

His deep, gravelly voice danced along her skin. The low rumbling timbre still made her want to do all sorts of naughty things with him.

Raven glanced at the box and the dark fae lord and then back at the box. Cole wore his "blending in with mortals" outfit today, but the hoodie failed to hide his powerful build or how he moved with the confidence of a well-trained fighter.

The package didn't appear so large anymore. Raven took the box from Cole's hands, rested it on her lap and tugged on the ribbon. Unless Cole has some sort of spell laid on the outfit, it couldn't contain the same kind of armour he usually wore—the box was too light. The ribbon unfolded with a whisper of satin fabric and fell to the sides of the box. She lifted the lid, releasing a billow of petal-scented air. Annoyance crept along her spine. Armour shouldn't smell like flowers. How could she possibly instill fear and respect if she flounced around smelling like she just walked out of a spa?

Raven looped her finger under a leather strap and lifted the garment from the box.

"Where's the rest of it?" She dangled the "court attire" from her forefinger. Attire. That was a misleading word. The "armour" barely qualified as a metal bikini with leather straps. Surely, Cole meant this as an undergarment for her badass outfit. Or maybe he had some kinky games in mind.

"That's it," he said, squashing both of the more appealing options running through her mind.

"Lloth got to wear a badass gown. With feathers." Saying the former Queen of Corvids' name still sent a wave of nausea through Raven's stomach and flashes of memory stained with blood sped through her mind. Raven wasn't a killer, but Lloth had planned to kill her to steal her powers and use Bear as a battery pack for the rest of his half-fae extended life.

"Lloth wasn't able to shift into anything. You need to have the freedom to transform without ruining clothing or getting trapped by it."

Raven's unique parlour trick involved transforming into a bunch of ravens. Technically called a conspiracy or an unkindness, her consciousness spread across the entire group of birds instead of being housed with one single bird over another. She could shift her focus to an individual bird, but if she lost a bird, her consciousness transferred and re-distributed amongst the remaining members of the conspiracy. Theoretically, if someone killed all her birds, she'd probably die. At least that's what she figured would happen. It's not like she planned to test the theory. Besides, with Bear back in her life and her conspiracy growing in numbers every day, someone, anyone, would find it difficult to kill her off that way.

Though she'd learned to travel by portal and keep her clothes, she hadn't quite figured out how to burst into a conspiracy of ravens and do the same thing. Cole wasn't wrong in assuming clothes would be cumbersome for shifting, which is why she usually wore baggy T-shirts and sweats, not bedazzled, armoured underwear.

"Lies." She dropped the garment in the box and pushed the lid back on. A whoosh of petal-scented air rushed from the closed space and fanned the already building fire inside her. "You're using this as an excuse to fulfill some half-breed dark fae dominatrix fetish."

Cole shook his head and reached forward. He slid one hand under the box and placed the other over hers on top of the bow. His hand radiated warmth and this close, his intoxicating forest scent curled around her. Shadows swirled through the room to caress her skin.

"It will be okay, *Einin*," he said, using his nickname for her—little bird in Irish.

Raven withdrew her hand, and he plucked the box from her lap. He tossed it on the nearby chair. The teal box smacked the worn leather and slid until it butted against the tufted backing.

"Knowing my luck, I'll end up in chains." She stood and stepped away from the chair.

Darkness flashed across his gaze. His hands slid up her arms, his rough callouses from wielding swords and daggers brushing her skin through the thin sweater.

"You're not going to wear chains," he said. "You're going to break them."

She smiled at the confidence in his voice and wished she could borrow some of it. "You sound so certain."

"Unlike Lloth, you don't leech your energy from corvids. You *are* corvid energy. You're made up of the very essence Lloth desired and sought to consume. You have the ability to be so much more than Lloth ever aspired to be."

"Can this court visit wait until after I've unlocked this next achievement level?" Assuming that was even possible. She still needed to find Pepe and learn enough badass queen skills to hold up her end of a deal she made with the Lord of War.

A few months ago, in exchange for Bane sparing her brother's life for breaking a thieving contract, she'd agreed to stop mortals from traveling to the Underworld for a period of forty-eight hours. Bane wasn't the patient type, nor did he understand what the word mercy meant. She was running out of time.

"Unlock the next achievement level?" Cole frowned. "You say the oddest things sometimes."

"Says the dark Patron Fae of Assassins who slums it with a mortal."

"Half mortal."

She sighed. "I'm still waiting for you to realize I've most likely peaked and there's probably no more leveling up."

Cole's handsome face split into an easy grin. "I'm

still waiting for you to stop talking nonsense and ask me about the dark fae court."

"Okay, fine. Please tell me, oh Great Lord of Shadows, about the big bad dark fae lords and ladies who wish me dead."

Cole's grin widened. A lock of black hair slipped in front of his face and he pushed it out of the way. "That's the spirit."

Chapter Three

"You don't have to go crazy to work here, we'll train you."

~ Unknown, but also Crawford Investigations

Raven closed the door to Crawford Investigations behind her and let the paper and leather scented warmth surround her. Pricks of pain stung her fingertips as the heat thawed her numb skin. Despite Canada's stellar reputation for igloo construction and housing Jolly Old Saint Nick in the North Pole, the Lower Mainland of British Columbia didn't get extremely cold. Nope. The city only suffered below freezing temperatures for a brief period of time, but it was a wet cold—a bone numbing, blood chilling, icicle stabbing her through the heart kind of cold.

And Raven was a wimp.

She wasn't built for the cold or the heat. Temperate weather was her jam and she missed the moderate climate usually blanketing the area.

Dad looked up from where he sat at the desk in the main room. Large bags underlined his eyes and his cheeks looked more sallow than usual. "Progress?"

"We have cameras set up for surveillance on both the neighbours and Mike's running background checks," she said. They'd spent all morning looking for Pepe and devising a plan.

"I already did the checks."

"Mike's looking into their correspondence," she clarified.

Dad hesitated and she braced for the inevitable lecture about professionalism, integrity and the private investigator code of ethics. Technically, what Mike planned to do wasn't a breach of a person's reasonable expectation of privacy, but he sometimes skirted that legal line when social media didn't offer what he needed.

Instead of the lecture, Dad nodded.

Okay, then.

"This came for you." He pushed a legal-sized manila envelope across the smooth desk surface, her first and last name printed neatly on the front with no return address.

"Slipped under the door?"

Terry nodded. "These don't tend to contain good tidings. Anything you need to worry about?"

Raven sighed, dropped her shoulders and stared at the popcorn ceiling. "Take your pick. Could be a death threat or maybe even blackmail." Not only had she become the Queen of Corvids, earning her an Underworld full of dark fae planning to use or kill her, but she'd also killed two people.

Two.

Images of blood flashed in her head. Her stomach churned.

"Thanks." She walked around the desk and opened the top drawer to extract a pair of latex gloves and a sealable, plastic bag.

Dad's eyebrows rose and he pushed away from the desk to give her more room. "A little overboard, don't you think?"

"With everything going on? Like you said, these don't tend to contain good tidings. No. Mysterious packages slipped under the door demand caution." She jammed her gloved finger under the lip of the envelope and ripped the seal. She'd never used an envelope opener in her life and never intended to. She'd seen too many murder mysteries featuring them as the weapon of choice. With her finger and thumb, she spread open the envelope and peered inside.

A photo.

Interesting.

And definitely not good.

She pulled out the photo—one large glossy close up of her family laughing at the dining table through the window overlooking the backyard. Cold icicles prickled up her spine, along the back of her neck and clamped on her skull. A silent, creepy threat to everyone she loved.

There must be something else. Something to indicate what they wanted and why they'd issue such a threat.

Raven opened the envelope again and looked inside. Nothing. She flipped over the photo. There, written carefully in block letters with black pen, someone had printed a time and location. Beneath the information they'd added: Alone.

Red hot fury rose up and melted away the ice. Alone. Luckily for Raven, not only could she shift into a conspiracy of ravens, the big bad Lord of Shadows had her back.

She took a picture of both sides of the photo and sent them to Cole.

I will destroy them. He replied by text almost right away, which meant he was in the Mortal Realm.

No, she replied. *You will let me handle this.*

She slid the photo back into the envelope and straightened where she stood. Dad's intense gaze bore a hole into the side of her face. She turned to find him waiting expectantly. Only his tightened grip on his pen gave away his worry.

"Everything okay?" he asked.

"It will be."

Chapter Four

"I'm an adult...but not like a real adult."
∼ Quote on mug of unknown origins,
but also Raven's internal dialogue

Raven stepped out of Crawford Investigations hours later and scowled. Sleet streaked through the air like the half-frozen sky-daggers they were. After locking up, she turned and stared at the empty parking lot. Maybe she should've gone home with Dad for Sunday night dinner instead of waiting for her younger brother Mike to pick her up in Jean Claude, her borderline-derelict Grand Am.

She pulled up her hood and shoved her hands in her pocket. Mike was late.

Next time he asked to borrow Jean Claude for a date, she planned to force him to buy the car from her.

Then again, if he showed up to his date with Jean Claude, he probably wouldn't get a second date. Not if the young woman was shallow. Raven grumbled and hunched her shoulders. She didn't wish that kind of person on her younger brother no matter how many times he corrected her grammar or fact checked her.

She waited under the protection of the overhang, the chill in the evening air cutting her face. Maybe she should find somewhere private like the forest out back and portal home. She could guilt trip Mike about it later.

Footsteps echoed through the parking lot, accompanied by the thundering sleet striking the pavement.

Raven tensed and pulled her hands from her pockets. Who would be out walking in this crap?

Two men rounded the corner of the strip mall from the back alley bordering the forest and walked toward her. Hunched under umbrellas, they wore almost identical long jackets and black pants. Raven gathered her Other energy.

No one had business on the backside of the strip mall. At least nothing legal. Besides loading docks for the complex, the only things were a bunch of trees, a narrow alleyway for the garbage dumpster and recycling bin.

The pit of her stomach told her they were here for her.

Raven tightened her hold on her corvid energy. She had options. Transforming into a conspiracy right now meant losing her clothes and leaving all her possessions, including the keys to the family business where she stood.

Pass.

She could use the dark pulsing energy of the Underworld and form a portal to another location.

Tempting.

But then she'd never know what these guys wanted and if they missed her here, they might check for her at home where everyone currently gathered for dinner. A fully loaded, target-rich home.

Pass.

Option three it was. She clutched her power and summoned the Scythe of Corvids from where it rested in her bedroom. The weapon's magic called to her own and sped through the ether of folded realities between worlds until she clutched the hard shaft in her hands.

Cold and deadly, the scythe granted her physical prowess and fighting skills she didn't normally possess. Its power vibrated down her arms and thrummed in her veins.

Her nude bra slipped from where it hung on the blade by its strap and flopped to the wet ground with a loud slap.

Raven winced and turned to the two men.

They lay on the ground, their backs hammered with

falling sleet.

Huh?

"You need to call the scythe quicker next time." A voice spoke behind her.

Rourke, a weapon warping dark fae, leaned against the door of Crawford Investigations under the protective overhang with his arms crossed and a long dagger in one hand. He wore a sports jacket over a sweater, jeans, and a bored expression.

"I was fine."

He uncrossed his arms and pointed the bloody dagger at the ground. Two more men lay face down on the pavement.

She hadn't even heard them.

"Any one of them could've slit your throat while your head was off in la-la land."

"I did not take that long."

He pushed off the wall. "For the summoning, no. For the decision making and then the eventually spinning and hugging your weapon, yes. We're not even discussing your undergarment."

Well, crap. Raven didn't realize she'd spent so long relishing her success of calling the scythe, and in the meantime, Rourke dispatched four men. He squatted near the closest one and used the man's clothing to clean off his dagger.

Her cheeks heated and she cursed her own stupidity. She wasn't one of those too stupid to live characters in a damsel-in-distress book. She was better than that. Smarter than that. Usually.

Wasn't she?

"I didn't realize you still guarded me," she muttered.

"I told you before how I utilized the element of surprise." Rourke twirled his weapon, the security lights reflecting off its shiny surface before making the dagger disappear. As a weapon warper, he could manipulate metal into a deadly weapon and ensure he aimed true.

"You could've told me." Banshee's tit, Cole should've told her.

Rourke shrugged. "I assumed you knew."

"Why would I?"

"Why wouldn't you? Has anything changed since you became aware of my presence?"

She learned to summon the scythe, discovered the meeting headquarters for an extremist hate group, stole the amulet of Othila from them, and killed her ex in self-defence after he abducted and tortured Mike.

"I'm a little more badass," she said.

Rourke's lip curled down.

She raised her hand and separated her forefinger from her thumb by an inch. "A little."

The Closers, the extremist group she stole the amulet from, dreamed of a world without Others, including dark fae like Rourke and Cole, and half-breeds like Raven. They would go to any length to see their dream come true. The amulet of Othila somehow blocked dark fae energy, rendering the fae powerless and therefore vulnerable to attack, and the Closers showed no reluctance in using it as a weapon.

Raven, with more luck and happenstance than skill, retrieved the amulet from the Closers, and now the deadly-to-fae accessory was safely stowed away in one of Cole's vaults.

"No offence, but I don't need you to guard me." Odin's shriveled berries, Rourke must be bored out of his mind.

"No offence, but I don't take my orders from you."

Ah yes. Rourke answered to Cole. He didn't always serve her lover. Once, Rourke had been a free agent, but he had the unfortunate luck of picking up a contract on Raven's life. He'd thrown a knife at her head. Weapon warpers rarely missed their targets, if Raven hadn't been shielded by Cole's magic, she wouldn't be standing here in the rain arguing with her former would-be killer.

Cole spared Rourke's life and in return, he now served Cole. Apparently, Cole had a twisted view on payback, because this assignment must be all sorts of torture for Rourke.

"Well..." Warmth spread up her neck and cheeks. "This isn't his decision. I'm supposed to be a queen for fuck's sake. He's overstepping."

Rourke nodded. "Of course, he is."

She glared. Cole wasn't wrong about Raven's need for a guard. She took issue with him making the decision without discussing it with her first.

Rourke shrugged. "I guess he'd rather risk that pissy face you're making at me than something bad happening to you. That really hasn't changed. If anything, Cole's desire to see you protected has increased."

Her head snapped up. "Why do you say that? Does it have to do with the dead guys on the ground?"

Rourke stiffened and shut his mouth, regret flashing across his gaze.

"What has he done?"

Rourke shook his head.

Argh. She'd get no more answers from him. Rourke may be a sarcastic pain in the rear end, but he was dependable, competent and loyal. Raven sighed. Cole desperately tried to give her space and independence, but given an inch, he'd wrap her in shadowy bubble wrap and lock her in a vault. He overstepped his boundaries, but she wasn't exactly in a place to take over her own defence. "I'll take this up with him."

"With who?" Cole's deep seductive voice caressed her shoulders and wound around her in an invisible hug.

She spun around. Cole stepped from shadows, the darkness parting like a curtain to admit him into the parking lot. Bands of shadow streaked above him, weaving an intricate shield and forming a protective barrier against the sleet which still rained down.

Her mouth watered.

Cole's black matte armour and cape blended in with the night and only his porcelain skin and chiseled features stood out. The moment their gazes met, his pupils bled out so his eyes appeared entirely black.

When she first met Cole, she'd called him Tall,

Dark and Dangerous—TDD. Not much had changed, except now she knew his full fae name, the intimate details of his body and the kindness in his heart that he hid from almost everyone else but her.

"Good luck with that," Rourke spoke somewhere behind her.

Huh? She glanced over her shoulder, but her metal-warping, dark fae assassin bodyguard had slipped into the darkness.

"Good luck?" Cole's full mouth widened to reveal his perfect white teeth. How someone who spent lifetimes blending in with the seedy sectors of society as an assassin could have such lovely teeth was beyond her.

"You don't need any luck with me," he said.

She toed an errant pebble on the sidewalk and fluttered her eyelashes at the big bad fae lord. "Are you saying I can't get lucky with you?"

He chuckled and stepped forward, his cape billowing in the breeze. His shadows extended and made a dry pathway to where Raven gawked like a hormone-plagued teenager. He focused on the dark shadows where Rourke had disappeared.

"Why do you look like you ate bad sushi?" she asked, following his gaze as he walked toward her. Why would he give Rourke's proverbial back such a dark look? "Rourke protected me, as you ordered him to. If anyone should be pissed, it's me."

His gaze twinkled under the security lights and he stopped in front of her. "Einin."

"Cole."

"I don't like that he gets to spend his whole day with you while I'm relegated to wait in the shadows."

Huh? "Are you...jealous?"

His mouth flattened.

"Odin's nutsack, you are."

He folded his arms in front of his chest. "I'm not jealous of Rourke. At least not in the way that you're implying."

"Good, because you don't need to be. He also has to hide in the shadows, and I haven't relegated you anywhere." Other than to her bed, and he was just fine there, thank you very much.

"Haven't you? You promised not to send me away, yet, you keep your distance." He held up his hand to stop her instant denial. "I understand you need to find your own feet. I honour and respect your independence, but it's hard to stand by and watch...this." He waved his hands at the bodies.

"Why did they attack me?"

"Why not? If they had an ounce of corvid essence and successfully took you out, they would've gained an entire court and all the benefits that come along with it. They had much to gain and probably figured they had little to lose. Not everyone lives contently in the Underworld, but I doubt they considered death a possibility. They underestimated you and Rourke."

"Doesn't that just warm the cockles of the heart," she muttered. "Are we going to just leave them there?"

Cole considered the dead bodies again. His shadows

swirled around the fallen men, lifted them from the sopping ground and carried them away through a portal he created. When the magic snapped shut, Cole turned back to her. "That's more consideration than they deserve."

"It's not them I was thinking about," she said, and meant it. They'd tried to kill her. She didn't feel sorry for them at all. "It's bad for business to have dead bodies littering the parking lot. Thank you for disposing of them."

Cole dipped his chin.

She hesitated and looked around the store fronts. "Are there going to be more?"

"Yes. I'm not trying to scare you when I say you're in danger." He ground his teeth.

"And yet you're standing back to give me space to grow and learn to handle things on my own."

He glowered.

"That must be frustrating."

"Exceedingly," he grumbled. "I don't like this. At all."

He didn't like watching her make mistakes. He didn't need to say those words, but she knew that's how he felt. It must infuriate him to have to hold back and not whisk her away or wrap her up in military grade protective gear. Sometimes, she wanted to let Cole swoop in and save her. It was an easier path, but also one that would most likely end up with her dead. She didn't need a hero to save her. She needed to save herself. "I guess we both have some things to practice."

Cole's gaze flicked to the scythe and briefly to where the dead men had littered the ground around her. "Did you summon your weapon?"

She tried not to straighten and puff out her chest. And failed. "All on my own."

His scent—a magical forest—curled around her and she inhaled deeply. He leaned to the side to look past her and hesitated. "Is that your bra?"

"Nope. Never seen that before in my life."

"You're a terrible liar. I recognize it. But bra or no bra, summoning your scythe is good news, Einin."

"Does it mean you'll pull my security detail?"

He laughed.

Guess not.

"It means we can finally solve one of your many problems." He held out his hand.

She stared at it—massive and covered with callouses, his hand had ended many lives, yet, it had also wrought all sorts of passion from her. How could she fear his hand? Or Cole? Quite simply, she didn't. Sometimes she worried she moved too fast, but only time would tell whether she made a mistake. Hindsight was always 20/20 like that. Right now, everything felt right.

"I can't go with you. Mike's picking me up."

Cole made a slow turn and surveyed the empty parking lot. "I think he stood you up. Text him."

The ride was a weak excuse anyway and Cole knew it. Raven didn't technically need a vehicle to get around anymore, but the anti-Other sentiment rolling through the community made her hesitant to flex her dark fae, portal-making muscle in the open near her parents' place where people might see.

Before she could think up another lame excuse for no other reason than enjoying the banter, a portal snapped open three parking spaces away. A large burly humanoid male stepped out of a swirling black cloud of sparkling mist and huffed at the cold air. The rain instantly doused his curly brown hair to his face, revealing short horns that protruded from his skull. Wearing a black shirt tucked into black leather pants, his outfit gave him away as an Other almost as quickly as the horns did. He scanned the parking lot and his black eyes blazed red when his gaze found Raven and Cole.

Cole leaned over. "Do you want to flex your queen muscle, or can I handle this for you?"

"Maybe he wants to talk?" Raven didn't resolve her disagreements with fights. She had next to nothing in combat training, unless kicking her brother in the nads to get out of a headlock counted.

Cole snorted and turned to the horned man. "Is she right? Are you here to talk, Frey?"

Frey snarled and unsheathed a sword strapped to his waist. "I'm gonna squash you and then rid the shadow realms of that abomination."

Raven pointed at her chest.

"Frey is one of Freyr's many bastard children," Cole said, very matter of fact. "His mom has a little corvid essence."

Frey roared and ran at her.

"Me or you, Einin."

"Me." She gripped her scythe and let its power flood through her veins. Banshee's tit. Why had she said that? Why did she choose now to strive for independence?

Cole stepped to the side, folded his arms and glared. He could stop this fight at any time.

Frey swung a thick rusted blade at her. She ducked out of the way. Heart in her throat, she shifted to the side and avoided another swipe. The scythe's power shook her core, taking over her body and moulding her into an elite fighter. She became one with the wind, one with the shadows, one with the weapon. Weaving, dodging, dancing around the large warrior, she moved with lethal efficiency. The scythe's blade sang in the cold, wet night. Rain pinged off the blade. The reflected glow from the security lights basked her in brightness.

Frey dropped his sword and flopped to the ground. The rain washed blood from his body, but he lay under the deluge of the winter shower unmoving.

Raven panted and clutched the scythe. With the imminent threat over, the scythe's power faded from her body and left her drained. She shuffled over to Frey and peered down at him. "Is he dead?"

Cole had walked over to stand beside her and peered down at the large hulk of fae left on the parking lot asphalt. "He'll live."

Relief swept through her body. She'd done enough

killing. She nudged the large body with her foot.

Frey groaned, but didn't move.

"You should kill him."

Raven tensed. Crap. Did she have to?

"Despite Frey having lots of brawn and a name meaning supreme lord, he's never had the mental capacity to obtain a position of power or understand the subtleties of life. He will come back and he might catch you unaware or at a moment of weakness."

She stared down at the motionless man who had stepped out of a portal moments ago with the sole purpose of taking her life. "I can't."

"I know."

Argh. "Then why did you say it?"

He leaned down and kissed her wet head. "Your respect for life and reluctance for taking it is one of the things I admire about you. It sets you apart from other fae. Some may view it as a weakness, but I think time will show your compassion to be a strength."

"I've never been called weak as a compliment before."

"You're not weak. I have no doubt you'd turn into a psychotic executioner if anyone was stupid enough to threaten your family, but you need to protect yourself as well. I told you he needs to die because you need to understand the realities of your new position. You may need to kill him."

"But not right now."

"No. Not right now."

But eventually, if Frey didn't get the message. She

shivered. She didn't want to turn into someone who viewed life as expendable, but she didn't want to die, either. Morals wouldn't keep her alive in the Underworld all on their own. She needed to come up with her own set of rules that she could live with, and still survive.

Cole's expression turned from serious to playful. He flapped his hand a little. "Come with me."

"You've said that before."

The shadows in his dark gaze danced. "And have I ever let you down?"

She didn't pause to argue about missing roast night. Instead, she clamped her mouth shut on any further protests because they didn't matter anymore. Cole mattered. She wanted to go with him. She wanted to let him make her body hum and her mind forget what just happened. Placing her hand in his, the world broke away.

Chapter Five

"Geology rocks, but geography is where it's at."

~Unknown, but also Raven's dad

S till clutching the scythe in one hand, Raven
stepped out of the glorious heat of Cole's body to
take in their new surroundings. Pillars and walls
made of black brick enclosed floors of midnight granite.
A black runner led to an empty throne constructed of
large metallic feathers. The last time Raven stood in
this spot, an evil queen sat on the dais in her gown of
black feathers and calmly explained her intention to rip
Raven's power from her body and use her twin brother

as a battery pack.

Cole brought her to Lloth's court.

Raven stiffened and a swarm of memories bombarded her. Fear, nausea, death.

Red moonlight bathed the ceiling-less hall and reflected off the granite under their feet. Wind blew through the empty hall. Spectators and guards no longer lined the black runner down the center of the room and corvids no longer perched on the ramparts in the hundreds.

Outside, the nearby ocean crashed against a rocky shore and seabirds and corvids called out to one another as they soared overhead. From memory, the castle perched ominously atop a cliff, which dropped down to the tumultuous water below on all sides save the entrance. There was only one way in or out unless using a portal.

"Why'd you bring me here?" Her gaze kept drifting to the crusted pool of blood where Lloth had drawn her last breath. Someone removed the bodies, but no one had cleaned up the mess Bane and Cole made when they disposed of Lloth's entire queen's guard while Raven killed their queen.

A shudder ran through her.

Cole stepped up behind her. He placed his gauntlet-covered hands on her shoulders and ran them down to hold her arms. His cloak billowed around them and whispered along the stone flooring to brush her legs.

"I brought you here because this is yours."

"I don't want it."

He squeezed her arms and leaned in, his lips whispering against her hair. "You will want this."

He wasn't talking about some kinky foreplay in the courtyard, yet, heat raced through Raven's body at the thought. She definitely had a few screws loose.

Cole released her arms, stepped beside her and reached down to hold her free hand. Despite the cold black matte metal of the gauntlet on her skin, she found the gesture reassuring.

"Trust me?" he asked.

She nodded and let him lead her through the grand hall with its eerie open ceiling view of the moon to a passage leading off the back of the courtroom behind the dais for the throne. Their footsteps echoed along the hall and down the passageway.

"Where are we going?" Her voice bounced off the black walls.

His dark gaze swirled with silvery bands of shadow. "You'll see."

"It's roast night."

Cole didn't need further explanation. Raven rarely missed Sunday night dinner, even when she hadn't lived at home. "It will be worth it. Promise."

She squeezed his hand and walked down the hall and through the corridors, down spiral stairways and finally to a large double door entranceway. The metal doors loomed over them with ancient runes carved into the framework.

"Do you think you can find your way back here?"

Cole asked.

"You're leaving me?" She squeezed the shaft of the scythe. Its power prickled along her skin.

His deep chuckle rumbled against her skin. "No, Einin. But I know how much you crave independence. You'll want to access this room on your own."

That didn't sound ominous at all. "I think so," she said to answer his question.

"Later, if there's time, I'll show you some of the other important chambers in this fortress. But one thing at a time." He nodded and turned back to the door. She mirrored his actions, the scythe getting sweaty in her grip and the Raven's Eye growing hot against her breastbone. The temperature was too high for an underground room.

"Is it just me, or is it hot in here?"

"It's just you."

"Thanks."

Cole turned to her again. "It's just you because the enchantments have sensed the presence of the Corvid Queen."

Oh.

"It's time."

"For what?"

"For you to open the door." He swept his arm out and waved at the large double doors. They remained closed and no less intimidating.

"Err. What exactly is behind the door? It's not going to eat me, is it? It's not Pandora's box?"

"Do you trust me?" he asked for the second time, his

35

expression turning serious all of a sudden, with a touch of sadness.

A few months ago, she would've screeched "no" because Cole was just another dark fae lord with a reputation as a ruthless killer, but things had changed since then. Trust was earned and Cole continuously acted with her best interests in mind. Underneath the love and trust, though, a smidgeon of caution remained from almost thirty years of programming, compliments of Mom. But Cole slowly chiseled that away, too.

"Yes," she whispered.

Cole smiled and squeezed her hand before releasing her. "Then open the door."

"How?"

He shrugged, his cape flowing out behind him. "Only the Queen of Corvids can open this door."

"Why tonight?" Missing roast night wasn't that big of a deal, but Cole knew how important her family was to her.

"It's the first night you've had off in a while and I thought you were ready."

Huh. Raven didn't want to dwell on why he thought she hadn't been ready before tonight, or how her dreams had been filled with memories of crushing Lloth in her giant bird beak, her ex's last moments, her part in his death, and her brother's pain from his abduction.

Cole leaned down. "If you hurry and open the door, we can go home and feast on the tender flesh of your mother's roast."

She squinted at him.

"That came out wrong." He winced and straightened. "I was hoping the promise of food would help motivate you."

He knew her well, but this time he'd overestimated her mastery of dark fae powers. They were going to be here for a while. "Did you bring something comfortable to sit in?"

Cole chuckled again. "Relax, Einin. Feel your power. Feel the energy from the scythe and the magic in these runes. They will guide you."

He sounded so sure and Raven kept wondering when he'd realize the severity of her incompetence.

"Take a deep breath and close your eyes."

She did as he instructed and reached for the corvid essence that swirled deep inside her. Dark, covetous and potent, the power rose to her call and swarmed her senses. The scythe in her hand pulsed in time, like a rhythmic drumbeat to the wingbeats of the birds in her mind. The ravens pushed against her skin, begging for release, demanding she burst into a conspiracy of ravens and take to the delicious night sky. The scythe cheered them on.

No!

Sweat dripped down her brow and her hand grew sweaty again.

No. She could control this. She had to.

With a deep breath, she pushed her magical awareness outward without breaking apart and scanned the magical doorway. The second her power, combined with the scythe, brushed the runes, they flared to life. A high-pitched keening flooded the chamber and echoed down the corridor behind them. The runes sucked in her magic, so hard and fast they almost ripped the power from her grasp.

She gasped.

Cole said something, but her pounding heart and the hammering in her head drowned him out.

This power is not yours, she told the door. Wrapping the corvid essence around her, she yanked her magic back. The keening stopped. Stone groaned and a strong gust of stale air with a metallic taste blasted past her.

Raven opened her eyes to see what the chamber revealed.

An unseen internal light illuminated a glittering room full of stacks upon stacks of gold.

Oooo. Shiny.

Chapter Six

"I may not have gone where I intended to go, but I think I have ended up where I needed to be."

~ *Douglas Adams*

Gold coins bigger and thicker than toonies toppled down the stacks with a clatter, sounding like a clinking wind chime.

"What am I looking at?" She turned to find Cole grinning, the gold in the room reflecting off his dark gaze.

"Gold," he said. "Lots of it."

She slammed down the end of the scythe's shaft on

the shiny black stone flooring and waited.

"Your gold," he said.

That didn't make any sense. "Bane said this job didn't pay."

"Bane's understanding of 'work' is limited. The idea of a queen working for anyone other than herself is unfathomable to him. This gold is not from menial labour. It's from bribes and payment thinly veiled as gifts."

"That's a lot of gifts." Her mind started running through calculations.

"The Queen of Corvids yields a lot of power. You wield a lot of power. You just haven't realized it yet."

She turned back to the glittering room with its tumbling towers of gold. "I don't have to work at the diner again." Her brother never had to work at Dan's either. And she could pay off Mom and Dad's mortgage. And get a new car.

Goodbye Jean Claude.

"This changes everything," she said. "Why didn't you tell me about the money sooner?" She had a lot to learn about her magic and the Underworld, but she also had to eat and pay her bills. Her need to survive her new role in dark fae society constantly warred with her need to survive in the Mortal Realm. As much as she would've loved to quit her job and focus on everything Cole had to teach, she couldn't afford to financially. Until now.

Cole sighed. "I didn't want you to pay the cost to get this money. Until you used the scythe to draw blood, this was all inaccessible to you." Cole stepped forward to stand beside her, his forest scent curling around her shoulders. "I didn't want to place that moral dilemma on you, either. This gold changes everything and yet nothing at the same time."

"Explain."

"We can transfer a large sum to your mortal realm bank, but I'd caution you on moving the entire fortune there. Mortal financial institutions are untrustworthy. You cannot count on them to tend your money. They will cheat, lie and steal. They'll charge you an outrageous conversion fee and will cap the amount of Underworld currency they'll accept. You will also need Underworld currency for your dealings here. The Canadian dollar is worth next to nothing to the dark fae."

"Hey!"

He shrugged. "Whether you like it or not, you are of both worlds and as such, you need to keep a foot in both worlds."

His words made sense, of course, but unease clenched her chest. If she left her money here, no one could access it without her presence. It would stay safe and contained as it had for Lloth.

An ugly thought bubbled up.

This was Lloth's money, but now it belonged to Raven. If something ever happened to her...

"I want my family taken care of," she said. "If something happens to me."

"They will be. You have my word."

"I don't want them to have just your word. You won't be able to access this money and shouldn't have to shell out from your own savings. I want them to have money."

"They will, Einin. I'll help you move enough over so they're taken care of."

Warmth blossomed in her heart. "You keep saying sweet things."

Cole leaned toward her, basking her in the heat of his body and the power of his gaze. "Only for you."

"Is there a way to covert the gold into Canadian currency without the bank?"

Cole's gaze flashed with approval. "The trolls."

"The toll trolls?" The trolls controlled the only bridge connecting Vancouver with the North Shore and, aside from their weekly toll-free Fridays, charged an obscene fee for those wishing to cross the Burrard inlet by foot or car.

"The trolls are so much more than that, but yes."

"Can I take enough to pay Mike's tuition, set up a college fund for Juni and take care of my parent's mortgage?" She held her breath.

"You can, and then have enough to pay off your loan, cover your own expenses and leave a buffer for emergencies or worst-case scenarios."

"I can get my own place again." Ahh. Freedom! No more socks on doorknobs. No more awkward situations involving Mike busting into her room without knocking.

Cole shifted the weight on his feet and looked away.

"What?"

"I'd advise against moving out."

She frowned. He disliked the interruptions as much as she did, though he seemed to find them more amusing than embarrassing.

"Why?" she asked.

Cole pressed his lips together.

"What have you done?"

"What I've always done."

She waited.

"Protected you."

Understanding clicked. He still had his men guarding her parents' place. If she moved out, he wouldn't pull his assassins from the Crawford residence because he knew how much her family meant to her, but he would want her location secure as well.

"I would add a second site to guard."

"Third, actually. I have men protecting your interests here at the Corvid Court as well."

"So, my choices are my parents' basement or the creepy castle of the woman I killed. Awesome."

"Or my place," he said.

"Did the Patron Fae of Assassins just ask me to move in with him?"

Cole shrugged again, but the indifferent gesture did little to hide the serious focus in his gaze. "You're there most of the time anyway."

She slid her hand along his cheek.

"I like waking up beside you," he said, gruffly.

"With messy hair?"

He nodded. "And drool."

She dropped her hand from his face. "Lies."

He chuckled, but otherwise remained still, waiting for her answer.

She didn't have one. Her whole heart leapt at the idea. Her skin tingled with the memory of his touch and the need to press against Cole made her body ache. Her pesky brain told her to slow down, wait and think about it. There was already a serious imbalance in their relationship, power wise. Her need for independence balked at the idea of becoming even more dependent on Cole. She should have her own guards. She should defend her own interests. But she also needed to know what in the Underworld she was doing and knew Cole merely shielded her until she could stand and fight on her own.

"So, I'm rich?" she asked to give her time to think.

He nodded.

"In the Mortal Realm and the Underworld?"

"In the Underworld, you're more upper middle class. Though you wield power and hold a coveted position, there are those who..."

"Could squash me?"

"Not the phrase I was looking for."

She stepped into his body, so close her shirt brushed his breastplate. "What are you looking for, Beul na h-Oidhche gu Camhanaich?"

A slow smile spread across his face and he ran his hands up her arms. "I've already found it."

The Lord of Shadows looked at her the way her birds looked at shiny things. She'd have to be a robot not to react to that look, full of need and want. And Raven was very much a mortal woman made of flesh and bones with her own desires.

"So, there's nothing you need?" She slid her hands along his shoulders and pressed her body against his armour. It was like trying to hug stone, but her intent wasn't missed.

Cole's gaze darkened and he gripped her hips. "I have everything I need right here."

"There's something I need."

"Oh?"

She stepped forward, forcing him to move back into a pile of gold. Coins spilled onto the stonework at their feet.

"You," she said. "I need you."

"That's a want."

She shook her head and rose on her tiptoes. "I *need* you."

His smile was pure wickedness. "Good."

Shadows shot out from the corners of the room and ran along her skin with their now familiar cool touch. Caressing her limbs and teasing her hair, the bands of darkness spread warmth through her body. Cole did naughty and delightful things to her with his shadows, proving some of the salacious rumours about dark fae, their devious exploits and tempting prowess.

Her body hummed under his touch, craving more, wanting more and tingling with anticipation of what was to come.

Cole's shadows wrapped around her and carried her to a pile of gold. She leaned back into the crumbling pillars, coins clinking to the ground and watched the Patron Fae of Assassins walk toward her. In full court armour, he looked like a magical creation from her fantasies. His black cloak flowed behind him and each step brought his flashing silver and black gaze closer. His hair had fallen in disarray, but he made no move to swipe it from his face. The shadows danced around him. Like thousands of servants' hands, the bands unclasped, unzipped and unbuttoned his clothing, peeling off his protective armour with each step.

He was breathtaking.

While he undressed, the other shadows continued to caress her skin, running over the flat of her stomach, flowing around the curve of her breasts and skipping up her legs.

He'd done no more than kiss her and she was ready for him.

Cole stopped at the base of the gold and raked her with his gaze. The coins pressed into her naked skin as she writhed with want. The shadows had undressed her as well, pulling off her clothing while seducing her with their magical touch.

Cole knelt between her legs and trailed his fingers up her naked thighs.

Please, now. Just take me now and end this torment.

Cole grinned, his lips curling against her skin as he kissed his way up her body, adding to the torture instead of ending anything. He pulled back, hovering over her body, bracing his weight on his forearms, and studied her. His gaze wild, the pupils had bled out so only black appeared, yet, in the bottomless depths, swirls of gray and silver danced.

"You never answered my question." His deep voice rolled over her skin.

"Is this how you torture for answers?" She panted and lifted her hips. *Come on. Now.* Give it to her now.

"Only with you." He pushed forward, pressing against her, but not enough.

It wasn't enough. She wanted more. More. She whined and writhed.

Cole leaned down and whispered into her ear, "I want you beside me. I want to wake up with you in my arms."

"Yes," she breathed.

He pushed in farther. "What did you say?"

"Yes," she said, louder this time.

He flexed his hips but paused again.

"Yes!" she screeched and clawed at his back.

Cole flashed her a smug smile and began to move.

Raven continued to scream yes, repeatedly, until Cole took her breath away entirely.

Chapter Seven

"Don't be afraid. I will sit with you in the dark and wait until the light comes."

~ Nadine Tomlinson

After becoming acquainted with her fortune in a way Raven never imagined, she needed to thank Mom for teaching her to never put money in her mouth when she was young. Elizabeth Crawford always claimed money was dirty. It turned out she was right. Money really was dirty. Very, very dirty.

Raven sat up in the large four-poster bed. They'd

missed roast night, but her body purred with satisfaction. So worth it. Cole sprawled out naked in the spot beside her, the moonlight bathing his pale skin. He didn't look any less lethal while sleeping. Instead, he reminded her of a dragon in slumber.

After the coin session, Cole had guided her through Lloth's castle—Raven's castle—and took her to the master suite. He'd taken the liberty of having everything replaced and the room cleaned. Just another item on an already imbalanced tally sheet, but no less appreciated.

The new, high thread count cotton sheets slid from her body as she stood from the bed. The night sky beckoned her. She padded to her clothes and pulled them on. Her scythe called out to her and she answered, pulling the power close. The weapon materialized in her hand and she walked onto the large stone balcony.

The wind curled around her, a little too cold to be refreshing, but scented with deep florals and something magical Raven couldn't quite describe. If pixie dust had a scent, the air smelled like dozens of barrels of glittery pixie dust had been released up wind.

She closed her eyes and inhaled. In the morning, she'd have to meet with the unknown photographer who liked to send threats in manila envelopes. She'd quit her job and pay off her bank loan. She'd also continue investigating both neighbours for their possible involvement in Pepe's disappearance and research ways to block portals to the Realm of War.

And somewhere in that schedule, she also planned to have one more Underworld Court prep session with Cole and gain the independence to stand on her own. Hopefully, Cole would impart enough knowledge that she'd avoid completely embarrassing herself or starting a feud.

But none of these things were what ate at her stomach.

Loss of purpose.

When she first met Cole, she barely kept her head above water, treading in place and dreaming of the day she paid off the debilitating loan so she could go to school and better her circumstances. Then she moved home to give herself enough financial breathing room to register for a couple of classes and work toward her goal of having a career that didn't involve running food to hangry customers. Originally, she planned to get a job as an investigator for Worker's Compensation of British Columbia and take enough business courses so she could help out Dad with the family PI business and eventually take it over when it came time for him to retire. Both the ultimate objectives of these plans were to put food on the table and keep a roof over her head while doing something she enjoyed.

But now what?

She had to weave some dark fae magic to appease the Lord of War, but assuming she survived that, what would she do with herself? What would fill her days? Feed her soul? Give her purpose? Not Dan's diner, that's for sure. She didn't need to work another day in her life and though Cole didn't say it, she could make more in one Underworld transaction than she could busting her ass for a year at an office job. She also couldn't ignore that she had some serious knowledge gaps regarding the Underworld, how dark fae society worked and who ran it all—thanks, Mom.

Raven took a deep breath and walked to the stone railing. She leaned the scythe against the stones and rested both hands on the cold surface. No, that wasn't fair. This wasn't Mom's fault. Not really. Not anymore. Mom only blocked the flow of information when they were minors. Raven could've filled in the gaps a long time ago. Her lack of knowledge was her own fault. Dang it. Life was so much easier when she had someone else to blame for her problems.

Now, she needed to step up her game. That's what she'd focus on. Becoming a competent Queen of Corvids.

She'd have to withdraw from the business courses. She needed to become an independent badass in the Underworld. The university probably offered courses on the occult, but traditional studies wouldn't cover the material she needed.

She glanced back into the bedroom where Cole still slept. Raven trusted him, but she couldn't count on him always being there to guide and mentor her. She shouldn't.

She tapped her fingers along the stones and looked out into the inky darkness of the night. The ocean crashed against the rocky shoreline below.

She needed multiple vantage points of her position in the Underworld to ensure she obtained well-rounded, unbiased information. Maybe a Wiccan apprenticeship? School for the dark arts?

Raven snorted.

The witches would never take her and the second didn't exist.

Or did it?

Raven had no idea, but luckily, she knew someone who might. Raven added calling Marcus to her list.

The breeze rolled past her, flicking her hair in every direction. The moon cascaded silver and red light onto the stones and lit the long drop to the ocean below. She'd never been here in daylight. Would these tall black spires appear as intimidating?

"It's not like Beul to leave his toys out." A deep rumbling voice spoke behind her.

At his first word, her hair shriveled into frizzy tight ringlets and her scythe pulsed in warning beside her.

She snatched the weapon and whirled around. A dark fae stood a few feet away. Standing at least seven feet tall, he wore plated black armour and a mask covering his nose and mouth. A black crown that looked more like the skeletal remains of a giant's hand rose up from his head and wings with feathers as black as the night spread out behind him.

Raven took in all the surrounding details in less than a second. Unlike most Others, his eyes weren't black, they glowed bright white and the long chain he held in both hands blazed with the same intensity.

Raven went right past outrage from him calling her a toy straight to fear.

"Who are you?" she asked. Her voice didn't tremble. Bonus points for her.

"Do you not know?" The gravelly quality of his voice sounded familiar, but she couldn't place it.

Raven groaned. Had she made a mistake by asking? Did he just gain some dark fae advantage over her? Or did he like to play with his food before he slaughtered it?

And where were the guards? Did Cole send them away for privacy?

The man's image wavered almost as if he contained more than what he showed, like his skin and armour were simply a cover for his true essence.

That didn't bode well for her.

"I'm Erebus, God of Darkness, son of Chaos."

Oh, shit.

Of course, she'd heard his name in history class, a long time ago. Erebus was one of Chaos' first batch of children born out of the primeval void who became one of the primordial gods. Legends said Erebus' dark mists spread over all the realms and filled every crevice within. His wife and sister, Nyx, the Goddess of Night, was also born of Chaos and held the power of gathering Erebus' darkness to create night. Or so the scholars said. Raven began to realize just how wrong the pre and post barrier collapse history was.

She stood in front of one of the first gods known in existence.

But that's not what intimidated or scared her. More recently, she heard Erebus mentioned by Cole and it made a lasting impression on her. When Cole had first introduced himself to her in his Underworld prison, he'd given his full name and titles, including bastard son of Erebus.

"You're Cole's—"

"Father." Cole's voice rumbled from the doorway to the bedroom. He'd pulled on some boxer briefs but did nothing else to shield his exposed skin from the cold air.

His father didn't flinch or turn in his son's direction.

"Is this what you sought to hide from us, Beul? A weak halfling. I didn't believe the rumours, but now I see it to be true."

The fear slipped away, and outrage resurfaced. First, he called her a toy, then a halfling. She gripped the scythe and the shadows stirred to answer her welling anger. Corvid energy rose from within. She pulled her power from her core along with the shadows and whipped the magic around her, ready to lash out.

"You are in my domain, Erebus, son of Chaos," she said.

Erebus dropped his head back and laughed. "You think to smite me? A son of Chaos? The God of Darkness. Not even Odin, your pathetic Allfather, could best me. His creation surely won't. These lords play their silly games for power. They are ants beneath my feet. You're a pet project to a dark fae lord and merely a grain of sand. What are lords, kings and queens to gods?" Power swelled within him, overflowing to smack her in the face. And he wasn't even trying as far as she could tell.

"I am darkness. I am the night and I am indestructible," he said.

Having a gun would've been nice right about now. He'd probably shut up if she put a bullet through his head.

And then who would be the monster? Shooting someone for speaking like a pompous ass? Ugh. Still, so tempting.

Her stomach churned, but she remained straight and rigid. She would not, could not, cower in front of this man. She bit her tongue, knowing better than to antagonize the God of Darkness.

"Why are you here?" Besides to lord his superiority over her. The words came out before she could stop them, harsher and blunter than she'd like. He probably expected platitudes, apologies, or cowering while using his impressive titles, but Cole hadn't covered court addresses in his etiquette lessons yet and she'd be damned if she'd grovel to this arrogant prick.

Erebus' eyes narrowed into slits—horizontal beams of glowing white light. He turned to his son, the feathers of his giant black wings fluttering in the light breeze.

"She needs manners," he said, the simple words little slaps to her ego.

Cole remained still, his hands balled into fists at his sides. Slowly, he dipped his chin. "She'll be ready."

"Why do you lower yourself for this abomination?" Erebus swung his hand out in her direction.

Um, hello? Abomination standing right here.

"You once *lowered* yourself, do you not recall why?"

Though he stressed the word in a mocking way, Raven would've preferred her lover not say he lowered himself to be with her at all, court politics and fae hierarchy be damned.

"Your mother beguiled me."

"Is that why you went mad with grief when Nyx killed her?"

Nyx sounded more and more like a goddess she didn't want to meet.

The wind howled and a band of pure darkness rolled past.

"Nyx freed me from your mother's spell." Erebus' eyes blazed. Bright orbs in the pitch black. The darkness cleared, leaving them cast in the soft glow of red moonlight once again.

"But you wouldn't let her free you from me," Cole said.

Though the God of Darkness had a covered face and glowing white eyes, he managed to convey a glower effortlessly. "A decision I often regret."

Cole folded his arms over his chest. "No doubt."

"See that she's ready. The council meets in seven days."

Cole nodded again, seemingly unfazed with Erebus' words and presence.

Cole's father turned to her once again, his wings

fluttering out to resettle against his back. "Heed his advice carefully, halfling."

Or what?

"Or die."

Had she said that out loud? She didn't think so. This must be one of those instances Cole mentioned where she wore her thoughts on her face. She clamped her mouth shut and bowed her head, copying Cole's gesture. Like she needed the stakes upped any more than they already were.

Another band of pure night rolled through and when it cleared, the God of Darkness disappeared with it.

She turned to Cole, the moonlight licking his exposed skin and playing with his rippling muscles.

"Council meeting?"

Chapter Eight

"Life is not a fairy tale. If you lose your shoe at midnight, you're drunk."

~ Unknown, but wise

Turned out, Raven's schooling lacked a lot of key information about the Other Realms, and she couldn't even blame the teacher. Nope. She had limited time for learning sessions and a lifetime of living with her head in the sand. Her own ignorance was at fault here. Sure, Mom raised her to stay away from the Underworld and kept secrets from Raven and her brother, but that shouldn't have stopped her from doing her own research. Ugh. If she had a time machine, she'd travel back in time and slap some sense into her younger self.

According to Cole's crash course in power hierarchy, Odin, the Allfather, might rule in the Underworld, but in terms of dark fae hierarchy, he was still a young adult, only now coming into his own. The first gods, the primordial deities, titans and cyclops that made it into mainstream mortal realm culture represented an even higher branch of power—one so powerful they didn't even care to hold court or break up fights amongst minions. Such banality was beneath them.

Raven was a child to these gods—both in power and knowledge. Yet, because she held the title of queen, she had a seat at the council with the other queens, kings and gods.

Cole wasn't invited.

"I'll die without you," she'd said when he'd explained the council meeting dynamics to her earlier. She wasn't trying to sound like a dramatic teenager, she really could die without his presence and advice. She was being realistic.

Cole's grim expression hadn't contradicted her assessment. "Your grandsire will be there."

Odin's presence did not inspire a lot of confidence and she'd told Cole exactly that. He'd nodded and scratched his stubble covered jaw. "It is wise to withhold your trust."

"Is there no way for you to come with me?"

A small smile cracked his serious expression. "There are a few ways, but you may not wish to pay the price."

She'd demanded more information, but he'd shook his head and waved her off. "You need to meet with the photographer with a penchant for vague threats. Unless you've changed your mind on letting me obliterate them?" He looked so hopeful.

But Raven hadn't changed her mind. She needed to fight her own battles and meet this mysterious person on her own. With a quick kiss and a promise to extract more from him later—to which he replied with a dirty innuendo—Raven had wrapped herself in corvid energy and shadows to transport herself to the meeting location.

The magic whipped away with the wind and Raven now found herself standing in a dark corner of a concrete parkade. She took a deep breath of mountain pine and hemlock. The grunge and dreariness set upon the Lower Mainland since the barrier collapse and subsequent wars didn't reach the top of Burnaby Mountain. The university perched on the top now boasted fantastic views *and* clean air—a novelty in this new era. Other institutions had to pay fees to fairies and maintained filters along the borders of their properties. But filtered air didn't smell as good as the naturally clean stuff.

Raven took another deep breath and smiled. The enjoyment was fleeting, and quickly overwhelmed by the twisting sensation from her stomach. She had no idea what to expect at this meeting.

Her blackmailers asked to meet her on the patio outside one of the busiest cafeterias. Fine with her. Lots of witnesses.

Raven rolled her shoulders back and walked through the parkade. Her sneakers scuffed the dry pavement and the cold air condensed her breath. She didn't need a map or directions. At one time in her life, she'd attended this prestigious university. Then Robert left her with a different kind of mountain—one of debilitating debt. Reality of her financial circumstances sent her toppling down, figuratively and physically.

She walked around the tables and the smell of fries and pizza pretzels. With exam time approaching though, most students shuffled along with dazed, zombie-like expressions. They wore day old jogging pants and pajamas. The latter fashion trend was something Raven never understood. If she wore pajamas outside the house during the day, what could she possibly look forward to changing into at the end of a long work shift? Pajamas had always played a part of her personal reward system.

Raven gripped the cold metal handles and swung open the heavy glass door to the patio. Cold air washed in.

A student popped her head up from behind a tower of empty pop cans and scowled. She pulled her sweatshirt's hood over her head.

Raven ignored the student and stepped onto the concrete patio, leaving the bustle of the cafeteria behind her. The wind rustled through the neighbouring forest and pushed away the mist clinging to the hill.

"I wondered if you'd show." A man stepped out onto the patio behind her. She turned to find Tony the Tooth standing between her and the exit with two guards. He studied her with his golden, unflinching gaze. The wrinkles lining his face suggested he laughed a lot but as with the first time she met him, he wasn't smiling. Though older and not the tallest, the well-cut jacket of his business suit emphasized a muscular build from years of street fighting and busting up peoples' faces. A thin, old scar ran along his jawline, so faint she hadn't noticed it the first and only other time they'd met.

Tony was the leader of the local hyena shifter gang, which, according to Bear, was rising in power, now biting at the ankles of the top two—the raccoons and jackals. Tony's hyena scent hit her face as if to emphasize that fact. They hadn't bothered to wear the scent masking charms today. Lucky for Raven.

A professional visit by the leader of one of the largest, most ruthless, shifter-run gangs in the Lower Mainland.

"You?" Why in the Mortal Realm would Tony the Tooth bother with such a plebeian like her? She'd already successfully completed a paid job for his daughter Sarah. Her fiancé, who also happened to be Raven's ex, Robert, kept disappearing on the second Wednesday of the month. Sarah suspected he was cheating and hired Raven to find out what he was up to. Turned out, Robert was a part of an extremist group of mortals called the Closers, who hated the Other Realms and wanted to restore the barrier between the realms. Sarah and her family weren't thrilled with the news, but they didn't fault Raven's investigation techniques or report, nor did they balk at paying the standard PI fees.

"Why would you threaten me?" she asked. They could afford to hire her, and she maintained confidentiality with each case. He had no need to threaten her family if all he wanted to do was meet with her. Crawford Investigations had standard business hours.

"Threaten?" he scoffed. "That's such an uncouth term. I make deals. Coming to an understanding is my bread and butter."

Great. Playing semantics was not Raven's favourite pastime. "What do you want?"

Tony sighed, obviously disappointed in Raven's unwillingness to play his battle of wits, or maybe he just found her blunt question distasteful.

"My daughter had an interesting tale to tell me about you," he said.

"I'm sure she did." Sarah had witnessed an anti-Other amulet lay Raven flat out on the ground. She may not know exactly what Raven was, but she knew Raven had to be part Other, and unsurprisingly shared this information with her father.

"I've done my own little investigation into you,

Branwen Crawford. You've let clientele and neighbours believe you're a fox shifter like your family." He paused. "But you're not, are you?"

Raven waited. His question was rhetorical, anyway. Finding out her birth name and drawing the obvious connection from Sarah's observations didn't involve any formidable investigation skills.

"You're something else. Something more."

She shrugged. Some would argue she was something less.

"Something Other. You exist in a time and place where it's dangerous to merely breathe differently. You're obviously aware of the prejudices and dangers, which is why you've tried to conceal your true nature."

Here it was. Wait for it...

"I could be persuaded to keep this information quiet..."

"Out of the goodness of your heart, I'm sure." She didn't even try to keep the sarcasm from her voice.

"Of course, and a favour. A simple one, really."

"If it's so simple, why resort to blackmail? Why not ask or if it involves some investigation, why not just pay my PI fee? It's not like you're hurting for cash." She waved at his expensive suit worth three times her car. A mental image of Jean Claude popped into her head. Make that five times.

Tony flashed his teeth. Not a smile. Showing his pearly whites to threaten her. Would he really try to bite her in a public place?

Raven glanced around the empty patio, surely not

here, but that wouldn't stop him from nabbing her off the street.

"Robert's gone missing," Tony stated.

Raven froze.

"Know anything about that?"

Images of blood and tissue flashed through her mind. Robert's lifeless body, the pool of dark blood, the sound his head made when it hit the floor, how the single swinging basement light glinted off her scythe's blood-soaked blade.

Her stomach rolled. She swallowed and forced her body to relax in front of the perceptive mob boss.

"You want me to search for Robert again? That's a standard PI case."

Tony shook his head. "I've already paid your fee once and this is not something I want a record of."

They planned to kill Robert once they found him. But he was already dead. If she told them the truth, they'd have more information to blackmail her with. If Robert was alive and she found him, she'd be a liability. They probably planned to take care of her at the same time or shortly after her ex-boyfriend.

Blood drained from her body.

She didn't know what to do, but she did know how to buy some time. She nodded.

A pleased smile spread across Tony's face.

"I'll look into it," she said.

Chapter Nine

"I can tell by your sarcastic undertones and no time for bullshit attitude that we're going to be friends."

~ *Raven Crawford*

Bands of tingling magic whispered against her skin and left her in the rundown hallway in an old apartment building. The threadbare, trodden carpet still smelled of stale popcorn, sweat and old man. After her Monday morning blackmail appointment, she'd planned to hit the bank and lift the burden of her atrocious debt from her shoulders, but when she'd actually met her blackmailer, plans changed. She refused to run to Cole with all her problems, but she wasn't going to stick her head in the sand or run off to do something stupid and misinformed. She needed someone's advice. Someone who also moved amid the underbelly of society and knew the exact position Tony held within the criminal world.

She took a deep breath, gagged, and knocked on Bear's door. She'd already texted her twin on the way over and he gave her a thumbs up. Though she wanted her brother's advice, she really just wanted to see him.

A few seconds later, which felt like eternity while holding her breath, the door swung open. Bear stood at the doorway and clear air laced with the smell of food washed over her. Dark hair, dark eyes and a large, muscular frame, Bear earned his nickname through appearance alone.

"Move." She pushed her way into his apartment and shouldered past him.

Kissa, Bear's demonic cat, screeched at her entrance and tore off to the bedroom. Some things never changed.

Bear shut the door and turned to her with an annoyed expression. "It's not that bad."

After a few gulps of clean air, she straightened and smiled. "You've grown accustomed to the stench. I think your building is getting worse."

He shrugged. "Inexpensive anti-theft device."

Born seven minutes and thirteen seconds before Raven, Bjorn "the Bear" Crawford arrived into this world with a chip on his shoulder. Already despising their absentee biological father from the Other Realms, he spent most of his life resenting his lack of magical inheritance.

Up until recently, he believed he hadn't received much of any supernatural ability—he couldn't shift into a fox like Mom and he couldn't "do any cool Underworld crap" like Raven. All he could do was call corvids to him, essentially making him the bird equivalent of a dog whistle—his term not hers. Turned out, his skill was coveted in the Other Realms and only the cusp of what he would learn to do. After the previous Corvid Queen, Lloth, abducted him, he discovered he could accomplish a lot more.

Bear was a private person by nature and his powers, or lack thereof, had always been a sensitive subject for him. He kept his new skills to himself, and Raven didn't push. Nobody did. They loved Bear no matter what powers he had or didn't have. Raven gleaned what he'd gained from observation alone.

The aroma of food intensified in her brain. "Poutine?"

Bear scowled. "Not according to Marcus."

"That's because he used regular packaged gravy instead of poutine sauce." Marcus walked into the hallway and draped his arm over Raven's shoulder. He leaned down and gave her a quick peck on the cheek. "Hey, Wenny."

Tall, lean and always smelling slightly of grease from his shop, Raven used to crush hard on her brother's best friend. Case and point, he was the only one who got away with calling her that ridiculous nickname. Though her crush had long since faded, it felt pointless to correct him now.

"Hey, Marcus." She looped an arm around his waist and squeezed.

"Sorry to break up this love fest." Bear scowled at them. "But poutine sauce *is* gravy."

Oh, for goodness sake. He was still stuck on that? She'd already moved on.

Marcus sighed and dropped his arm from Raven's shoulder. He turned and walked to the living room, leaving them to follow him.

"All poutine sauces are gravy, not all gravy is poutine sauce," Marcus said.

Bear growled.

"He has a point, Brother Bear." She held up her finger to stall his fake outrage. "We've all endured bad poutine."

"Gravy is French for sauce." Bear folded his arms.

"No, it's not." Marcus placed his hands on his hips. "Sauce is French for sauce."

Bear snapped his mouth shut and glared. He breathed heavily through his nose before speaking again. "Gravy is just a word referring to a sauce made from meat drippings. Ergo, poutine is made with cheese curds and gravy."

Raven turned her head side to side, her attention bouncing between the two men as they continued their spat. She didn't have time to watch television dramas anymore, so she may as well take a break from the stress of her reality and enjoy this moment.

"And again, I'm not refuting that, bro, but poutine must be made with a specific type of gravy—as in poutine sauce—and you didn't select the right kind. *Ergo*, this poutine sucks."

Bear needed to work on his death glare. Marcus didn't even twitch.

"I'm surprised you didn't grow a beard. You could've brought over a special comb to brush out the *gravy* after eating poutine," Bear said.

"Are you calling me a hipster?"

"A poutine snob."

"And we all have beards in your deranged imagination?"

Raven stepped between the men to pick up the empty gravy package on the counter. "You used chicken gravy?"

"Everyone's a fucking critic," Bear growled.

Raven shrugged. "I don't have a beard, either, so there goes your stereotype." Raven dropped the package beside the untouched plate of steaming poutine and turned to her brother and Marcus.

"I'm glad you're here, Marcus. I need to talk to you about something, too." Her brother's friend was lower on her priority list, but as Mom always said, no better time than the present.

The smug expression slipped from the mechanic's face and he glanced around the room. "Err..."

"Do witches ever take non-witch apprentices?"

His eyes widened and he rocked back on his heels. "Not what I was expecting, but no. Not that I'm aware of."

What in the Underworld was he expecting? And drat. She'd hoped for a different answer.

"Why do you ask?" Marcus shoved his hands in his pockets.

Bear grumbled and walked behind the counter. He picked up a plate of poutine and dumped the contents in the compost. The plate went in the dishwasher.

Marcus and Raven stared at each other, pointedly not looking at Bear while he cleaned up the defective poutine and definitely not commenting on it.

"I need to learn more about the magical power I wield," she said.

Marcus' eyebrows shot up. "I thought your big, bad dark fae boyfriend was teaching you."

Heat crept up her neck and cheeks. "Yes, but I want an unbiased vantage point."

Darkness clouded his vision. "If you can't trust him, why are you with him?"

More heat spread across her face.

Marcus scowled. "Don't answer that."

Bear opened the fridge and pulled out some beer.

"I know your mother already warned you about the seduction of the Underworld," Marcus spoke slowly, as if carefully selecting his words. "Dark fae are overwhelming, obsessive and know how to use their power and looks to enthrall mortals."

Cole was definitely overwhelming at times, and she

agreed with the obsessive part. He was heavy-handed and didn't consult with her when he thought he knew best. And although she'd heard countless stories of poor mortals seduced by dark fae for nefarious purposes, Marcus' last point didn't fit Cole. She'd tried to resist her magnetic attraction to him, but she never got the sense he tried to use that against her. If anything, he held himself back, letting her come to him.

Maybe she was just a sucker. Time would tell and hindsight was always 20/20.

"I do trust him," she said. "But our mom also raised us to not put all our eggs in one basket."

Bear pulled out a bottle opener and popped off the lids. He threw the opener back in the drawer, loudly, and slid it shut. Kitchen utensils clattered and bumped against each other. Was he still pissed about the poutine or had something else set him on edge?

"I think seeking additional opinions and alternate instruction is wise." Bear handed Marcus a beer and offered the other one to Raven.

She shook her head.

"Has he..." Bear frowned as if trying to find the right words and failed.

"Has he what?"

Bear shrugged and took a swig before speaking again. "Cole's knowledgeable and powerful, but if this has to do with what I think it does, your solution might lie in science or witchcraft from the Mortal Realm."

Marcus choked on his beer. With a forced swallow, he took another drink before commenting. "You're going to try to reinstall the barrier?"

Was he pleased or sad at the thought? Despite knowing him for almost her entire life, she couldn't read his expression right now. Wary, maybe.

She shook her head. She had no intention of recreating the divide that once separated the Mortal Realm from the Other Realms. "No, but I want to understand what it was. I need to put up something similar."

"Temporary or permanent?"

"Temporary."

His shoulders relaxed and his death grip on his bottle eased. So, Marcus wasn't a Closer. That was good. She couldn't handle two of her friends, her only two friends, secretly hating Otherkind.

Megan's face popped into her mind and her stomach sunk. Raven hadn't spoken to her best friend since she saw Megan wearing the symbol of Othila. An extremist group of mortals obsessed with segregation and the destruction of Others had appropriated the symbol from Viking runes for its representation of separation. Her ex had been a part of the group, and now it looked as though Megan had signed up for their hateful agenda as well.

Her stomach twisted harder and she mentally gave her head a shake. She had to deal with that at some point, but not right now. Raven narrowed her eyes at Marcus.

"So?" she asked.

"So what?"

"Is there some sort of school for the dark arts or Wiccan apprenticeship program for non-witches?"

Bear went back to the fridge and opened the door to the freezer. Cold air flowed around him as he stared at the contents.

Marcus sighed. "Not that I'm aware of, but I'll look into it for you. I'd offer to help, but I can't think of any spells or books that fit what you need."

She nodded. "Thanks."

Bear pulled out a box of frozen pizza and shut the freezer. "Are you poutine snobs up for pizza?"

"Of course," Raven said.

Marcus nodded.

"Rayray?" Bear didn't look at her and instead ripped open the box.

"Yes?"

"Why are you here? I know it's not for lunch, it certainly wasn't for poutine, and you didn't know Marcus was here until you arrived."

"I just wanted to hang out." And that was mostly true.

Bear waited.

"And I need some advice." She sidled up to the counter and sat on one of the counter-height stools.

"On what?"

"How to handle a bully."

Bear sucked in his breath. "Let me smash him."

She shook her head. "No. I need to handle this myself."

"What kind of bully?"

"The blackmailing kind."

Chapter Ten

"Life is short. Smile while you still have teeth."
~ Unknown, but also Raven's Mom

Full of pizza and Bear's advice, Raven walked to her local bank and formulated a strategic plan to check off her long list of tasks.

Show them your teeth. Raven repeated part of Bear's advice over and over as she turned down the street to her bank. She was pretty sure Cole's advice would be to just kill them all, but that didn't work with her conscience.

Before she could approach the building, a meaty

hand dug into her jacket and hauled her into the alley. Raven stumbled into the darker space and tripped over a garbage bag that had fallen to its side. She flung her hands out to break her fall and awkwardly rolled onto the pavement. *Ouch.*

"You should've killed me, bitch," a man snarled.

Raven squeaked and rolled over to see Frey stalking toward her with a long dagger in his hand. His curly brown hair framed his face and tumbled to his shoulders.

Her heart started to punch the inside of her ribcage, as if she needed a warning system of imminent danger. She scrambled to her feet, embraced her Other energy and called her scythe. The weapon snapped into her waiting hand in time to block Frey's first attack. The power of the weapon spread through her body. She danced out of the way and deflected Frey's strikes. He kept coming. Over and over again. Battering down her defences. He was strong. Raven was not.

She panted and ducked under a nasty swipe.

Should she call Cole?

Frey swung and missed lopping off her head.

The scythe flowed like blood in her veins. She pulled her essence and wove it around the scythe's magic, side-stepping Frey's attack as she did so. She became an eruption of power, forcing Frey back, beating him into submission.

"How did you find me?" she snarled. He didn't have a blood connection with her, and she didn't summon him.

"Locator spell." He swung at her again.

"You need to stop attacking me."

"Never, you whore!"

Ugh. What did her bedroom activities have to do with this guy trying to kill her? "Listen, you idiot. I will kill you."

Her next attack sent him sprawling back. He looked up at her, gaze wild and growled. He pulled out a lodestone, threw it on the ground, and stepped into the portal as soon as it opened.

She could've attacked him before he got away. Heck, she could've followed him. Instead, she watched the portal snap shut and fae magic dissipate and sighed in relief. Phew. Another day without killing something. Gold star for Raven.

She banished her scythe back to its corner and headed back to the bank. She swung open the door. The few people waiting in line looked over to the entrance, saw her, and froze. An elderly woman clutched her purse and a contractor straightened, eyes wide.

What was their problem? She took her phone out and used the camera to see what she looked like. Oh. That. Hair wild, scratches along her neck, and flushed face, she looked like she'd been out rolling in the trash cans out back. In a way, that wasn't far off.

Raven stuffed her phone away and used her fingers to smooth down her hair as best as possible. She joined the line for a teller and ignored the curious stares.

Make them realize it's too costly to mess with you,

Bear had said. Would that advice work for Frey as well? If he didn't fear possible death, was there any cost that would make him back down?

Raven tapped her foot and deliberated options for Tony and Frey. With everything automated these days, the bank didn't staff their front counter well and it took entirely too long for Raven to make it to the front of the line. At least she had time to think.

Lucy, her financial advisor, stood off to the side speaking with a co-worker. She glanced up and recognition flashed across her face.

Raven waved.

Lucy said goodbye to the co-worker and walked over to where Raven waited. "Ms. Crawford, how are you?"

"Much better since our last meeting." Last time they spoke, Lucy had confronted Raven with the harsh reality of her finances and the realistic life choices she'd have to make in order to claw her way out of debt to reach her, now-pointless, dream of a degree. "How are you?"

"I'm so glad to hear you're doing well. I'm fine. Thank you for asking. Is there anything I can help you with?"

Raven glanced at the one teller behind the counter and the older woman standing in front of Raven who now used her walker as a seat to get comfortable.

"Actually, yes." Raven turned back to Lucy. "I wanted to inquire about your Underworld to Canadian currency conversion rates. I couldn't find anything on—"

"Shh." Lucy's hand clasped onto Raven's arm. She pulled Raven out of the line and into her nearby office. After she shut the door, Lucy turned to Raven with wide eyes. "Are you crazy?"

Raven frowned. While some might pose solid arguments regarding her mental state, she highly doubted she'd lost it. All she wanted to do was check with the bank before going to the trolls to convert her money. Not only did she want to ensure she got the better deal, she didn't want to get ripped off. A number of internet searches didn't tell her a damn thing. "No...I don't think so."

"Do you want everyone to know you're Underworld royalty?" Lucy hissed. "The Mortal Realm is not a safe place for you."

Raven straightened. That was twice in one day someone felt the need to share a fact she was already well aware of. "How would they know that from my question? Plenty of people have business dealings with the Underworld. And wait...how did you know that?"

Lucy folded her arms and leaned back. "First, I wasn't completely sure, but you just confirmed it. Second, I always suspected. Your eyes kept doing weird things every time we discussed your loser of an ex-boyfriend, and three..." She took a deep breath. "Only Underworld royalty have enough coins worth converting. The mortals who do business across realms usually work solely in one currency or the other. The conversion rates suck, and they'd take too much of a financial hit with each transaction."

Raven's brain misfired and she had to go through Lucy's words one more time. An image of Robert's headless body surged up and made her stomach twist.

Show them your teeth.

Raven straightened her spine and lifted her chin. "Not true. Trolls also work with multiple currencies."

"Are you really trying to convince me you're a troll? And even if you were, trolls are also from the Underworld."

And there was a growing hatred for all things and beings from the Other Realms, Raven finished Lucy's unspoken words. She threw up her hands in defeat. "Does the bank convert Underworld coins?"

"Yes, but they'll flag your account and you'll find yourself audited and your funds seized."

Raven dropped her mouth open. "That's bullshit."

Lucy nodded.

"Are...are you going to report me?"

A genuine smile broke out across Lucy's face. "Of course not. I've been on your cheering squad since the moment we met. You're not the only one who's been screwed over by some loser."

Oh, thank baby Odin. Raven could use a friend.

Megan's face popped into her mind again, and the sinking feeling in her gut returned. Raven still didn't know what to do. Her friend had no idea Raven's biological father hailed from the Other realms, and Raven kept the secret from her their entire friendship.

Raven shoved thoughts of Megan to the side and

focused on the present. "What do you suggest I do?"

Lucy's expression was grim. "You'll have to go to the trolls."

Crap. That's what Raven was afraid she'd say.

Chapter Eleven

"I cannot afford to waste any time making money."
~ *Louis Agassiz*

Grease clamped onto her skin the second Raven stepped into the thick warmth of Dan's Diner. Meat sizzled on the grill, customers either barked or glared at each other, the oldies stations—soft listening for the over sixties—crooned over the static speakers.

Suzy looked up from a newspaper splayed open on the counter and frowned. "You're not scheduled on tonight."

"I know. Is Dan in?"

Suzy squinted at her. *Geez, woman.* It was okay to let another woman talk to your boyfriend. An image of Suzy and Dan bumping uglies in a sweaty heap popped into her brain. She shuddered. *Thanks for that one, brain.*

"He's in the back." She jerked her head toward the kitchen doors.

"Thanks." Raven dodged a bickering couple as they walked to the exit, too absorbed in their hot debate of whether 2020 or 2021 was the start of the next decade to notice they almost plowed her over.

Suzy tracked Raven's passage past the counter to the back of the restaurant but didn't say anything more. Okay, then.

Pushing through the swinging doors to the kitchen, Raven watched her step on the greasy floor. Dan had propped open the door to his single-desk office.

Raven clutched the envelope containing the tri-folded paper and walked into the office.

Shoved into a corner sat a small leather loveseat. Opposite of the dubious seating option was a desk crammed against the wall covered in stacks of paper and receipts. A man sat at the desk, his back to the door, hunched over his computer. His thin polyester blend shirt pulled tight over his broad back.

"Dan?"

The boss straightened, minimized the window and swiveled around in a seamless move more worthy of a ballet studio than a rundown diner in North Burnaby.

Pushing fifty, Dan would've been a handsome man twenty years ago, sixty pounds lighter with a full head of hair. Heck, he could still be considered handsome now, but there was something always slightly off in his expression. Mike said Dan had dead eyes, and it fit. Though Dan had never crossed any lines, not one single employee at Dan's Diner, not even Suzy who was banging him, would be surprised to learn he was a serial killer. He looked like one.

Images of blood and a severed head surged up like bad indigestion.

No, Dan might be a greasy, dead-eyed owner of a questionable establishment who looked like what everyone thought serial killers should look like, but if anyone in this room was a serial killer, it was Raven.

Well, now. Wasn't that a pleasant thought?

"Raven." Dan frowned and glanced at the schedule. The single fluorescent light gleamed off the top of his head. "You're not on today."

"No. I'm not." Raven pushed back her shoulders and held out the envelope. "I'm here to give you this."

Dan scowled and snatched the envelope from Raven's outstretched hand. "What is it?"

"My two weeks' notice," she said. "Thank you for the opp—"

"You're quitting?"

Raven snapped her mouth shut and nodded.

"You think you found something better?"

Dan didn't need to know she came into money. Nor did she owe him any explanations. "You could say that."

Dan's lips peeled back from his teeth. "You're a waste of good legs and nice tits. You could've really done something, but instead you're going to throw away any chance because you suddenly think you're too good for this place? You're not. You'll find out soon enough, but I won't take you back when you come crawling in here begging for a job."

Wow. That escalated quickly. Raven opened her mouth to respond, but Dan kept going.

"I worked around your schedule. I gave you nights off. I hired your useless brother. And this is how you repay me? Don't bother coming in for the rest of your shifts."

How dare he call her brother useless. He was worth more than this entire business. Banshee's bastard. Where had this come from? Mike and she had always been polite and respectful. She didn't deserve this lashing and Mike was too good for this sleaze to mention.

Dan wanted to screw her over, that was clear. Most people needed those two weeks of pay, especially if the next job didn't start right away. His decision to drop her shifts would've broke the bank if she was moving on to another low-paying job.

Yup, he was trying to financially ruin her. And he insulted her baby brother while doing it.

"That's a lot of words to say you have a small penis," she said.

Dan blustered. His face turned red and he shifted

his belly to stand up.

Raven reached over, clamped a hand on his shoulder and pushed him down. Luckily, gravity was on her side. "You're a worthless piece of shit. Have fun covering my shifts."

She turned and stomped out of the office.

"Come back here!" Dan stumbled to the doorway and yelled at her. "Your whole family is scum and we all know it. You should be taken out like the trash you are. Tell that worthless brother of yours he's fired, too."

Raven lifted her arm in the air and extended her middle finger to wave goodbye.

Chapter Twelve

"In my defence, I was left unsupervised."

~ *Raven, all the time*

Raven stepped into Mike's room and stopped in her tracks. What in the Underworld was going on here?

Mike looked up from the keyboard he hunched over and turned to her. Dark red hair and a lean frame hinted at his fox shifter nature, but her nineteen year old brother who attended university to become a software engineer had started to fill out in the last few months. His brown eyes with specks of gold focused at her as code continued to scroll along the double screens on the desk. "What's your problem?"

Raven took in his made double bed, freshly vacuumed carpet and organized desk. "I didn't know this room had a floor."

"Ha, ha."

"No, seriously. I forgot what colour it was."

Most people were surprised to learn natural foxes competed with skunks for the greatest stinker award. Not only did natural foxes secrete a pungent oil from their sweat glands, they used it as a cologne of sorts to identify themselves, convey their status in the skulk and mark their territory.

Fox shifters weren't quite as bad as natural foxes because they had their human nature to override the baser instincts of the fox, but some shifters, adolescent males, especially, struggled with personal hygiene.

Mom and Dad gave up trying to get Mike to keep his room clean long ago. For much of the same reason their parents left Raven to flounder and find her financial feet, the Crawford's believed in "hands off" parenting and let Mike wallow in his own filth. They were happy he showered, contained his fox-stinking tendencies to his room and didn't urinate in the house to mark his territory.

"What gives?"

Mike shrugged and turned back to his computer.

"No, seriously, Mike. What's up? This place is usually a cesspool."

"Maybe I'm comfortable with who and what I am

now that I no longer need to mark my territory."

That was a load of bullshit. Dad said he lived in filth until he met someone worth overriding the fox impulses for.

Raven froze. "You met someone, didn't you?"

Mike cringed. "No."

"Liar." He had a date yesterday and it must've gone well enough for him to be late picking her up. "Did you bring her back here for Sunday night dinner after meeting for coffee?"

"No."

"Did you want to, but couldn't, because of the state of your room? Or was it because of the family? Oooo! That woman who texted you when we were casing the Closer house. What was her name? Rebecca...Becky...Becka?"

Mike turned to her again and pushed away from the desk. "Don't."

"Don't what?" Nailed it. Her name was Becka.

"Don't do some psychotic big sister PI crap and scare her away."

Raven's grin grew all on its own. "Mikey's got a girlfriend."

Mike lunged from his seat and dove for her. She stepped out of the way. She might not be a natural fighter, but she'd tussled with brothers her whole life. It would take more than a half-ass tackle to take her down. "Shame, shame, double shame. Now I know your girlfriend's name."

"What are you, twelve? Please, drop this." Mike's

gaze frantically shifted side to side. He held out both arms in front of his body and waved them up and down as if trying to calm a wild animal. "And keep it down." His panicked gaze drifted over her shoulder to the door behind her. "I don't want Juni to know."

"What's it worth to you?" Raven pretended to examine her nails. She never really got the gesture. If she truly had zero fucks to give, she'd simply walk away or play on her phone, not examine her cuticles.

"I'll owe you."

Raven relaxed her fingers and shoved her hands in her pockets. "Deal."

Mike released a long pent-up breath and dropped his hands.

"And I'm going to collect on that favour right away."

Mike narrowed his eyes at her. "What did you do?"

"I quit my job."

Mike straightened. "At Dan's?"

Of course, at Dan's. They both knew she'd never quit the family business. Crawford Investigations for life. "Yup."

"Did you get a new job?"

"Nope."

"Did Dad get a bunch of new cases?"

"Nope." She rocked back on her heels. She hadn't converted her money yet, but she had to trust Cole would help get things done.

Grandma Lu's nagging voice joined Mom's in her internal dialogue in some off-beat song of clichéd life quotes: *Look before you leap. One bird in the hand. Dooooo dah. La, la, la.*

Maybe she should've waited before quitting.

Shit.

She definitely should've waited. Sure, she planned to meet Cole next to visit the trolls, but Mom practically raised the Crawford kids on the "One bird in the hand is better than two in the bush" motto. Mom's life lessons tended to surge up and kick Raven in the gut whenever she did something stupid.

Mike's mouth dropped open to form a perfect "O". "Did you lose your mind?"

"No, but I need to focus on my Underworld position right now and I need you to trust me on this."

"Okay..." Mike shifted his weight onto his other foot. His phone buzzed on the desk and a message bubble popped up on his screen. He didn't look over. In fact, he made a concerted effort not to glance at the screen and maintain painful eye-contact with her.

"Do you need to get that?" She jerked her chin in the direction of his phone.

"Nope. I'm good." Red crept up his face.

Oh, this was too good to pass up. She stepped toward his desk. "You sure? I could—"

Mike growled and stepped to the side to block her path.

Raven raised her hands in mock surrender. "Okay, okay. No need to go feral on me. Geez."

"Is there anything else you need?" Mike asked, voice strained.

"As a matter of fact, yes. I need you to research the barrier collapse and find out anything you can on the Closers and their plans. Do you still have access to Robert's computer?"

Mike's annoyed expression disappeared, wiped away by a face-splitting grin. Of course, he still had access.

"Can you search it for Closer stuff?"

"Will that be all, Your Highness?" Mike asked.

She jabbed him in the chest with a stiff finger and used his own phrase against him. "Don't."

Mike snorted and folded his arms across his chest.

"Have you been working out? Pumping some iron to impress the ladies?" She reached out and squeezed a bicep. He'd definitely been working out.

"No," he lied and brushed away her hand. "I would've done all of this for free, you know. You didn't need to trick me into some favour-owing set-up."

She cleared her throat and looked away. "Yeah, about that. This stuff isn't what I'm calling in for a favour."

Mike glowered.

"This is where that favour comes in." She wrung her hands together.

Mike waited, still glowering.

"You need to keep all of this from Mom and Dad—the job, the Closer search and what I tell you next."

Mike nodded.

"And you can't get angry."

Mike pursed his lips.

"And you have to trust me that I will fix it."

"Stop stalling and spit it out already."

Raven gathered magic around her for confidence. "I accidentally got you fired from Dan's."

Mike's eyes widened.

"After Dan got all feisty with me about my resignation, I *may* have insinuated he had a small dick and then he fired you. Don't go back. You don't have any more shifts." She wrapped the Other magic around her tighter and called to her next location. "Maybe hold off on more dates until I get things sorted out."

"Fuck, Raven," Mike growled. "I needed that job."

"I also flipped him off." Her magic carried her away. Yup, she definitely should've converted her money first before quitting and getting Mike fired. He would've been much more receptive to the news.

She didn't travel far, she only needed to get away from Mike before he lost his temper. Redheads, geez. She materialized in the alley behind the house and the cool air brushed over her skin. Mike's shrieks of outrage traveled from the house.

Cole looked up from a prone body lying at his feet. He flicked blood off a long dagger and straightened. His sour expression softened, and he stepped away from the dead person. "Shall we go to the trolls now?"

Chapter Thirteen

"Every man is guilty of all the good he did not do."

~ *Voltaire*

Raven remained frozen while Cole walked toward her. His black cape billowed behind him and whispered against the ground and dead body like a feathery parting kiss. He used a ripped piece of cloth to clean his blade and with a flick of his wrist made the deadly weapon disappear somewhere in his clothes.

Cole wore what Raven mentally referred to as his

casual assassin court clothes, the matte black armour and cape too fancy for the regular daily grind of an assassin, but not as flashy as the formal armour he wore to important court appearances.

Frankly, he could kill anyone at any time, no matter what he wore. And this look happened to be Raven's favourite.

He held his hand out to her. "Shall we?"

"Are we not going to talk about the dead guy?"

Cole raised a dark eyebrow. "Do you not remember where you portalled to?"

Raven glanced around and her stomach sunk. Of course, she remembered. They'd agreed to meet in the alley after she spoke to Mike. She whipped back to where the prone figure lay face down in a half-frozen puddle. A dagger lay a few inches from his outstretched arm.

"He planned to kill us?" A pointless question, really. The evidence clearly indicated an answer. Why else would a dagger-wielding stranger lurk in the alley behind her parents' home?

Cole's lip curled up. "He planned to try. This particular cut-throat was Lloth's nephew with perhaps a smidgeon of corvid essence. He likely hoped he had enough for the corvid mantle to pass to him after he ambushed you."

She gulped. "Exactly how many Others possess corvid energy in the Underworld?"

"Too many." Something dark flashed across Cole's expression. He stepped forward and slipped his hand around hers. "I will protect you."

"I want to protect myself," she said. "And my family."

He nodded. "And you will. I'm just a bandage you'll rip off and discard once you come into your own."

She squeezed his hand. "You promised to never let me go."

His smile was sad. "I did. And I won't."

"Then why do you look so sad?"

"Because, Einin, once you embrace your power and stand amongst the denizens of the Underworld, you'll realize there are beings more powerful than I."

"Like your father?"

He nodded.

"He dropped by the castle to kill me."

Cole barked out a short laugh. "He didn't have that kind of slaying in mind."

"He called me a toy."

"And he would've treated you as one." The shadows swirled around him, pulsing with anger. "Like he did my mother."

Oh. What could she say to that? She squeezed his hand again and let the silence fall around them.

"But I wasn't actually referring specifically to my father. There are others who will want you. They will seduce you and tempt you with offers of more power."

It was her turn to snarl. "They will try."

Cole pulled her into the heat of his body and slipped his hand up her neck to cup her face.

"Seriously, Cole. They can try, but they're not you.

All I want is you."

"A bastard with the lowly title of lord. You could do better than me. There are those that can offer higher, better connections."

"I don't care about your connections, parents' marital status when you were born or conceived. And I definitely don't care about your titles, Cole. Now shut up and kiss me."

Cole smiled and leaned down. His full lips pressed against hers in an almost chaste kiss.

"Let's visit the trolls tomorrow." She growled against his lips.

He laughed, kissed her again and showed her how the dark fae could seduce the common sense out of the most sensible mortals.

Chapter Fourteen

"Knowledge is knowing a tomato is a fruit. Wisdom is not putting it in a fruit salad. Philosophy is wondering if that means ketchup is a smoothie."

~Unknown philosopher

Raven should be researching how to block portals, but the Lord of War hadn't been around to nag her for a progress report and she wanted to get her finances sorted first. If blocking mortals from the Underworld somehow incapacitated her, or Bane killed her for failure, at least her family would be taken care of.

The air outside the troll domain smelled fresh and clean, like an unspoiled forest with a fast-moving stream of mountain run-off flowing through the middle. The surroundings gave no indication they were about to enter the section of reality controlled by the trolls. Cole had explained how this domain was a little different than the others, how it existed between the Mortal Realm and the Underworld, kind of like the Shadow Realm, but instead of filling the spaces in between, it was more like a dark, murky tunnel.

It didn't look or smell like a tunnel, so Raven struggled with Cole's analogy and once again cursed her own ignorance.

Chin up, Crawford. You'll figure this out.

In addition to the troll domain acting like a tunnel, mortal realm phones worked occasionally and fae magic was inconsistent and unreliable. Trolls considered portalling into their land a mortal offence and killed any offender without a trial, but portalling out was considered a hasty departure bordering on rude, not worthy of murder.

As they picked their way down a path made more for mountain goats than humans, Raven debated whether the risk of the portalling death sentence was worth it.

"What do you know of the jotun?" Cole stepped over a log and paused to offer his hand to help her over.

She took his hand, even though she could've easily hopped over on her own. "The who?"

"Trolls. They're known as the jotun. This is the

name they identify with. What do you know about them?"

"Aside from what you just told me about their realm tunnel thing, which I still don't quite get, by the way."

"Yes, aside from that."

"I'm well aware of their greedy monopolization of the only physical point of access to and from the North Shore, their ruthless enforcement of bridge tolls, and their capitalization on reg vulnerability, dependency on physical transportation and lack of power."

Cole's lips twitched. "Besides all that."

"Not much. I don't like how they take advantage of powerless regs."

"Trolls are often very misunderstood."

"Ooooo. Do I get a lesson?" She batted her eyelashes at him.

"Yes, you do."

He stepped over another log and when she shook her head at his offered hand, waited for her to clamber over. "The jotun are offspring of Ymir, the primordial giant from your Norse legends."

"Is that where the whole giant troll idea came from?"

Cole nodded.

"I remember reading some old, pre-collapse books that said trolls were giants and wondered how they could've gotten them so wrong."

Cole shrugged. "Those legends were recorded before the barrier collapsed, as you said, but there's always some grain of truth. The legends and myths are steeped from reality, but a lot of misinformation was spread. If you heard a giant had children, wouldn't you assume they were giants, too?"

"Point taken. Please continue."

"Also contradictory to some mortal realm legends, Ymir's body wasn't used to create the world as you know it. His skull didn't become the sky, nor his flesh the earth. His blood didn't form the seas or lakes and his teeth and bones are not the mountains. Instead, when Odin bested him in battle, his body broke apart and created the original jotun."

"So, he didn't really die?"

"More like reborn."

That didn't match with the basic history she'd learned in school or what she'd read online. "I'm confused."

"You have to remember, the world before the barrier collapse was infused with folklore, mythology and religion based on the echoes of reality from the Other realms. As I mentioned before, there's a lot of misinformation still out there. Sometimes understanding is easier if you forget what you think you know and start fresh."

That didn't sound daunting. No, not at all. "Why did Odin and Ymir battle?"

Cole shrugged again. "Why do any gods fight?"

"Power?"

"Exactly. Once Odin defeated Ymir, he assumed control of the Underworld and to this day rules the jotun and the dark fae lords.

"The jotun have never taken to Odin's command. They multiplied in numbers and have their own black magic as a source of power. They are not content with the status quo and constantly push back against Odin's rule and the dark fae." He turned and offered his hand to Raven again.

She slipped her hand in his.

"You must remember that, Einin." He pulled her close. "The jotun have no love for our kind, especially Odin and those who carry his blood."

She gulped. "And you're voluntarily walking into their domain with Odin's granddaughter?"

He smiled and nodded as if this decision made perfect logical sense. "In dark fae, troll translates to magic. The jotun represent not just magic, but more specifically, the forces of chaos within magic."

"Chaos," she whispered. "Like your grandfather."

Cole's mouth moved into a tight smile. "My grandsire is the embodiment of everything the jotun understand and admire. We have a similarity. I'm the product of chaos and they wield the chaotic forces of nature."

Raven might know little about the jotun, but Cole had nothing in common with them. She pondered on the information he shared with her. "I thought troll translated to monster or fiend or something like that." Her translations seemed more fitting.

"Maybe in one of your ancient dialects it did. To the dark fae, raw nature is synonymous with fiends and monsters. In fact, the dark fae believe they represent culture and civilization, the antithesis of the jotun. They are constantly at war with them as well."

Cole stopped along the bank of a slow-moving river and turned to Raven once again. "Do you feel that? Can you sense them?"

Raven shook her head. "My hair isn't even curling. Maybe they're too far away?"

Cole shook his head. "The jotun are not dark fae, remember. They're Otherworlders, but their energy and power are different. Close your eyes. Extend your magic outward. Try to feel where the environment around you feels more potent and rough. It might vibrate more for you."

Raven closed her eyes and followed Cole's directions. She reached inside and found her corvid essence, now completely entwined with the shadow magic she inherited with her crown. Instead of embracing the power and pulling it forward to burst apart into a new form, she sent her magic outward, like letting water slip through her fingers. Thin wisps of power danced along the rocks of the path and caressed the trees and leaves. She knew precisely where Cole stood, even with her eyes closed. His power intensified and called to her own. Dark, potent, like an endless abyss, her magic wanted to explore the depths and run along his skin.

Cole sucked in a breath. "Focus, Einin."

"I like how our magic feels together." She trailed whisper-like tendrils of power along his chest.

"Einin," Cole growled. "This is not the place to feel

me up."

She was going down, not up...but whatever. She abandoned Cole and the tempting pull of his energy and pushed her power outward again. It crashed against a heavily vibrating rock—prickly, raw, rough...wrong.

Raven gasped, pulled her magic back and opened her eyes.

A large boulder along the side of the path rumbled. She poked it with her magic.

Cole shook his head and grimaced. Did he pull a muscle in his face?

The boulder rolled and unfolded—there wasn't really any other way to describe it. The circular rounded sandstone morphed into a gray-skinned troll. His thin upper lip peeled back in a scowl to reveal uneven teeth and black gums. Two ribbed horns protruded from his temples and his black-eyed glare focused on her.

With a twisted body and gangly wart-covered limbs, the troll only stood to Cole's shoulders, yet, radiated fiendish brutality. She refused to look down where vine-like fuzz covered his genitalia. Nope. Not eyeing troll junk today.

She had no wish to call him on the nasty look he gave her or pick a fight. She'd never come across a troll outside a toll booth, but stories spoke of their vicious behaviour when crossed. No thank you. She liked her limbs where they were.

The troll flicked his oversized ears and rounded his

humpback to study her while looking pissed-off at the same time.

She glanced at Cole. He shook his head and chuckled as if he followed her entire mental dialogue. He probably did. He read her like she read smutty romance novels—with voracious focus.

Cole turned to the scowling troll. "Greetings, Nerthach."

Nerthach's lips peeled back even farther...in a smile? A deeper scowl? Raven couldn't tell.

"Why are you here, Camhanaich? And why did you bring a play toy?"

"I'm no one's toy." Swinging her scythe at the troll to wipe away his smug grin would feel really good right about now. Maybe she should summon the weapon now.

Cole placed his hand on her shoulder and shook his head.

Oh, for fuck's sake.

The troll smirked. "Why else would you come to this place to magically grope the grandson of Chaos?"

Heat raced up her neck and face. Well, fuck. She hadn't realized others could follow her magical fondling. She glanced at Cole again. He nodded and his lips twitched.

Odin's pink poke hole, he was trying not to laugh at her.

She placed her hands on her hips.

His shoulders shook.

Gah.

She focused on the troll and fixed him with her best death stare. "I'm not a toy. I'm the Corvid Queen and I'm here to complete a transaction. Camhanaich has been kind enough to act as my guide."

If it were possible for the troll to appear anymore hostile, this one basically flipped the switch to vibrate with hatred.

What was his problem?

"Odin's granddaughter."

Oh. Yeah. That.

She took a deep breath before continuing. "More like freakish daughter of his creation, but yes."

"Creation versus birth carries no difference to us, halfling," the troll spat. "You are of his blood and he's claimed you. You represent his house." His tone left no room for misinterpreting his feelings about that.

"Something you should keep in mind in your dealings with the Corvid Queen," Cole interjected.

The troll stiffened and dipped his chin.

Great. Point for her team, but it felt like a loss somehow. She flicked her long black hair off her shoulders and straightened. Caving to the hatred, trying to play nice, or revealing her insecurities wouldn't be a good idea right now. She had to appear strong, collected and borderline sociopathic or the trolls would try to manipulate her.

"Is it a large transaction?" the troll asked, his tone not quite as condescending as before, but not exactly friendly, either.

"Yes," Cole said.

The troll's expression closed down, resembling more of his rock form than his mobile one. "Follow me."

Chapter Fifteen

"You're only given a little spark of madness. You mustn't lose it."

~ *Robin Williams*

Raven and Cole followed Nerthach the troll as he herded them through a series of underground tunnels until the last one opened into a cavernous room.

A rotund troll with similar features to Nerthach turned at their entrance. He gulped down whatever he was eating. His gaze bounced between Raven and Cole, his scowl deepening with each bounce. Maybe he hated dark fae on sight. Maybe he'd already met Cole, and she was guilty by association. Or maybe he already knew who she was.

"Camhanaich," the troll spat.

Guess that answered one question.

"Gwawrddur." The name rolled off Cole's silken tongue with ease while Raven still contemplated how in the Underworld she'd spell that. Let alone how she'd tie her tongue in knots trying to pronounce this troll's name.

"I thought we had a business relationship," Gwawrddur grumbled.

"We did," Cole said. "And we still do. Though your son's welcome suggests otherwise."

The troll cast Nerthach a dismissive look. "They say my children were sprung from the Highlands of the Underworld. Do you know what they say about me?"

Who was "they?" Historians? Dark fae paparazzi? The gods? Raven waited, sensing a story. She liked stories and this guy didn't need or want a response anyway.

"The Y Gododdin says I glutted black ravens on the ramparts of Odin's stronghold," Gwawrddur growled.

That threat wasn't even subtle.

Gwawrddur scowled. "The translator equated ravens with my enemies." He turned to her then, finally acknowledging her presence. "And he wasn't wrong."

Oh, this got better and better. Nothing like quoting the oldest surviving Welsh poem in history that contained elegies to a bunch of warriors to liven up the intimidation factor.

"Yet, you brought her here," Gwawrddur continued. "The Queen of Corvids and granddaughter of Odin. Yes, I know who she is. I don't need my idiot son to tell me."

"You can call me Raven," she said. She whipped her magic out and stretched it through reality. The scythe pulsed and waited. She gripped the cold shaft with her power and tugged the weapon to her side.

Gwawrddur and Nerthach hissed and shrank away from the Scythe of Corvids. Silence descended on the cavern, a slow drip of water acting as percussion somewhere down one of the many off-shooting tunnels that led away from this awkward encounter.

The scythe continued to pulse with magic, and she relished having the weapon in her hand again. Her power vibrated and intensified. That weird awareness, the one gifting her the ability to fight like a battle-hardened warrior, rolled through her veins. The weapon yearned for release.

Just a little slaughter, it begged.

"So, it's true." Gwawrddur glared at Cole. "You're backing her."

"Yes." Cole's shadows pooled around the room. "And we wish to make a transaction. We have no quarrel with you."

So much more was going on here, but she knew better than to start spouting off all the questions popping into her head.

"How much?" Gwawrddur asked.

"Three million Canadian."

Raven almost squeaked. She swallowed the involuntary reaction and choked on the air.

The men turned to her with varying looks—Cole's amusement, Gwawrddur's annoyance and Nerthach's anger.

She cleared her throat and nodded.

"That will cost six million gold," Gwawrddur said.

If Raven's eyes could pop out of her skull, they would've flown across the room.

"You're being petty. Three point five," Cole said.

"You're being unrealistic. Five point nine."

"Now you're just insulting me. Four, or we walk."

"Go ahead," Gwawrddur snorted. "What's the alternative? Do you think you can get a better deal through one of those banks? Four point five or we start charging stupid tax."

"Deal." Magic whipped around the room, binding the words like a written contract.

Cole turned to Raven. "You're up."

Instant sweat sprung from her pores and her hands grew clammy. She took a deep breath and reached for her magic again, this time using it to reach through the realms and past her vault's defences to access her fortune instead of her scythe.

After their playtime in the coin room earlier, Cole had shown her how to group the money and made her practice how to haul stacks of coins from place to place.

She looped her magic around the piles of

Underworld gold, threading and weaving shadow and corvid essence until it laced together and formed a secure magical mesh. Once completed, she tugged, and the gold appeared in the room. She released her magic and the power flittered away, sparkling in the under lit room. A wave of dizziness flowed through her. Cole gripped the back of her arm to steady her. She blinked a few times to clear the waves and straightened.

The trolls scowled, apparently unimpressed with her success. They didn't appear to notice Cole's helping hand. Thank baby Odin.

She wanted to beam or jump up and punch the air with pride, but she couldn't. She had to remain stiff and formal and let these feral creatures believe hauling four point five million Underworld gold coins was no big deal to her.

"It's done," Gwawrddur spat.

Huh? How was it done? Where were the black duffel bags stuffed full of Canadian hundreds?

"The money is wired to your account," Nerthach said, tone dry enough to turn grapes into raisins.

"I didn't provide you with my banking information," she said.

"We don't need it," Nerthach said, holding up a tablet. "We're connected to every financial institution across the globe."

Raven dug out her phone from her back pocket. "I'd like to confirm."

The trolls hissed in unison.

"You question our integrity?" Nerthach said.

"No, I'm confirming. I've never completed a transaction with you before and I'm not going to leave four point five million gold coins with you and walk away." She clicked on her banking app and the account summary page popped up.

The balance stared back at her. She sucked in a breath. That's a lot of money.

Don't squeal. Don't squeal.

She took a screen shot and swiped the screen away.

A text message from Bear popped up on the screen before she put her phone back in her pocket. She hit the icon and read the message.

The trolls are the source behind the shell company Robert paid off before joining the Closers.

The blood drained from her face. A few months ago, she discovered her ex-boyfriend, Robert, remortgaged his home and dropped a large sum of money on a faceless shell company before he started disappearing on mysterious monthly excursions with the Closers. Bear couldn't find any direct link between the Closers and this shell company, but they knew they had to be connected because of the timing.

The Closers were bad news. In addition to their hate, they had possessed the amulet of Othila that blocked dark energy and brought Raven to her knees. Even the Lord of War got his panties in a bunch when the group was mentioned.

If the trolls were behind the company, it meant the trolls either led or financed the Closers. Or both.

Her blood cooled. Bad news just got worse.

"Is everything okay?" Gwawrddur asked.

She shoved her phone in her back pocket and forced her mouth into a smile. "The money is in place. Our transaction is complete."

Gwawrddur and Nerthach grunted.

Cole frowned at her but instead of asking a whole lot of awkward questions in front of their audience, he wrapped his arm around her waist and carried her away with his shadows.

Chapter Sixteen

"While most puns make me feel numb, mathematics puns make me feel number."

~Unknown, probably a mathphobe

Raven's family gathered around the table and waited for the bomb to drop. With Cole leaning against the wall, her entire heart sat in this room. And it wasn't even Sunday night.

Mom, still wearing her fall office attire, poured herself three fingers of whiskey and swallowed it in two gulps.

"You paid off our mortgage?" she rasped.

"Yes. I paid the mortgage. I paid off my bank loans. I paid Mike's tuition and set up college accounts for Mike and Juni."

They blinked at her.

Someone say something. Anything. Sweet baby Odin, this was torture.

"I guess I can forgive you for getting me fired from that health hazard diner, then..." Mike grimaced. He must've shouted some pretty foul things at her as she portalled away. He looked very guilty.

"Sweetheart, it's not that we're not thankful..." Mom started. "We are. Immensely. We just have so many questions." Mom set her empty glass down on the coaster and looked wishfully at the source bottle.

"This is quite a surprise," Dad said.

"Well, I'm stoked. Any chance I can get a clothing allowance, too?" her sister asked.

"Juni!" Mom hissed.

Juni shrugged.

"What did this cost you?" Bear asked. His grim face, brooding body posture and clenched hand indicated he wanted to break something instead of celebrate.

"Aside from an atrocious exchange rate, nothing." She paused to fight back the nausea from a surprise attack of memories involving lots of Lloth's blood. Gaining the former Corvid Queen's vault of gold cost her a little of her soul. She had to take a life to gain entry after all. Sure, Lloth had planned to kill Raven and she'd acted in self-defence, but the memories still plagued her at inconvenient times. "Nothing I hadn't already paid."

They blinked at her again.

This wasn't going the way she planned.

"The money came with the Corvid Queen title. I inherited a vault full of gold," she said. "If there's any perk to my job, it's that I can take care of you guys."

"That *job* may cost you your life," Bear snarled.

Juni's face paled. "I'd rather have you alive than a clothing allowance," she whispered.

"Or tuition free school," Mike added, his mouth flattening into a thin line.

"Well, quitting isn't an option, okay?" Raven said. "I don't have a choice. I'm already the queen. There's a high probability I won't hold up my end of the bargain I made with Bane. Even if I somehow survive that, I will constantly face the dangers and assassination attempts that come with the position. I may very well die, and then all that gold in the vault will go to my murderer. At least, this way, regardless of what happens to me, I know you will be all right. I know..." She broke off, her last word a half-sob. She took a deep breath and with a shaky voice, she continued. "I'll know at least something good will come from all of this."

"If anything happens to you, we will not be *all right*," Mom hissed.

"Financially." Raven ran her hand through her hair. "I thought I was doing a good thing. I thought we could have something to celebrate. I set up a trust fund as well, so if the worst does happen, you'll inherit some of the money instead of it all going to the next Corvid Queen."

"Your murderer," Bear growled.

"It is what it is," she said, suddenly weary with thoughts of her bed plaguing her mind. Maybe she should've waited for tomorrow to tell them, but she'd been excited to share the news. "You guys are a serious buzz kill, you know that?"

"Won't you need to keep some to grease those fae elbows in the Underworld?" Juni asked.

"I'm not sure they grease elbows, but don't worry about that. There's plenty of gold left in the vault."

They blinked at her again. Trust her family to be the only family pissed off to find out their financial woes had been taken care of.

Argh. She loved them all so much. "I don't have what you guys have to offer this family. Let me do this."

"What in the Underworld is that supposed to mean?" Mom snarled.

"I'm not the brilliant one, like Mike, or clever like Dad, or strong like Bear, or fierce like you, Mom."

"Um, hello?" Juni waved.

She smiled. "Or sassy like Juni."

"You're the full deal," Mike said to Raven, expression serious.

Huh?

"Don't you get it?" Mike said. "You have a little of everything."

That was a funny way of saying a whole lot of

nothing, or only somewhat smart...

"You're the well-rounded one," Mike finished.

"Resilient," Mom said.

"Loyal," Dad said.

"A pain in the ass," Juni and Bear said at the same time. They looked at each other and high-fived. Ugh. Siblings. The only enemies she couldn't live without.

"Does this make it easier for you?" Dad asked. He'd been fairly quiet through the whole exchange. "Does knowing we're taken care of and you've helped us financially make facing the dark fae nobility, all the dangers and the unknown easier?"

"Immensely," she said. *Please don't fight this.*

Dad took two steps to reach her and wrapped his arms around her. "Thank you, Rayray."

Mom's arms were suddenly around them both. Her whiskey breath brushed Raven's face. "We're so proud of you."

"Group hug!" Juni bulldozed into them from the side. She looked at the remaining people in the room. "Get in here."

Mike chuckled and joined in.

"I'm good," Bear and Cole said in unison and then proceeded to glare at one another with their arms crossed.

Oh, family time. It was the best.

Chapter Seventeen

"Do not judge my story by the chapter you walked in on."

~ Unknown, also Raven Crawford

The cool air wrapped around Raven and tickled her nose as she left the house. She shot a short text to her friend, Megan, to see if she wanted to go for coffee. With the bills taken care of and no waitressing shifts to run off to, Raven could focus on the four outstanding items on her "to do" list—prepare for ominous dark fae council meeting, figure out how to fulfill her promise to Bane by blocking mortal movement to the Underworld, confront Megan about her Closer membership and find Pepe.

With her main, credible source of information and tutelage, Cole, off to tend to his own business, the first two items would have to wait. That left the latter two, one of which she wanted to avoid. Megan was her best friend and the idea she could be secretly or not-so-secretly a hater of Others hurt Raven's heart.

Maybe she should focus on locating Pepe instead. He'd been missing for more than five days and no one had delivered a ransom note or demands for his return.

As if receiving a subliminal message, an elderly woman hobbled along the sidewalk in front of her parents' house and paused to scowl at Raven and the house. Revealing her glaringly white dentures along with her hatred, Mrs. Humphreys continued on her way.

Perfect.

Raven crossed the yard, stepped onto the same sidewalk and shut the gate to her parents' place.

"Mrs. Humphreys," Raven called out.

The old woman froze. Her head ducked down and she hunched her shoulders forward, apparently stuck between proper etiquette and disgust.

The woman's hatred would overrule polite neighbourly behaviour, but before Mrs. Humphreys could come to her familiar decision, Raven walked up behind the woman and placed a hand on the gate to her yard. "A moment of your time."

Mrs. Humphreys slowly turned to Raven. Her gaze

darted between Raven's face and the gate.

That's right bitch. You have to talk to me.

With thin pale wrinkled lips, a large nose with large pores, and blue eyes that bordered on white, Mrs. Humphreys stood at five foot nothing and appeared frail and weak. Raven would normally scold someone, anyone, who tried to intimidate or harass an elderly person. But this was Mrs. Humphreys. This woman had set traps in her yard when the Crawfords moved in next door with the hopes of catching her parents along with Raven's nine and six-year-old siblings in their fox form. Children. She wanted to catch children like vermin. Those traps could've snapped Mike or Juni's necks at that age.

Mrs. Humphreys may have missed out on catching a fox shifter, much to her dismay, but she caught a lot of other animals in those traps. The old woman had little care for the innocent raccoons, squirrels and cats she caught and killed instead. She'd also called animal control and the cops for "vermin sightings," "rampant pest infestations" and "suspicious behaviour" so many times the whole family lost count.

Even Mike. And that boy was obsessed with numbers and kept records on everything.

Mrs. Humphreys might be a contender for the monthly pin-up model of an elderly magazine, but inside, housed beneath her paper-thin skin and wrapped around her frail bitter bones, she hid a hateful, spiteful and cruel soul.

"Let me pass," Mrs. Humphreys hissed through her

lips.

"After you tell me what you did with Pepe."

The old woman scowled and narrowed her near-blind eyes at Raven. "Who?"

"My dad's goat. What did you do with him?"

The old woman scoffed, a cruel smile twitching her lips. "I had nothing to do with that walking meal going missing, but I'm glad it's gone. Foul creature." She leaned in. "I'm only sad the person who took him didn't invite me to the cookout." She smacked her lips, closed her eyes and moaned.

Raven recoiled and took a step back. "You're a truly heartless woman."

"And you will rot for the disgusting perversion of nature you are." She jabbed her forefinger in the air toward Raven. "We know what you are. We see you coming and going in the shadows accompanied by the Underworld spawn. You will get what you deserve. Retribution is coming and all the Others will feel the true wrath of regs."

"If you know what I am, then I guess there's no point in hiding, is there?" Raven called her power to her. Fueled with the rising anger inside, dark fae energy swirled around her and the scythe materialized in her hand.

Mrs. Humphreys' eyes widened, and she took a step back. For the first time in the history of Crawford-Humphreys confrontations, the woman appeared genuinely scared.

"Your day of reckoning is also coming, old woman,

and you've forgotten who controls the passage to the Other realms." Raven gripped the scythe and leaned forward. "You will stop harassing my family." She swung the blade slowly, so the edge hovered in the air a foot away from the woman's neck. "You will leave them alone. If you don't, just remember, elderly or not, I will not spare you and you will not get to stick around to see anyone conquer the Others."

The woman's lips trembled.

"And if I find out you stole or hurt Pepe, you will experience what my wrath feels like."

"I didn't take the stupid goat," Mrs. Humphreys spat. She flung out her arm and pointed down the street. "Why don't you ask that hoity-toity neighbour of yours what happened and leave this old woman alone."

Raven banished her power and the scythe disappeared—returning to its position in the corner of her bedroom to act as a bra-holder. Luckily, it hadn't appeared with any of her undergarments since that one time.

Raven took another step back, away from Mrs. Humphreys' gate. The old woman, collected her hatred and confidence, lifted her chin, swung her gate open and shuffled up her walkway toward her front door.

Raven turned in the direction Mrs. Humphreys had pointed and considered the two-storey house on the other side of her parents' property, asking, for the second and no less disturbing time, what would a nudist want with a goat?

Raven stepped toward Tarzan's home and her

phone vibrated.

Megan.

Her bestie had replied to her text. *Can't. Got plans. Rain check?*

Raven hesitated. Megan's plans usually revolved around her kids' nap time, her yoga class and any outing that involved wine and friends.

Raven checked the time on her phone. Unless Theo changed his schedule, it wasn't naptime. It wasn't yoga time. And drinks with friends happened in the evening after everyone got back from work and Megan's husband could look after the kids.

It was Wednesday.

A chill ran along Raven's spine. Wednesday had been a regular meeting time for Closers.

Busy on a Wednesday? Coincidence?

Raven's PI training and experience taught her coincidences were rare and most often not the case. Last time Raven followed a Closer, they'd led her to a house in the Hastings-Sunrise area. After they'd rescued Mike from her belligerent ex, Robert, she'd returned to the house with Cole only to find it abandoned. And it stayed that way as if the Closers suspected the place was now under surveillance.

Raven changed direction on the sidewalk and trotted down the walkway to her home. Her stomach twisted in a knot. Pepe's whereabouts remained a mystery, but she couldn't pass up the opportunity of finding the new Closer meeting location, even if it meant following her best friend.

A gust of air blasted past her, carrying the scents of exotic winter blooms from the Underworld. She spun around and called her scythe back from its resting place.

"Arrrgggghhhh." Frey ran at her, a weapon resembling a supersized medieval pickaxe hoisted above his head. His brown curly hair bounced with each crushing stomp on the sidewalk.

She side-stepped and deflected the blow. Instead of fear gripping her heart, annoyance spread through her body. When would this guy give up? And why now? She didn't have time for this. She needed to get to Megan's house in time to follow her.

Frey continued to attack her, and she continued to dance out of the way. She reached for her magic. Instead of embracing it or using it to shift or portal, she sent it outward, wrapping it around the large fae. Bands of black and purple magic wound around Frey. Huh. She wasn't sure that would work. She spun the corvid magic around the fae, weaving in threads of her newly acquired shadow magic. Around and around and around.

"You bitch!" Frey snarled.

She slapped magic across his mouth.

Frey struggled against the binding, bucking back and forth. He toppled over and thrashed on the sidewalk.

She knelt beside him. "I don't have time for you to kill me today."

Opening a portal to the Corvid Court, she pushed

Frey through the gateway with her magic. Hopefully, if she did things right, he'd end up in the dungeon. Maybe some time cooling off in a near-empty fortress would give him some much-needed clarity.

Chapter Eighteen

"We've all met someone who speaks fluent bullshit."
~ Raven Crawford

Ice cold slush splattered the feathers of Raven's conspiracy as she hunkered the birds down outside a house in North Burnaby that overlooked the inlet.

As far as Raven knew, Megan didn't have any friends in this area, and the diverse crowd of norms filing into the cozy dwelling with a large bay window confirmed Raven's suspicions—Megan attended a Closer meeting.

The cold dreary weather matched the sinking feeling threatening to overwhelm the entire conspiracy. Why? Or more realistically, what? What would bring Megan to join such a hateful group? She understood Megan's concern for her children as much as someone without children could, and she definitely understood fear of the fae, as she held her own healthy dose for the calculating and often cruel and malicious group of Others. But this?

Answering fear with hate and murder and attacks?

Megan wasn't a bigot. She didn't hate blindly, so this just didn't make any sense. Unless...unless she didn't know her friend as well as she thought, or Megan had somehow successfully hidden that part of herself all these years.

Raven couldn't get mad at that, either. It wasn't as though she hadn't kept her own secrets.

Megan skipped down the front steps, light on her feet as if relieved from whatever weight she'd divested from her shoulders and shared with her group of fellow Other haters.

Raven gathered her birds and sent them aloft into the dark and dreary day to find their way to Megan's house. Before she lost her nerve to confront her friend and unearth both their secrets. The only awful unknown was whether Raven would still have a friend at the end of the day, or another enemy.

Raven sat in the dark living room in a borrowed sweatshirt—she still hadn't mastered keeping her clothes when she shifted into a conspiracy—and waited for Megan to enter the house, close the door and flick on the lights. It wasn't nighttime yet, still early afternoon, but the dreary gloom outside blocked the sun and cast the Lower Mainland in darkness.

Megan must've made a stop before heading home because Raven not only had time to change, but to call Cole on Megan's home phone. She'd told him about Frey in the dungeons and he'd laughed and laughed. And then assured her the homicidal maniac was stuck there. He promised to send over one of his staff to "take care of the details." Hopefully, that just meant securing Frey and feeding him.

Megan turned the deadbolt on the front door.

"Hello, friend," Raven said.

Megan yipped and spun around. With wide eyes, she clutched her chest with her hand. "Raven! For Banshee's sake, you scared me."

Funny, Megan scared Raven a bit, too. Sure, Raven could use some practice delivering a surprise greeting, but Megan's recent activities and the absence of her much-loved family concerned Raven.

"Where's the family?" she asked.

"My mom took them for the day to give me a break." Megan set her purse on the nearby stand, hung up her coat in the hallway closet and stepped farther into the living room. "What are you doing here?"

Raven pushed herself out of the plush couch

cushions and stood. "We need to talk."

Megan folded her arms. "About how you've been lying to me our entire friendship or about how I joined the Closers?"

Raven stepped back, her calves bumping the couch. "B...both?"

Megan nodded and walked past Raven and into the kitchen. "This will take some wine."

Raven stumbled after her friend, her feet suddenly heavy and numb at the same time.

"How long have you known?" Raven asked,

Megan didn't answer right away. Instead, she set two large wine glasses on the table and opened the fridge to pluck a bottle of white from inside. She walked back to the table, twisted the cap off the bottle and proceeded to pour generous portions.

"Since I dated Bear."

"He told you?" She'd kill him. She'd rip his—

"He said nothing, but I figured it out."

Raven dropped her plans to kill her brother, but then her brain short-circuited. Megan dated Bear in high school. "You've known this entire time?"

Megan nodded and finished pouring the wine— almost to the brim and well past the standard five ounces.

"How?"

"Bear's eyes."

Odin's nutsack. Other eyes bled out during intense emotions, most notably when the individual became aroused. The news that Bear's interest in her best friend outed them both shocked and disgusted Raven. Ew.

"Why didn't you say anything?" she asked.

Megan plucked the wine glass from the table and took a long drink. "Why didn't you?"

Raven sighed and pulled out a chair to sit down. Her butt hit the thin cushion. "I was raised to keep my mouth shut and my powers hidden. The Mortal Realm is not a welcoming place for Others."

"And later? When we were older. Why not tell me then?"

Raven shrugged. "Old habits die hard, I guess. It never seemed like the right time and I worried I'd lose you as a friend, especially after you started collecting Regulator pamphlets and spouting anti-Other sentiments."

Megan pursed her lips. "You didn't trust me."

Raven picked up her glass and drank. Not too dry, not too sweet, Megan served her favourite, yet, she wasn't in the right mind to enjoy it.

"You've known me since we were thirteen and shared a homeroom with Mr. Elliott. How could you doubt my reaction or loyalty?" Megan continued.

Raven placed her glass back on the table. "You said you feared Others and what they would potentially do to your children."

"And I still do." Megan set her glass down on the table a little too hard and some wine sloshed over the side. She let it run over her hand and down the stem to pool at the base. "Do you blame me? I have no natural defence against Others. Why wouldn't I want some sort of barrier? Why wouldn't I want some way to protect those I care about most? I also fear speeding cars, those communal play areas in fast food restaurants full of bacteria, and trampoline gyms."

"Do you fear me?"

"Of course not." Megan waved her question away. "You despised Mandy Penner at the height of pubescent rage, yet, you never hurt her."

Mandy Fucking Penner. Raven had despised Mandy, especially when she dated Marcus when Raven still crushed hard on her brother's best friend. The truth was Raven hated the other teenager's easy popularity when Raven spent most of her adolescent years withering on the inside with her own insecurities and low self-esteem. She never paused to consider other girls might be doing exactly the same thing, despite how well-adjusted and confident they appeared. Mandy hadn't done anything to Raven except thrive in an environment Raven would've preferred to outright avoid. Megan had been her salvation through those tough years. Megan, Bear and Marcus. Being a teenager had been hard, and Raven thanked sweet baby Odin she didn't have to go back in time.

"You've never shown yourself to be a killer or someone who intentionally hurts people," Megan continued. "But there's so many Others who wouldn't think twice about squashing us if we had something they wanted, or we were merely in the way."

"Some would argue mortals share that trait." Raven squirmed in her seat. She'd killed twice using her powers. Completely self-defence, but would Megan see it that way? Would Megan fear her then?

"Is that why you joined the Closers?" Raven asked. "To help re-establish the barrier and gain protection from the Others?" And somehow look past the painful point that Raven might have to live on the other side. It made sense, really. Raven would never fully understand the fear of Others that Megan had to live with every day, but she could empathize. Vulnerability and fear never felt good.

"Of course not," Megan said.

Raven stopped drinking her wine. Not what she expected.

"I joined for you."

Raven choked. Wait...what?

Megan smirked but something sad crossed her expression when she took a seat across the corner of the table from Raven. "I know you think I'm useless, but I could do this for you."

Raven straightened in her chair. "What? Why in Odin's twinkle berries would you think something like that?"

Megan looked into her glass. "You're always so...I don't know...dismissive whenever I ask you questions about your investigations."

Raven opened her mouth to deny Megan's statement while her brain frantically replayed the past—a particular moment when Megan hung out with

Raven on a stakeout flooded her memories. Raven snapped her mouth shut. "Well, damn..."

Megan took another sip of wine.

"That's not...I'm not..." Raven took a deep breath. "I didn't speak to you like that because I think you're useless."

Megan folded her arms and leaned back in her chair.

"For once in my life, I felt knowledgeable myself. In my family, I don't experience that feeling often. I guess it came across as douchebag instead of wise. I'm sorry. I never meant to make you feel that way."

Megan grumbled, but her forehead frown lines eased away.

"But why the Closers?"

Megan sighed and her shoulders dropped. "I saw how those Regulator pamphlets upset you. I left them out on purpose to get you to confess." Megan looked away and bit her lip. "But you didn't, and I wanted to know more about your world, so I started going to the Regulator meetings. And then we watched that woman, Kelly, for your PI case. The one who made a fraudulent work injury claim. She showed up at the next meeting I went to and actively recruited for the Closers. You're always saying there's no coincidences in the PI business. I saw an opportunity and agreed to go."

Raven took another drink of wine. It slid down her throat, cool and smooth. "What did you find out?"

"They know about you. At least, they do now. You

need to be careful, Rayray. I think you're a target."

Oh, goodie. "They can join the club."

"Don't be glib. They might not be Others, but they're still dangerous."

"I'm not being glib. I'm exhausted and the novelty of having some Big Bad after me has worn off a little." Wasn't that the sad truth?

Megan fixed her with a blue-eyed glare. "You need to be careful," Megan repeated. "They're planning something, and I think it involves you somehow. My group has been more focused on some lord from the Realm of War."

Raven straightened in her seat. "Bane?"

Megan nodded. "Yeah, that's him. They won't shut up about how they tricked him into helping the cause."

For the third time in this conversation, Megan surprised her, and Raven's brain short-circuited. The words coming out of Megan's mouth made no sense. Bane hated the Closers and wanted to form a temporary barrier against them, and Closers hated any kind of supernatural, which included Bane. Why would either willingly work with each other?

They wouldn't.

Which meant Megan's information was valid. The Closers had to have tricked Bane.

Huh.

No wonder he hated the group and no wonder he was constantly on her ass to put up a barrier. He wanted her to take care of his business so no one discovered his blunder. Dark fae lords hated appearing weak. It invited more attacks and attempts on their position of power.

But why would Bane demand a barrier? How did that help him? He was the Lord of War. Why not just obliterate the group himself? Unless...

Unless the agreement somehow bound him in a way that prevented him from retaliation and the barrier allowed a workaround.

Did Bane even want a barrier, or did he want his promise to the Closers fulfilled so he could exact punishment?

"What did Bane agree to?"

Megan smiled. "In exchange to access the Murdoch Manual, he granted access to his realm every Wednesday with a lodestone and the promise of no retaliation or harm to any group members."

The infamous Murdoch Manual was created by one of the former physicists responsible for discovering the force of magic, Fm, and for bringing down the barrier. "What in the Underworld is in those manuals? And more importantly, why would Bane care about the research of a mortal physicist?"

Megan shrugged. "I'm not allowed near the manual, so I can't answer your first question and as for the second, Bane hasn't exactly confided his inner motivations to any of us, not even the Travellers. I've never actually seen him, although I hear he's quite something to behold."

"Travellers?"

Megan downed the rest of her wine and eyed the

bottle as if she wanted to drink straight from the source.

Raven reached forward, picked up the bottle and filled Megan's glass.

Her friend raised it in a silent salute and took another drink. "The Travellers are specially chosen Closers who venture into the Realm of War to test various hypotheses for reconstructing the barrier. Apparently, the manual hints that the key to powering the barrier comes from outside the Mortal Realm."

Odin's shriveled noodle, the Closers were more of a threat than anyone realized. What if they succeeded? What if she was stuck in the Underworld and separated from her family? She gulped. What if she was stuck here and cut-off from Cole?

At least Bane hadn't agreed to help with the barrier.

Wait...

"So, Bane didn't promise to help resurrect the barrier?"

Megan frowned. "Why would he do that?"

Excellent question and more importantly, if the barrier wasn't part of his agreement with the Closers, why did he want or need to block portals. Had the Closers done something to his realm? Did he need to cut off their travel because they were close to discovering a method to build a magical wall? Or did he need them blocked for another reason?

And did his motives even matter? The truth wouldn't let Raven off the hook for her own deal with the dark fae Lord of War.

Megan watched her process the information. Calm,

yet grim, her friend always adopted that patient expression while she waited for Raven to come to her senses or realize the stupidity of her current course of action.

"Thank you for the information." Raven pushed her wine glass to the side. "Are we good?"

Megan pursed her lips. "I don't know. Are we?"

"I want to be," Raven said. "You're my best friend."

Megan flinched as if Raven's words hurt. "Am I?"

Raven's stomach twisted before taking a swan dive. "I never meant to hurt you and I didn't want to put you in a position where you'd be at risk for your knowledge or for having to choose between your beliefs and our friendship."

"Bullshit. You were scared to come clean."

"Of course, I was scared!"

Megan straightened in her chair.

Okay, maybe she should ease up on the wine.

"Of course, I was scared," Raven repeated, dropping her voice. "You're my friend. You're family. I didn't want to lose you and feared telling you the truth would result in exactly that."

"And I'm pissed at you," Megan seethed. "Pissed that you thought I would give a shit about what flowed in your veins over who you are and what you are to me."

Well, damn.

"I fucked up," Raven said.

"Understatement of the year."

"Can you forgive me?"

"I'm not sure."

Rave dropped her head and tried to summon some will power to walk out of the house with her chin up.

"Can you show me some of your super-secret dark fae powers?" Megan asked.

Raven lifted her head to find Megan's intense gaze sparkling with intensity and a wide smile flashing her teeth.

"That's something I can arrange," Raven said.

"Then we're good." And as short and simple as Megan's words might seem to an outsider looking in, they went deeper and meant more to Raven than any long drawn out flowery speech, because Raven knew her friend and she believed her. Everything else in Raven's life might be a chaotic mess but her friendship with Megan would endure and that made Raven feel invincible.

Chapter Nineteen

"Chocolate doesn't ask any silly questions. Chocolate understands."

~ Unknown, fellow chocolate aficionado

Bolstered with new found confidence from her still intact friendship, Raven beckoned Rourke from the shadows to join her on the sidewalk. She'd given Jean-Claude to her brother and hadn't had time to purchase a new vehicle—if she decided to get one. She planned to buy Mike a car, too and retire the Grand Am for good, but she had to stay focused. Her friends and family were taken care of. It was time to get down to business. No more distractions. No more delays.

She'd finally heard back from all the surrounding animal shelters and the animal control bylaw officers. No sign of Pepe. Mike had run searches to scour the web to see if their spite goat had been advertised for auction or for sale. Again, no sign of Pepe.

Which meant she needed to shift her focus to the other big ticket item on her list. Time to settle her debt to Bane. And in order to do what she planned, she needed someone to watch her back and a place where she wouldn't be interrupted by Mike barging in to quiz her on useless trivia, Juni trying to sneak in to steal clothes, Mom nagging about her lack of progress in life or even Dad with one of his Dad jokes.

"Is this where I whisper something incredibly lame like, 'where to mistress?'" Rourke scowled in case she didn't pick up on his current mood.

"Of course not. I'm on the good side. Those sorts of lines are reserved for the villain's henchmen."

"There's no such thing as good versus evil in the Underworld. I'm assuming this rule applies to your world, too."

"Everything is just shades of gray?"

Rourke nodded, completely missing the reference. "This is why some people argue the Shadow Realm is the most powerful of all."

"Whatever." She held her hand out.

Rourke eyed her palm as if it carried anthrax powder.

She flapped her hand. "Come on. I'm taking us to the Corvid Court."

"Your court, you mean?"

"Yeah, sure." She still thought of the large, empty castle with gloomy nooks and open courtyard as Lloth's and no amount of redecorating would change that.

Rourke scowled at her outstretched arm. "And you want to hold hands?"

"Look. Unless you have another way to get us there, you need to hold my hand so I can form a portal for both of us."

"Camhanaich—"

"Is far superior with his powers than I am, but he's not here and I need to rely on myself to get places. Grab a hand, Dorothy. We're going for a ride."

"My name is Rourke." He deadpanned. "Are you all right?"

"No, I'm not all right. Not only does my evil henchman not catch my random references, but I finally have an idea how to complete my obligation to Bane, the confidence to carry out the task and my trusty sidekick is balking at a little friendly hand-holding."

"I'm not a sidekick," Rourke grumbled and snatched her hand, his callouses rough against her skin and his palm surprisingly warm. "Or an evil henchman."

"So, you're not always at my side and weren't formerly employed as an assassin for hire?"

His scowl deepened. "You need to give Bane advanced warning."

Balls. She forgot about that detail. Good thing Rourke reminded her before they travelled to the Shadow Realms. Hopefully, Bane was slumming it on the mortal side. She dug out her phone with her free hand and hit Bane's contact information.

He picked up and answered without any flowery greetings. Not a shocker. "Bane."

"This is your requested notice. If what I have planned works, the blockade will be erected in an hour or so."

"About time." He hung up and gave zero appreciation to Raven for using the word "erected" in a sentence. Adulting was not very fun when everyone took it so seriously.

Whatever. At least Bane was somewhere in the Mortal Realm when she called. There were no cell towers where they were headed and the idea of paying Bane a house visit in the Realm of War didn't provide any warm fuzzy feelings.

Rourke shifted his weight on his feet beside her. What was his problem?

He raised his arm, swinging their clasped hands together. "As much as I relish the idea of the Patron Fae of Assassins catching me holding hands with his mortal lover while she casually chats on the phone with his sworn enemy, we should go to your lair now, so you can hatch your evil plans for world dominance."

"You're so dramatic."

"I'm not dramatic. I'm realistic. You're about to flex your magic muscle to prevent an entire group of people from travelling to or from the Mortal Realm."

She scowled but said nothing. If she dished it, she had to take it, too. "I'm not planning to dominate the world. Only make good on a promise to a war mongering sociopath so he doesn't smite me."

Rourke rolled his eyes so perfectly Juni would've approved. "He wouldn't smite you. You're too valuable to destroy and even if he had corvid energy to assume your position, he doesn't want it. He'd just enslave you until you worked off the debt."

Raven opened her mouth and then closed it again.

Rourke raised his eyebrows, taunting.

What should she do or say first? Object to Rourke referring to her as if she was a top hat or iron in some sort of weird-ass board game or... "What in Odin's left nut is the price tag attached to my debt?"

Rourke shrugged. "Probably life."

"And what would I have to do to work it off?" That didn't sound ominous. No, not at all.

"Knowing Bane, he'd probably make you scrub floors with a toothbrush or keep his boots clean. He's not a sociopath. He's cruel and calculating with a wicked sense of humour."

Raven narrowed her eyes at her companion. Bane? Sense of humour? "Exactly what is your history with the Lord of War?"

Rourke's expression closed. "Nothing that pertains to the scope of this job."

"And if he attacks me, your history won't prevent you from defending my life?"

"I'm insulted you would even have to ask that."

Argh. So close. She'd pry the truth out of him eventually.

"Your Queenship?" Rourke swung their clasped hands again. "Shall we?"

"Fine." Raven embraced the dark Other energy constantly swirling inside of her and shifted them to the courtyard of Lloth's—her—castle. Time to honour a promise and excise one foul fae from her life.

Chapter Twenty

"Do you ever start crying about something and then the next day you get your period and you're like, I knew I wasn't a weak ass bitch."

~ Unknown, but hilarious

The cool night air washed over her, oddly comforting like a caress despite the icy wisps along her skin. The last time she'd roamed these halls, she'd been with Cole and his father had paid them an unannounced visit. Awkward didn't begin to cover that family reunion.

Two slivers of twin red moons basked the stones in

warm muted light and a raven's croak in the distance drifted on the silent night air unanswered.

Raven shrugged off the unease tingling along her skin and stalked up the stairs to the entrance as if she owned the place.

She flinched.

She did own the place. This grand fortress was purchased with Lloth's blood. Nobody else seemed to have a problem with this except Raven and it didn't help to remain hung up on it. She didn't want to lose her humanity or empathy, but she needed to adjust her way of thinking if she planned to survive this new role.

"Where to?" Rourke trailed behind her.

"Cole showed me some of the rooms last time we were here. Lloth had a ceremonial room with a strategic placement that allowed for a magic user to pull directly from the realm's lay lines while being bolstered by the position of the stars and moon."

"The *seomra cumhachta.*"

She heard Rourke's nod more than saw it since he seemed determined to stay two steps behind and to the right of her. He probably followed some sort of fae court etiquette to show respect or deference, but it just annoyed her. She wasn't royalty and getting treated as such made her feel like even more of a fraud.

"Rourke?"

"Yes, *mo bhanrigh?*"

"Can you not walk beside me?"

"No."

She sighed and continued down the hall that lead to

the seomra cumhachta.

"Raven?"

"Yes?"

"Do you not wish to call Camhanaich?"

Raven sighed. She'd thought of doing just that. She'd feel more confident with him by her side with his strength, knowledge and support, but... "How would it look if the Queen of Corvids always ran to her boyfriend for help?"

He'd helped her out so much and needed to catch up on his own business. The last thing she wanted to do was call him for more help.

Rourke's grunt behind her was answer enough because they both knew exactly how it looked, even if neither of them agreed with it.

"Stupid, if you ask me," Rourke muttered. "There's no one else here but us and it's not as though I'm going to run off to gossip."

The idea of Rourke flipping his hair over coffee while eager listeners waited for him to dish the latest "deets" about the new Corvid Queen made the corners of her lips twitch.

"No, you're not one to run your mouth, but Cole has been tutoring me on the ways of the fae and despite what he might tell you or what you might think, I do pay attention."

"Sometimes."

"Sometimes," she agreed. "And what I've learned is some fae are so powerful, they don't need a spy physically present to unearth secrets or keep tabs on events." Raven stopped at the end of the hall and turned to her bodyguard.

"That is true." Rourke reached past her and opened the door.

"But we can also agree that the fae with those abilities can probably determine your weaknesses and incompetence with or without Cole present for whatever it is you have planned."

She curled her hands into fists. "Banshee's left tit, Rourke. I want to do this by myself. I have to do this by myself. Cole can't always stand beside me, nor can I count on you to always have my back. I have to learn to stand on my own. Truly on my own. Having Cole standing by to jump in at a moment's notice is like riding a bike with trainer wheels on. He's been teaching me how to use my magic for months. At some point, the training wheels have to come off. And I have to show others I can function independently."

Rourke clamped his mouth shut with enough pressure his lips turned white and his jaws clenched.

"What?" Great. How had she managed to piss her shadow off? Or did he not get the biking reference?

He shook his head and waved his arm toward the open door. "Nothing, my queen, but if this goes—how do you mortals put it? Sideways?—I'm summoning Cole."

"Fine." She walked past him. "If I can't do it or need help, call Cole."

"Fine," he repeated and followed her in, closing the solid door behind them.

Cool air swirled around the room from the open ceiling. Moon and starlight basked them in an ethereal glow. Their boots struck obsidian tiles. An inlaid design of a rune decorated the floor along with gutters and channels that must collect rainwater and direct it toward the drain in the center of the room.

The first time Raven stepped foot in this room, she felt as though she'd entered some sort of mystical funnel made for giants, the circular shape to the tower and sloped floors only added to the aesthetic and if the sky spat a torrent of rain, she wouldn't be surprised if she got sucked into some vortex to another dimension. Despite the surreal feel to the room, dark energy pulsed. Bouncing off the stone walls, the large embedded rune on the floor and her, with each ping, the magic intensified until it hummed in her veins and left a metallic taste in her mouth.

"Are you going to start doing magic now or just continue to stare at the sky?" Rourke asked.

She hadn't realized she was staring into the night. "Shh." She flapped her hand at Rourke and willed him to go away. "I need you to be quiet and do your guard thing. Probably smart to stand outside the rune, too."

"You don't say..." Rourke's dry tone could've sucked moisture from a prune. She turned to find him standing outside the rune with his arms folded.

"Try to contain your excitement."

"Go team." He slow-motioned a fist pump in the air and the move looked all kinds of wrong on him.

Closing her eyes, she shut out her surroundings,

including her bodyguard and his giant attitude, and embraced the potent power swirling in the room. Magic answered her call right away, slamming into her and almost knocking her off her feet. She staggered but remained upright. She ground her teeth and locked her knees. No. She had to do this now. No more delays or having Bane's threat of collecting a debt owed hanging over her head. She promised to block the movement of all non-Others for a period of forty-eight hours. This whole time, she'd wracked her brain trying to figure out how she'd home in on the mortals and prevent any and all attempts they made to travel out of the Mortal Realm.

When the solution hit her, she'd almost groaned at the simplicity. She needed to block non-Others. She never promised to not block anyone else. Instead of trying to narrow down the restriction to any particular group of people and each individual attempt at a portal, she could cease all travel—an embargo on portals.

Frankly, that should make everyone happy. Bane didn't want mortals to travel, mortals didn't want Others to travel and Raven didn't want to end up dead or cleaning the crud off the bottom of Bane's boots with a toothbrush. The only downside was if this worked, she'd end up stuck in the Realm of Shadows for forty-eight hours.

Would it be that bad? She could always stay with Cole. He'd find something for them to do to pass the time.

Focus, Crawford.

Her body shook with magic of the Underworld. She expanded her awareness toward the edges of the realm. Pops of power punctuated her consciousness. Portals. If she were some sort of jelly dessert, the Travellers felt like greedy little children poking their fingers into the surface when their parents weren't looking.

Gathering her vibrating energy, she pushed it out, and out...and out. Forcing the fingers out of the dessert and hardening the surfaces so no more could penetrate.

Heat built inside her. She pushed on, keeping her focus on the borders of the Shadow Realm. Pressure built in her head, threatening to combust.

Raven?

She ignored the voice. Sweat dripped down her face. The shadow realm was huge. Too huge. Did she have enough power to cover all of it? Could she push her awareness this far from her body and still reclaim it later?

Raven!

Pain sliced through her body as more power eked out from her core, funneled from the deep reserve within her.

Almost there. Almost enough.

She spread her magic through the shadow realm's farthest corners.

No more pops of power. No more dirty little kiddie fingers poking through.

She did it! It was done.

Now she had to hold it for forty-eight hours.

Sweat poured down her face. How in the

Underworld would she manage to hold this for two days?

Once, she made the mistake of going to the gym with Bear. He'd given her an "easy" weight to press up and hold. Holding her magic like this felt like holding those weights above her chest, but so many times worse. Instead of only her arms and chest muscles shaking, her whole body shook, and she wanted to puke. Her head grew light and she swayed. The slashing pain intensified. She'd extended herself too much.

Panic trickled into her thoughts. Her tenuous hold on the realm faltered. Magic pushed back. Her chest burned and burned as if someone held a hot poker to her breastbone.

The room around her darkened and the smell of a midnight forest flooded the room.

Cole.

Rourke must've summoned him. How long had she been at this? She couldn't break her focus away from...whatever it was she was doing.

"What the fuck?" Cole's deep voice exploded.

"She's been like that for hours," Rourke said. "I can't get her attention."

Hours?

Sweat continued to pour down her face. She couldn't look at them. She couldn't demand to know what time it was or why Rourke was exaggerating. She had to stay focused on her task.

A familiar magic tentatively pressed around her,

poking her work.

Cole cursed.

"Is it bad?"

"She's extended herself too much."

Rourke swore.

"You were supposed to stop her from doing something monumentally stupid like this," Cole said, voice cold.

"Yeah, sure. Control Raven. Tell me, oh master. How has that worked out for you?" Rourke said.

Silence answered Cole and descended over the room. A warm hand slid over her shoulder. Cole's familiar energy tingled along her skin. Instead of snuffing out her power like Others, Cole's magic played well with hers.

"Einin." Cole's tone softened from when he spoke to Rourke. "I know you can hear me. Don't try to respond. Keep your focus on your magic just as you've been doing. Don't let go. I can lend you a little of my power. Only a little. Like Bane did when you faced Lloth."

"I thought—" Rourke's voice cut off. "I thought that was decided."

"No." Cole's answer hung in the air.

What was decided? She swayed and her hold slipped. She scrambled and grabbed onto her magic, pushing it back in place. Argh.

Cole's hand squeezed her shoulder. "You need to use this extra power to tether the spell."

"Cole." Rourke's voice cut in again.

"Not now."

"Camhanaich. You can't let her do that. She'll be cut off from her magic. She might never get it back. You'll render her powerless."

Odin's nutsack. That didn't sound good. Her hold wavered. She bit down and swayed, pushing her back into place.

"That's a small probability," Cole said. "At least she'll be alive."

Oh no...she definitely fucked up this time. What if she just let go? She could try this again later and fix whatever she got wrong this time.

"But what about..." Rourke needed to work on finishing his sentences.

"I don't care about that. I care about her. Even with tethering, she may not make it, but if she lets go now without the proper spells in place, she will definitely die in the backlash."

Okay, then. Definitely not letting go. Her hold trembled.

"Get ready, Rourke. Once she tethers the spell, I'm taking us to the Mortal Realm."

"How? All portals will be blocked if she did everything right."

"Splicing."

"Splicing?" Rourke sounded as if he gagged on the word. "You can't splice out of here."

"Yet we can't stay, either."

"You'll both be powerless."

"Which is why you need to be ready. We're

counting on you. Or did you not mean it when you made your oath to her?"

To me? What did that mean?

Rourke growled. "You know I did."

Cole's arms slid around her waist and pulled her back into the heat of his chest. "Einin, I'm going to lend you as much power as I can. You need to take it and tie off your magic, so your spell stays in place. Do you remember practicing this with me?"

She whimpered in response. He made her practice the tie-off skill with her portals multiple times. It should work for this, but the spell was a lot bigger than a regular portal.

Pain continued to slice at her mind and her hold on the realm shook. Her whole body shook.

Cole held her close. His familiar power pushed into her awareness, vibrating in perfect harmony with her own. She latched onto it and tugged.

Cole's grip tightened, but he didn't let go and continued to send her his magic as she pulled and tied off her own power.

"Time to cut it loose, Einin," he whispered in her ear, his deep rumbling voice a soothing caress.

She gulped, closed her eyes and cut the tether of magic connecting her psyche to the spell. As if she'd played an invisible game of tug-of-war and her opponent let go without warning, sudden weightlessness from cutting the tether sent her physically flying backward.

Immediately following the short-lived freedom was

a wave of pain. It slammed into her raw consciousness and started shredding her nerves. Raven shrieked and thrashed. Her back arched away from Cole.

Too much. It was too much.

Strong arms anchored her in place against a solid wall of muscle. A vortex of wind swirled around them.

Rip!

Shockwaves danced through the air as Cole tore a seam through the very essence of the Shadow Realm and stepped into the abyss, carrying her with him.

The wind stopped howling. Warmth surrounded them along with the smell of pizza.

"What the fuck?" Bear's growl had never been a more welcome sound. "What have you done to my sister? I'm going to kill you."

She tried to open her eyes. She tried to tell him it wasn't Cole's fault. That it was hers, but everything was going to be okay. That she loved him. She tried to wave him off, but the only thing she managed was a low moan.

"Save the threats," Cole said. "She did this to herself. You need to fix her."

"Me? How?"

"You're her soulmate," Cole said.

She pried open her eyes to find the men staring at each other. The only sound in the room was her own whimpering.

"I'll show you," Cole said. "And let's hope it will be enough."

Chapter Twenty-One

"I want the part of you that you refuse to give anyone."
~ *Unknown*

Raven rolled over on the bed. A thin cotton sheet slid along her skin. Though clothed, the contact cut at her raw senses. Her chest ached, sore and tender as if recovering from a severe sunburn.

She nuzzled into a warm chest—Cole. His familiar and reassuring forest scent surrounded her along with...the wooded glen scent of her brother.

"Bear?"

She rolled back to find her brother sprawled out

beside her. His eyes fluttered open and he turned to her. "Hey, Rayray. You had us worried there."

"Um."

"Cole explained what you did. Without backup. That was dumb."

"I really don't feel like you're in any position to chastise me about life choices." She sat up and rested against the headboard. "Is there a reason we're all crashed in the same bed?"

"Not my idea. Trust me." Bear stretched and sat up beside her. His wrinkled T-shirt spread across his chest. "I have better things to do than snuggle my twin with her dark fae play toy."

"Love you, too, brother dearest." Something pinched her chest. She winced and pulled the chain of her necklace from her shirt. The Raven's Eye glinted at her and pulsed with magic. It rested right against the sore spot on her breastbone. It must've burned her during the spell.

Bear scowled at her, but he was tired because it was a half-assed one.

"Why?" She waved her finger between the two of them. They were close, but not creepy close. Not cuddling in the bed kind of close.

"Because he's your soulmate and close proximity and contact helps restore and bolster your Other energy." Cole grumbled into the pillow. His disheveled hair fell into his face. She liked this messy look of his the best.

"Einin." Creases she didn't remember seeing

161

around Cole's eyes made him appear more tired and more human than he was.

"Yeah, I'm out." Bear flung back the sheets and slipped from the mattress. "Don't fuck in my bed."

Raven sighed and dropped her head back on the tufted material. "Good talk, bruh."

Bear paused at the door and turned to her. "I'm glad you're not dead."

"Thanks." *I love you, too.*

Bear grunted and slipped from the room, closing the door quietly behind him.

Cole remained lying on his side. He'd reached out to run his hand along her leg, almost as if he needed to touch her, to reassure himself she was actually there.

"So, Bear needed to give me some hugs so I could replenish enough energy to restore myself to a functional human being? Why are you here? Not that I don't want you here, but Bear has a couch and you don't particularly like my brother and he's not your biggest fan either."

Cole's hand tightened on her thigh briefly before he let go with a sigh. "I helped him actively synch his energy with yours."

"Helped him?"

"I showed him how."

She straightened. "By demonstrating?"

"Yes..."

"Was Chloe here, too?" She was missing something important here, but even though she'd asked about Chloe, she doubted the missing piece had anything to do with Cole's twin sister. Months ago, Bane hired Bear to steal the Claíomh Solais from Cole. Bear had taken the job, but refused to deliver once he realized the "object of power" was Chloe. They'd gone into hiding, and Raven had been left to deal with two pissed off dark fae lords with no clue of what was going on. It worked out in the end, sort of. And though Bear was extremely private and protective of his relationship with Chloe, Raven knew this romance was something different for her brother. Something special.

"I demonstrated with you," Cole said, looking cagey as fuck.

"If you can synch your magic with mine, why couldn't you replenish my power yourself?" Yup, still missing something.

Cole shut his eyes to take another deep breath. To his credit, he'd woken up three minutes ago and forming complete sentences without caffeine.

"Let me guess. It has to do with blood?"

"Yes." He looked away. "And even if I could, I wouldn't have had enough to give. I'm tapped from splicing us to the Mortal Realm."

He must've felt it was too dangerous to stay at the Corvid Court. She didn't have to grill him on the decision later. He would've made the choice based on what he felt increased her chances of survival and right now she needed to stay focused. "So, you can't replenish my power, but you can lend me a little of your magic and you can synch your energy with mine?"

Cole clenched his jaw and looked as though he

debated not answering. "Yes."

"Usually, when an Other touches me, they nullify my power. But not you."

His dark Other eyes blazed with wild emotion, deep pools of tormented shadows. "Not me," he conceded.

"Why? What makes you different? Is this something you're able to do with anyone?" Nope. Definitely did not like that idea, but she'd kiss a Banshee's butt before she voiced all her insecurities.

"No, Einin. What we have is rare. I've already told you that."

"But not unheard of."

"No. You will meet others your magic is compatible with. Odin and Huginn Muninn, for example."

Raven stiffened. "You said we weren't related." She flapped her finger between them.

Cole chuckled. "We're not. Magical compatibility is not all the same. There are varying degrees. You used some of Bane's magic to defeat Lloth, did you not?"

Raven shuddered.

"Yet, you're not related to him nor do I think you harbour any romantic feelings for the Lord of War." Cole's gaze sparked and his lips twitched.

Ass. He knew she had zero interest in that giant douche canoe.

"Your magic was compatible enough with Bane's."

"Ew."

Cole ignored her and continued. "But he still nullifies your power when in contact, doesn't he?"

"He nullifies a lot of things when he touches me."

Cole smirked. "I'm glad to hear I don't have to compete with the Lord of War for your affections."

"Stop deviating from the topic."

"The problem is the Mortal Realm has been plagued with whispers of the truth for so long that concepts like soulmates and magical compatibility have been romanticized when there's nothing overtly romantic or sexual about either of those concepts."

She frowned. "But how do you explain us then? I was drawn to you the moment we first met."

"My dazzling personality, no doubt?"

"Naturally."

She ran her hand down his arm, relishing his strength and presence. He was here. She was here. Everything was okay. "I know it's not because we're clandestine soulmates because you've already ruined that concept for me along with a number of paranormal romance books. And now you're telling me it's not because of magic compatibility."

Cole chuckled. "Soulmates are a different thing for fae as you've discovered but the whole mate concept still holds true for werewolves, so read your little romance-loving heart out."

She glared at him.

The bastard winked back.

"Please tell me what's between us isn't some weird twisted love spell, fated mate instalove or some sort of unavoidable dark fae magical mojo voodoo crap."

Cole sat up and drew her into the heat of his body. "No, Einin. None of those things."

"Then what?" She wasn't dropping this.

"Haven't you spent time searching for something, but when someone asks you about it, you can't really remember what it is, what it looks like or feels like? And then you suddenly find it, and everything clicks? You get your memories back and everything makes sense about why you were trying to find this thing in the first place?" He pulled back a strand of hair from her face and tucked it behind her ear. "I've been searching for you my whole life but didn't realize it until the night we met."

"When you abducted me, and I punched you in the face?"

"Not in that order."

"Not in that order," she agreed. She'd punched him first.

"Yes. Everything makes sense now. You make sense." He ran his finger down the side of her face. "There's no special name for it. No label. But I don't think it needs one other than love."

"You want me to believe you saw me in that cheap polyester blend blouse and those serving pants and instantly fell in love with me?"

"Love? No. That came later. Lust and like, absolutely. Your ass looks great in those pants, by the way." His gaze heated and scalded her body. "Your ass always looks good." He reached over and scooped her up by the hips, dragging her across his lap.

His erection dug into her thigh.

"Good morning to you, too." She leaned down and

kissed him.

Cole chuckled against her mouth and pulled her closer.

"I said no fucking in my bed," Bear screeched from the living room on the other side of his apparently paper-thin walls.

Raven flailed to the side. "Bear, you asshole. Why are you eavesdropping?"

"It's a shitty apartment and it's not exactly hard to hear you two lip smacking. Get decent and get out here."

She flashed the bird at the closed door and rolled off Cole.

"Aren't you the same age?" Cole mused.

"That means nothing to Bear. He's seven minutes and thirteen seconds older and that means he will be bossing me around when we're old and gray." Raven slipped from the bed and straightened her clothes—a baggy T-shirt and an old pair of Bear's shorts. Someone had changed her. She pulled the neck of her shirt out and peered down. She still wore the same bra and presumably underwear. A large red sore marked the center of her chest where the Raven's Eye had burned her.

"If you weren't wearing the Raven's Eye or if I hadn't arrived in time to lend you a boost of power, you would've burned up."

She turned to find him clenching his jaw and looking like he wanted to punch something. Not her, of course, but she'd hate to be the first person to get in his way and piss him off right now.

Her stomach growled and a wave of light-headedness passed through her. She wavered.

Instantly, Cole stood beside her, his large hands on her waist to steady her.

She took a deep breath and pulled herself upright. This wasn't her. She wasn't a swooning lady in distress. She didn't faint on an empty stomach. She cursed. Sometimes she angry-cried, and not in that pretty kind of way. But not this. She might not be a badass combat-trained lethal weapon, but she took care of her business, cleaned up her own mistakes and got things done.

Raven stepped from the heat and seduction of Cole's body, opened the bedroom door and stepped into Bear's living room unassisted.

Bear and Rourke looked up from where they sat. The warm light did nothing to hide their pale, drawn faces. Dark bags underlined bloodshot, tired eyes.

She turned and studied Cole. Not as weary looking as the other two men, more lines creased his face and if a dark fae lord could look tired, well, Cole looked exhausted.

"What happened?" she asked. "Did the blockade fail?"

"It worked," Rourke muttered. "But you almost tore yourself apart to complete it."

"Oh."

"And you almost died using what remained of your power and the little boost I gave you to tie off your spell." Cole slid past her and walked to the kitchen, flicking the switch on the coffee maker and pulling out mugs. The man was a saint.

Almost died? She hadn't realized it had been that close. Or maybe she had but was too mentally fried to fully comprehend. "Oh."

"And you almost died again after Cole ripped a seam through the realms to bring you to me." Bear turned to Cole. "Please don't do that again. Scariest shit I've seen."

Cole pulled the milk from the fridge, shut the door and glared at her twin. "I'll do it again if I have to."

If she needed him to.

Cole turned to her, face solemn, gaze intent. His unspoken words hung in the air.

"At least my promise to Bane has been fulfilled," she said. "What happens now? Can I leave the spell tethered and recoup my power without taking it back? Do I have to cuddle Bear some more? Can I wait for the spell to dissipate? Or do I have to untie the magic and somehow suck it back up?"

Cole looked away and poured milk into the mugs.

That couldn't be a good sign.

"What you need to do is rest and eat something," Bear said. "You've been borderline comatose for almost two days. I can hear your stomach from here."

"Two days!" She jerked back. "The forty-eight hours are almost up."

Bear nodded. "And Bane's not going to be happy."

She turned to Cole because acknowledging the

impending rage of the Lord of War was not something she could do right now. "You need to answer my question. What happens now?"

"The first two options you listed are not really options at all unless you want to forfeit your life. If the spell becomes untethered and you're not magically fortified for the backlash, your own power will rip you apart. The spell will not dissipate and leaving it as it is raises a whole new level of complications you don't need. At best, you will alienate the majority of the Underworld and piss off the gods and lords." Cole spoke dispassionately, voice cold, and slightly off, but his flashing gaze gave away the turmoil simmering within.

She gulped. "At worst?"

"At worst, one of your many wannabe competitors will get past my wards, work through your magical knot, untether the magic and absorb your power for themselves. They will then be able to use your own energy to track you down, kill you and assume your position in the Underworld as the Corvid Queen or King."

Geez. She'd really screwed the pooch on this one.

"So, I have to untether it."

Cole nodded.

"And soon."

He nodded again.

Raven flopped into Bear's armchair and faced the three tired men in the room. She didn't need to reach for her corvid essence to know very little would answer her call. Would she even have enough to shift into a single bird? She felt drained and her energy stretched too thin. Like trying to blow a bubble with overly chewed gum, she inherently knew if she attempted to use her magic right now, it would fail—like air ripping through thin mint gum.

"How will I gain enough power to do that?" she asked.

Bear and Rourke turned to Cole and glared.

Raven straightened. What had she missed? "Not that I don't appreciate a good death stare in my defence, but why are you two directing them at Cole?"

Rourke cleared his throat. "Because there's a simple solution to this if his lordship wasn't so stubborn."

Her brows rose involuntarily. Cole was stubborn, but he normally went out of his way to protect her. He must have a good reason for holding back...whatever it was he held back.

Cole clenched his jaw and his large hands curled into fists. "I wanted her to have a choice."

"Fat lot of good that did her," Bear growled.

"And did you even ask her?" Rourke asked.

The room darkened and the lights flickered. "I didn't want to back her into a corner where she had no options or felt forced. Nor did I want to take advantage of a dire situation where she'd resent me later." Instead of looking at her, he looked everywhere else in the room.

"Um...she's right here." Raven waved.

"She's backed into a corner now, anyway, despite

your best intentions," Rourke said,

"Not exactly helpful, weapon warper," Cole growled.

"Yup, that's me," she said, dropping her hand. "Helpless damsel in distress. And to add to the insult of my predicament, I'm also clueless. Unless one of you would like to tell me what the fuck is going on?"

Cole finally turned to her. His hard expression softened a little and his shadows brushed along her skin. "Einin..."

Before Cole finished his sentence, the energy in the room exploded. Stinging magic travelled up her body, raising every hair along the way. A strip of red slashed through the space between her and Cole, splattering blood on Bear's carpet. High-pitched wailing erupted from the slash through the realities and ricocheted through the room.

Bane stepped through the splice and straightened. The slash snapped out of the room as if sucked back into the other side, cutting off the wailing. Bane scoured the room with his flashing, murderous gaze until he saw Raven.

Odin's dried pancakes, this couldn't be good.

Chapter Twenty-Two

"If you can't convince them, confuse them."

~ *Harry S. Truman*

Raven stood from her armchair, coiled in Cole's protective shadows and watched fury dance along Bane's expression. Normally full of menacing energy and the promise of annihilation, Bane's posture still radiated anger effectively, but lacked the normal oomph she'd come to associate with his presence.

He was tapped from splicing realties.

Well, hallelujah, sweet baby Odin. Finally, some

good news.

"We had a deal," Bane seethed.

"And I met my end of the bargain. I have fulfilled my promise to you and consider our arrangement completed." Magic tingled in the air. A knotted rope slid from the inside of Bane's jacket pocket and remained suspended in the air between them as if an invisible guest grabbed both ends and held out the rope horizontally for them to behold. Magic danced and wrapped around the knots, untangling the glowing rope without any guidance. When the last end slipped free, the magic disappeared and the rope fell to the ground, no longer animated or glowing or wrapped in Underworld magic.

The release of energy was satisfying like a slide cut at the salon or a really good massage. It *felt* great and Raven almost wanted to make another deal to feel it again. Almost. Then the almost dying memories crashed her back to reality.

"Looks like the rope agrees," Raven said.

Bane held up his finger to shush her. The room darkened and Cole gathered more shadows around them.

"You were supposed to block the movement of all non-Others into the Underworld," Bane said, his tone dangerously low.

"And I did," she said.

"You blocked everyone!"

Raven shrugged. "You never specified I couldn't block anyone else, nor did you say I had to leave travel open for anyone. That simply wasn't part of our deal."

The air crackled and Bane took a menacing step forward. "I'm going to wipe that smug smile off your Odin-loving face."

"I'd advise against that," Cole said.

Bane sneered. "You're just as tapped as I am. What are you going to do?"

"Admittedly, not as much as I would like." Cole shrugged. "But I'm not alone and as you pointed out, you're also tapped."

Rourke and Bear stepped in front of Raven to emphasize his point.

"And we're not tapped." Rourke flicked a dagger out of nowhere and did that flashy spinning trick, the dagger somehow reflecting the little amount of light remaining in the room.

Bane pulled back at Rourke's words. "You would defend your master's...woman...with your life?"

"Yes, I'm her *caomhnóir*," Rourke said.

Bane straightened and shut down the fury of emotions streaking across his face, so he resembled a stone more than a man. "I see."

Bane turned on his foot and stalked toward the door. Instead of turning at the last moment to dramatically announce this wasn't over or some other cheesy, cliché line, he slipped from the room and closed the door with a soft click behind him. The reality was way more disturbing.

Raven would've preferred the theatrics, personally. Growing up with three other siblings, she was used to them. Cold civility was just plain creepy.

Rourke sagged into the couch. "That went well."

It did. Thank...Wait a minute. Why did Rourke's tone sound sarcastic? She turned to the weary-eyed weapon warper but blanked on what to say.

"How'd he find us? He doesn't have a blood connection with any of us, does he?" Bear glared at her.

That look was completely uncalled for. She might've made some dumb choices, but she wasn't that dumb.

"No, but he's been here before and it takes only two brain cells for Bane to figure out where we'd go after Raven expended that amount of power," Cole said.

When Bear had gone missing, Bane had picked the locks on the front door to the building and to this apartment to search for Bear and Chloe. Those inciting events felt like a lifetime ago, when in reality it had only been a few months.

"He knew I'd have to mend with my brother," Raven finished Cole's explanation, though it didn't look like anyone else in the room needed her to.

Bear looked pissed off. He must've realized his place was searched when he disappeared, but getting the reminder probably made his sanctuary feel violated all over again.

"You have to tell her," Rourke said to Cole.

"So do you," the Lord of Shadows snapped.

Rourke rocked back on his heels and scowled.

"As much as I love cryptic speeches and vague references I can't catch, I'm right here, so why don't the two of you start dishing?"

The men, including her traitorous brother, sighed in unison.

Nope. Not liking that response at all. She pegged Rourke with a "tell me now or I'll break your legs" stare, but it was completely ridiculous. In a battle between the two of them, she was more likely to break something on herself. She jabbed her finger in the air at Rourke. "What's a...keevenoyr...?"

"Caomhnóir."

She glared.

Rourke glanced at Cole.

"Oh, no you don't. No checking with Daddy for permission first." Raven placed her hands on her hips. "Besides, he already told you to tell me."

"A caomhnóir is a sworn protector of fae nobility. Blood sworn. It roughly translates to guardian."

Wait a minute... "To me?" She jabbed her chest with her finger a little too hard and winced. Cole stepped over and handed her a coffee.

Rourke nodded.

"Shouldn't I have been present for this oath?"

"I have made my blood oath, *mo bhanrigh*." Rourke used the fae term for "my queen" and smiled when he said it. "You can either accept or deny me, but my pledge will remain."

"But you're sworn to serve Cole."

Rourke nodded. "He released me so I could protect you as your caomhnóir instead of as his minion."

Raven turned to Cole. "You shouldn't have made

him do this."

"I volunteered," Rourke said.

Raven's mouth dropped open. "Why...why?"

Rourke shrugged. "I'm a weapon warper and thrive on battle. Keeping you alive will prove much more challenging and entertaining than being one of Cole's many assassins. Besides, I was assigned to protect you anyway. May as well take the glory and prestige that comes with the caomhnóir title."

Huh. That kind of made sense. A lot of what the fae did now made sense and that should scare her more than it did. "Let me guess. To fully accept you as my caomhnóir, there's blood involved."

Rourke flashed his jagged teeth at her. "Of course." He turned to Cole. "I think she gets us."

Oh no. Mike must've let him watch television. He was using mortal phrases and it sounded all wrong.

Cole grunted—an agreement, rebuke and exasperation all in one.

"Your turn," Raven said to Cole. "What miraculous solution do you have to my magic problem that you don't want to tell me about? And don't try to stall again. I don't think Bane is planning to barge in here a second time to save you."

Rourke shoved her brother's shoulder. "That's our cue to leave."

"This is my home," Bear grumbled.

The two men glared at each other.

"Do you really want to be here for this conversation?" Rourke asked.

"Fine," Bear grumbled. He pointed his finger at Raven. "No fucking in my bed."

The men filed out of the apartment leaving Raven alone with Cole in her twin's apartment.

Cole took her untouched coffee from her hands and placed it on the nearby counter. He sat down on the couch and patted the cushion beside him.

"I think it's best if I stay over here," she said.

"Don't trust yourself to behave?"

"Not at all and this is my brother's place." She shuddered.

A lazy grin spread across Cole's face. "He said no fucking in the bed, he never mentioned the couch."

"Cole!" She snatched a nearby pillow resting on the armchair and chucked it at Cole's head.

Instead of using his shadows to bat it out of the way, he swatted the pillow from the air with his hand before it made contact. Huh. He must really be tapped to resort to manual labour.

"I've known since day one the overwhelming attraction I felt for you was different and chalked it up to your dark fae nature and ridiculous good looks."

He nodded. "That's part of it."

Modest man. "And our magical compatibility."

He nodded again. "A little of that, too."

"But you've assured me this isn't some fated mate compulsion fae bull pucky. We're able to exercise choice."

"Of course."

"And I chose you."

His lips tugged into a smile. "Yes, you did. Repeatedly."

"So, why are you afraid to tell me whatever it is you're not telling me? Does it have to do with the initial attraction? With the magical compatibility?"

Cole sighed. "Yes and no. I think the initial attraction was a combination of many factors, none of which are bad or part of some 'bull pucky' compulsion. I also think you might share a little more of your sire's and grandsire's magical abilities than you think— thought, memory and foresight. I think your initial attraction to me was not created but magnified because some part of your psyche recognised how important I'd be to you in the future and the manner of which I'd be important to you."

"Okay..." Damn. Grandma Lu always lectured the Crawford kids not to fall in love with a person's potential, and here she was, failing her lesson.

"I can lend you a small boost of my power, just as I did before to help you tether off your spell, and just as Bane did to help you fight off Lloth while under attack, but power boosting has its limits and I'm not sure it will be enough for you to untether your spell and shield you against the backlash. You'll need to gather your power and slowly reel it in without getting overwhelmed by the magical tsunami."

"But there's another way?"

He nodded.

"And let me guess...blood?"

He cracked a smile and chuckled, the deep rumbly

chuckle she loved to listen to when she lay her head against his bare chest.

"Yes, Einin. It's called *anam cara*. It's a blood oath and bond that allows us to exchange power and draw each other's magical essence. I do not offer this lightly."

"Do you want to offer it at all?" Maybe that's why he was reluctant to make this option known in the first place.

Cole's gaze blazed. "I've wanted you as my anam cara since our first night together."

"Is that what you've been so cagey about this whole time? Oh, don't give me that look. You might be the Lord of Shadows, but I've been a spurned woman and I'm also a PI. I know when truths are skipped and danced around. I kept asking you all these questions about our connection because I knew there was something you weren't telling me. This whole time you were trying to avoid telling me about the possibility of this bond."

Though he often had the best intentions, she was sick of Cole holding back information. Sure, she had a lot to learn. Sure, he couldn't dump it all on her at once. Sure, he had to prioritize. But this seemed like a big-ticket item that he should've shared with her sooner. "Why? Why didn't you want to tell me?"

Cole sighed. "Because you're still so naïve of the fae ways. Even though this is something I want, and feel is your best course of action for the position you're in, I didn't want you to feel pushed or tricked into something you didn't fully understand or might not want. I planned to broach the topic later, after you were more accustomed to our world, had gained more equal footing to me power-wise. And after I wooed you some more."

Wooed? People still did that?

"Because the anam cara is a marriage of sorts and it is not reversible. I'm not as savvy about the Mortal Realm as you, but I know no one talks about marriage on the first date. Not if they want a second one. I didn't want to scare you away."

Wait a minute. "Are you proposing?"

Cole's expression softened. "The anam cara bond doesn't have to be sexual in nature, but it often is. I already know my heart, but I'm not so sure you do. I will wait until you are confident of your place, power and my intentions."

"My place?" Oh look, words. She still knew how to voice them.

"Your place in the Mortal Realm, your place in the Underworld, your place in between and your place in my heart."

She licked her lips. "Let me see if I'm getting this right. You're suggesting a platonic magical marriage of convenience that will strengthen both of us magically and help me secure my kingdom, while we continue to pursue a romantic relationship?"

"I'm not sure I like how it sounds summarized so clinically," Cole grumbled. "But yes, that's what I'm suggesting."

"And what if it doesn't work?"

"The anam cara will work."

"What if we don't work out?"

Cole narrowed his gaze.

"Hope for the best, plan for the worst..." Raven looked away and tried to ignore the knot in her stomach.

"Then we go our separate ways. I'm not going to coerce you through a magical bond to stay. It goes against my personal code of ethics and the anam cara is a two-way bond. You could use it against me, too."

A shiver ran up her spine.

"We'll have to make some ground rules if that happens, but I'd very much prefer not to go down that path at all."

"Okay..."

"I want to be transparent with you. There are other options. We can bring Bear and other fae and hope energy boosts from us will be enough. We could also solicit the witches for help. Maybe they have a spell or incantation that can boost your levels or take care of the tethering or shielding."

"But?"

Cole shrugged. "Every course of action carries its own reaction. This is about you. The choice is yours. You need to select the option you can live with and accept the consequences and backlash, whatever they may be."

Raven had already made up her mind. Maybe she did possess a little of Odin's precognition. Maybe she always knew her path led to Cole. She never claimed to have good intuition and frankly, if she did have future-deciphering skills, it must be faulty because she'd wasted too many of her "good years" with Robert.

"I'd like to pursue the anam cara."

Cole's face split into a large smile—not a conniving smile, or one hinting at the satisfaction of a successful manipulation, not that she expected to see either of those—but one of unrestrained happiness. If she had any doubts remaining of Cole's character or intentions, this reaction alone laid them to rest. Cole continuously showed his feelings by competently placing her and her safety first and foremost and even now, with something he so obviously wanted, he ensured she knew all her options and gave her possible outs.

Swoon.

Something he said earlier, though, gave her another idea. "There could be another way."

Cole's expression shuttered.

"It's not that I don't want the bond, I do, but I would prefer to complete the ritual on our own terms, not forced."

"What do you have in mind?"

"Trust me?" she asked.

He smiled and ran his finger down her face. "Of course." Cole held out his hand and waited.

She stared at the open palm. "Bear said..."

"I know what your twin said." Cole flapped his hand. "But if you don't stop looking at me like that, you'll just have to prepare an epic apology. Or...you can take my hand and we can go to your place."

"You can portal us to my parents' place?"

Cole shook his head. "With a temporary barrier blocking the shadow realms, even portalling on the same side of the barrier is unreliable. I can still manipulate shadows, but portals require access to the Shadow Realm as do the full extent of my powers."

"I really fucked up, didn't I?"

Cole shook his head and kissed her forehead. "You did great. I'm so proud of you. You just didn't consider your leave."

Raven's eyebrows shot up. "A billiards reference? Really?"

"Why not?"

"After this is over, did you want to play?"

"A date?" Cole's smile grew. "Absolutely."

"Great. I can show you just how well I can position your balls."

Cole laughed, grabbed her hand and continued chuckling the entire way out of Bear's apartment, pausing only to say goodbye to Bear. Rourke trailed behind them, his expression changing between bored and incredulous, like he'd never seen the Lord of Shadows stuck in a giggling fit.

What an odd gathering they made tramping through the streets of North Vancouver to where Rourke stored one of his sleek cars—a weapon warper pledged as her personal, royal guardian, the Patron Fae of Assassins and Lord of Shadows who would soon enter a marriage of convenience with her, and then Raven, the queen-in-training, PI, ex-waitress, and half-fae raven shifter. Yes, definitely odd.

Then again, this was an odd new world.

Chapter Twenty-Three

"All my life I thought air was free...until I bought a bag of chips."

~ Unknown, also Raven Crawford

The door swung open and Raven stood face to face with her brother's best friend. Marcus's eyes widened and he stiffened in the doorway.

"Raven!" He glanced at Rourke. "You keep odder company by the day."

"You're being rude." Although she mentally noted the oddity of her group, someone else voicing it out loud was offensive.

After they made their way across the last-standing bridge to the Lower Mainland from the North Shore, they dropped Cole off at a random corner of the street—for a purpose unspecified—so her only odd company this time was Rourke. Knowing he'd pledged his life to her, she automatically felt defensive and protective of him.

Of a weapon-warping dark fae assassin turned guardian.

Rourke's amused smile taunted her.

Oh, shut up.

Marcus turned back to Raven. "An unexpected house call. Should I feel special? Are you here to ask me to join your special group of misfits?"

"I tried calling. Three times. You didn't answer and when we swung by the shop, they said you took a sick day. I was actually worried, you jerk." She tilted her head and studied her long-time friend, his dark hair was messier than usual, and his clothes more dishevelled, but he didn't look sick. From his apartment, a faint smell wafted into the hallway. It reminded her of...

"Is that alfalfa?" She wrinkled her nose. "Are you brewing potions?"

"Yes. Spell gone wrong. Don't ask." Marcus slipped into the hallway of his apartment building, closing the door to his place behind him. "This isn't a good time, Wenny."

Rourke growled.

She waved him off. "I'm sorry to interrupt whatever

potion play time you're having in there, but I need your help."

Marcus straightened and pulled his shoulders back. "I have a few fae-deterrent spells."

Rourke snarled, like that would somehow help change Marcus's opinion of his kind. Their kind.

"No. No, it's not that."

Marcus's frown deepened as she explained her current predicament.

"Do you have anything?" she asked after finishing a summary of events. "Something to boost my power or shield me from the magical backlash long enough for me to safely reabsorb my magic?"

Marcus's forehead wrinkled and his eyebrows bunched together. He tapped his chin. "Maybe..."

Something crashed in his apartment and he flinched.

"Do you...have someone over?" Raven asked. Normally, he wouldn't have answered the door, but that would explain the unanswered calls. Ever since Bear and Raven mercilessly teased Marcus about dating Mandy Penner, for two completely different reasons, he'd been private about his love life.

"Give me thirty minutes. Where should I meet you?"

"My parents' place," Raven said. She tried to relax her face and prevent a full-face frown. She'd grown up with Marcus. She used to have a crush on him. There was a time she would've walked around his place and helped herself to food and the remote control as if it were her own place. Sure, they didn't see each other as often anymore, they weren't as close, and he certainly didn't owe her anything, but something was off with him. "Blink quickly if you need help," she whispered.

Marcus rolled his eyes and shooed her away. "I'm fine. Just—"

Something shattered. Marcus cringed. "As I said, just give me thirty minutes. I'll be right behind you."

"Fine, fine. Who am I to argue when you're doing me a favour?" She walked away with Rourke at her heels but couldn't shake the feeling something else was going on with Marcus.

Chapter Twenty-Four

"I love sleep. My life has the tendency to fall apart when I'm awake."

~ Ernest Hemingway

Cool air flowed over Raven as she stepped from Rourke's sleek sedan with tinted windows and onto the sidewalk. She should've made him chauffeur her around when Cole first assigned him as her guard detail.

"Those toll trolls have never been so nice," she said, thinking about their earlier crossing before meeting with Marcus.

Rourke shut the driver's side door and joined her on the sidewalk. "Would you talk back to the Lord of Shadows?"

Raven turned to her guardian.

He groaned. "Of course, you would."

"But others wouldn't, especially when we paid their ridiculous toll in Underworld coin. I get your point."

"Those bastards are greedy. They hiked up the fees again. You'd think they were part goblin." Rourke locked the car and did the same disappearing trick with the keys as he did with his weapons.

Raven shrugged. She'd never met a goblin, so she had no knowledge to draw on. "Well, if you're not going to tell me what you dropped Cole off to do, why don't you tell me a little about goblins?"

Rourke smiled and flashed his jagged teeth. "Have you never met one? Not surprising, I guess. They like to lurk in the shadows, counting their coins and coveting the gold of others."

"That's not exactly ne—"

"Ms. Crawford." A familiar man stepped from between two parked cars and blocked their passage on the sidewalk. Tony the Tooth.

Before Raven could respond, Rourke flowed from his spot beside her to stand in front. Two long daggers appeared in his hands. He needed to show her that trick because it was pretty impressive.

Though she couldn't see Rourke's face, his snarl broke the silence. Tony wasn't alone, but his guards remained perched behind the nearby trees and parked cars. Amateurs.

Tony's lips curled down as he studied the fae guardian in front of him. "Call off your dog, Ms. Crawford. I'm here to talk."

To emphasize just how non-confrontational this meeting was, three hyena shifter goons stepped out from their "hiding" places.

"I merely want a progress report." Tony said. "Besides, fae aren't immune to bullets and you're out numbered."

Raven rocked back on her heels and reached for her magic. It sputtered and flowed away. Tony had picked a marvellous time to approach her. She'd planned to put him in his place next time he paid her a little visit, but that would have to wait. Luckily, she had absolute faith Rourke would and could defend her.

But at what cost?

She wouldn't sacrifice her friend and one and only caomhnóir to avoid a tense chit chat with a crime boss.

"It hasn't been a week, Tony. I have little progress to report. Robert belonged to a fanatical group of Regulators known as the Closers. After the meeting where Sarah confronted him, he disappeared. He hasn't accessed his bank accounts, he hasn't shown up for work, he hasn't retrieved any of his belongings from his shared dwelling with Sarah and he hasn't contacted his mother." Of course, Raven hadn't confirmed any of these details. She didn't need to. When Robert kidnapped and beat her baby brother, he'd signed his own death certificate.

Her stomach churned and her brain chose this inconvenient moment to flood her head with memories filled with blood and pain.

Raven swallowed the lump in her throat.

Tony studied her face for a long minute before speaking again. "What's your take? You must have one."

"He might be on the run or hiding."

"But?"

"But that would mean he's either supplied by Closers or he had a pre-organized exit plan complete with a nest egg. Robert has never been good with looking ahead or being well-liked, nor have I discovered any skill or attribute of his to make him invaluable to the Closers. I don't see either of these explanations fitting. Plus, he never goes more than three days without calling or seeing his mother. She's in quite a panicked state right now."

"So?"

"So, I think someone else beat you to it. I think he's dead."

Tony somehow managed to narrow his eyes more. "That would be most unfortunate. His life was ours to take."

Raven shrugged. She couldn't turn back time.

"You will find out who killed him and locate his remains."

Rourke snarled.

Tony spared him a glance. "He's rather impressive. Where did you get him?"

Raven ground her teeth together and waved Rourke away. She didn't want to tip off Tony to her fae status or hopefully soon-to-be reinstated powers. Having a dark fae guardian with jagged teeth would raise some flags and suspicions. The last thing she needed was Tony the Tooth taking an interest in her background and conducting his own investigation. He would discover all her dirty dark fae secrets and adjust his plans and manpower accordingly. She preferred it if the gang leader underestimated her.

"I will continue my search," she agreed.

Tony's face remained expressionless. Without another word, he nodded at his goons and walked away. Their cologne drifted in their wake, surrounding Raven and Rourke in a cloud of perfumed air. Their expensive shoes glinted underneath the winter sun and slapped the cold pavement.

Raven stood with Rourke in silence, waiting until the hyenas loaded into their vehicles and pulled away from the curb.

"I'm not a dog." Rourke had seethed the entire time they watched the hyenas, tightening and relaxing his hold on the dagger hilts. "And they shouldn't speak to you that way, mo bhanrigh."

Raven shrugged. It wasn't that big of a deal. Her life as a waitress gave her plenty of experience at being mistreated by others. Her skin had thickened over the years. She could take Tony's small insults.

Rourke turned to her. "You should've killed them for their insolence or let me do the honours. Letting them go makes you look weak."

Raven sighed. Dark fae and their obsession with appearances. "I am weak, Rourke. Or did you forget I drained all my powers?"

"I could've taken them down for you."

She nodded. "At what cost? I wouldn't want you harmed for protecting me from something as silly and mundane as assholes talking shit."

"Wouldn't want me harmed?" Rourke sputtered. "You underestimate my skills."

"Good. Let me be pleasantly surprised when you have to protect me. But for now, I prefer those goons to underestimate *me*."

Rourke's expression softened with understanding. "As you wish, mo bhanrigh."

They walked in companionable silence down the sidewalk toward the house while the cold wind tried to cut open their faces. When Rourke opened the gate and held it for Raven to step onto the walkway to the house, a loud croak erupted. The eerie boom of sound sent tremors down her body.

Rourke reached out and gently gripped her forearm to stop her.

Two large ravens launched from the tree in the front yard, the branches groaning and creaking from the pressure.

Raven let out a long breath, the warm air condensing into a puff of white. She patted Rourke's hand. "Huginn Muninn."

Rourke gaped at her. "You mean Huginn *and*

Muninn."

She shook her head. "Watch."

As they studied the birds aloft in the winter sky, they collided and reformed into an imposing man dressed in formal court attire, complete with knee-high metal shielded boots, breastplate, gauntlets and a billowing cape made of raven feathers.

"Raven." His deep voice rumbled down the path, sounding more akin to his ravens than a mortal man.

"Father."

Rourke released his grip on her arm but did not relax his stance.

Her biological father's gaze flicked to her fae guardian. "Your caomhnóir?"

She nodded.

"A wise choice." He dipped his head to Rourke and turned back to her.

"I wasn't aware I had one," Raven muttered, though she felt safer in Rourke's presence and wouldn't have chosen anyone else, a little annoyance pinged her brain at decisions being made for her. Again.

"How are you here?" she asked. Passage between realms was blocked after all.

"I was already in the Mortal Realm when you formed a blockade."

"What in Odin's shriveled nuggets is going on out here?" Mom shrieked from the doorway behind Huginn Muninn.

Her biological father stiffened and slowly turned from where he stood.

Raven couldn't see his face, but she had a clear view of Mom's. All the colour drained from her cheeks and her mouth dropped open.

"Hello, Lizzie." Huginn Muninn bowed.

"Hugie?"

Chapter Twenty-Five

"Boobytrap backward is partyboob. Carry on."
        ~ Unknown, obviously a genius

ugie? Raven puked in her mouth a little.

"Time has been kind to you, Lizzie." Huginn Muninn's voice dropped lower. The wind swept through the front lawn and rustled his thick cloak. Feathers brushed against his armoured boots and the corners flapped in the air.

"You...you can't be here." Mom drew herself up, her face somehow draining of more colour.

"You freaks need to find a better meeting place!" A

weathered voice screeched from the property beside them.

In unison, they all turned to the elderly woman shaking her fist at them from her deck. The cold wind almost knocked her over, but the old crone clutched the guard railing with her skeletal fingers. Apparently, distance and the illusion of protection the bannister offered were all Mrs. Humphreys needed to bolster her confidence.

Rourke leaned over. "Shall I stab her for you, mo bhanrigh?"

Oh, if only she could say yes. She didn't recall telling her guardian much, if anything, about her bigoted neighbour, but he'd guarded Raven for months now and must've witnessed enough to come to his own conclusions.

Raven snorted and swatted his arm. "Knowing our luck, she'll just stick around and haunt us."

Rourke grumbled but relaxed his stance beside her.

"Get inside," Mom said, her tone resigned and annoyed at the same time.

Huginn Muninn turned to leave, but Mom's voice stopped him in his tracks.

"You, too," Mom said.

They filed into the house while Mom stood guard and glared at the neighbour. Pretty sure she flashed her the one-finger salute before retreating into the warmth of the house. After the door clicked shut, the entranceway became very crowded with four adults, one of whom was a large fae warrior in full armour.

"The living room is over there." Raven lifted her arm and pointed to the matching sofas with a coffee table placed in between.

Huginn Muninn, or Hugie hesitated and glanced down at his boots. The metal creaked.

"Don't worry about those," Raven said. "Go right in."

Mom peered around Hugie's large frame and glared at Raven.

She shrugged. Did they really want to stand around waiting for him to pull off his armour? This was awkward enough.

Hugie stalked into the living room and contemplated the two sofas. He opted for the one facing the large window that looked out to the front yard and placed his back to the wall with all the family photos.

Mom drew in a deep breath and pushed past Raven to sit on the opposite sofa.

Raven glanced at Rourke and then the door. Maybe they could sneak away and give these two some privacy.

As if reading her mind, Rourke shook his head and jerked his chin toward the sofas.

Good point. They might need a referee more than privacy.

Or a witness.

Raven mentally pulled up her big girl socks and joined Mom, sitting on the far side of the same couch, so she could watch both her biological parents, the front yard, and the entrance where Rourke remained. Though she had Mom's back, one hundred percent, she chose her position because Hugie took up almost the entire other couch, so there wasn't much choice.

"We have children," Mom said, more in a whisper.

He nodded, stiffly. "They are beautiful. I am very proud of both of them and the life you have given them."

"Have you always known?"

Hugie hesitated and glanced at Raven.

You're on your own, dude.

"I knew."

"All along?"

He nodded again. "I was aware of your pregnancy and the moment they were born. I felt my essence expand and split."

Huh. Though Raven knew Hugie was aware of their existence early on, hence Odin's orders to have Mom killed if she ever entered the Underworld, but she hadn't known about the essence splitting.

"You left me to struggle," Mom said.

"You persevered."

Mom clenched both hands into fists and rested them on her lap. "I was young and dumb and suddenly a mom of unruly twins with special abilities. Help would've been appreciated."

"And help you received, though you may not have realized it."

Mom clamped her mouth shut. She took long deep breaths as her gaze darted back and forth. "The small inheritance from the mysterious great aunt?"

Hugie dipped his head.

"The sudden vacancy at the rent controlled apartment building?"

He nodded again.

Mom pursed her lips. "Thank you, but I needed emotional help. Companionship. Support. Did I mean nothing to you?"

"You meant everything to us." Hugie's gaze flashed. His voice came out in that dual tone and sent shivers racing down Raven's skin. His dark Other energy rippled off him and cascaded from his body to flow over the room. "We loved you and we still do."

Raven squirmed in her seat, but Rourke shook his head at her again. Argh.

"Then why?" Mom asked.

"I told you why." His dual tone disappeared, and his voice hardened. "My father ordered your death if you ever stepped into the Underworld again."

"Because I was pregnant? I hadn't told you yet. How did you—Oh, never mind. That doesn't matter, does it? I always assumed I couldn't enter the Underworld because Odin didn't approve of me. I assumed he'd find out about the children or sense them somehow if they entered the Underworld. I tried to hide them because I knew if he didn't approve of me, he wouldn't approve of them. I forbade Raven and Bear from entering the Other Realms to keep them a secret from the mighty Allfather." Mom sagged into the couch. "And he knew the whole time."

Hugie didn't respond. He didn't have to. Mom was correct about everything.

"You could've stayed here with me," she said. "With us."

Hugie shook his head. "Odin would never let us go. He would've changed his orders. We were lucky he included your presence in the Underworld as a requirement for your death sentence. It provided a loophole."

"And if he hadn't?"

Hugie stared at her.

"And if he hadn't?" Mom demanded. "Would you have carried out his orders like a good little creation?"

Hugie looked away.

Mom stiffened. Her lips trembled and her brows pinched in. "I was obsessed with you. There was a time I would've followed you anywhere."

Raven shifted on the cushion again. Now would be a good time to be anywhere else but here.

"But not now." Hugie's smile wasn't exactly sad, but it wasn't radiant either.

"Not now." Mom shook her head. "I found someone else to love. Someone worthy of my love."

Hugie nodded. "Terry Crawford is a good man and has been a better father to our twins than I ever would have been. There is a reason I was meant to be sterile. My life is not well-suited for babies."

Mom pursed her lips and the skin around her eyes tightened as if she was about to say something catty and then thought better of it. Juni got the same look.

"You should have told me what you were. What you are."

Hugie tilted his head. "Would it have changed anything?"

"Between us? No. But the information would've been handy for raising the twins."

Hugie's face split into a genuine smile this time. "They turned out all right."

That wasn't what Mom meant and everyone in the room—including Hugie—knew it. She didn't peg him as the type to deflect.

Raven had always been grateful for Mom, but she never quite realized or acknowledged what an absolute rock star she was. Without hesitation, Raven could recall all the crappy stuff that happened in high school, which somehow ended up being Mom's fault even if she wasn't there, but Raven never reflected much on the earlier years. Elizabeth Crawford had been a young, first time mom with a set of rambunctious babies.

Damn.

Mom needed a hug. Some chocolate. Wine. And a thank you.

Before Raven could think of something, anything, to say, footsteps thumped up the entrance stairs and the front door swung open with a familiar creak.

Crap! She hadn't been watching the front yard. She glanced at Rourke. His wide eyes and flat mouth gave her a millisecond warning before Dad turned the corner and halted abruptly at the wide entrance into the living room.

Awkward.

"Hey, Dad." Raven gave a half wave.

Mom closed her eyes, probably mentally preparing some sort of exit strategy or conflict resolution speech.

Hugie swept to his feet and bowed to Dad.

Dad frowned and rocked back on his heels. He wasn't purposefully being rude, at least Raven didn't think he was, he'd probably never had anyone bow to him before in his life.

"Sorry, who are you?" Dad asked.

Hugie straightened. "My names are Huginn and Muninn, thought and memory, Odin's creation and sire to Bjorn, Commander of Corvids, and Branwen, Queen of Corvids."

What in the Underworld was that? He added her and her twin to his title? Name dropping was one thing but bragging about "siring" children was a whole new level of ick. All sorts of ew rippled along her skin.

As if sensing her unease, Hugie turned to her with a tender expression. "I apologize. Adding you and Bear to my title was not my idea."

Dad crossed his arms in front of his chest and scowled at the large fae warrior in front of him. "Then whose was it?"

Hugie turned back to Dad. "Odin's. He felt the inclusion of Raven and Bear in my title directly following his own name would help remind the Others of your children's court connections and dissuade some of the less-than-scrupulous fae from trying to kill either of them."

Dad grumbled, but he didn't look nearly as pissed off anymore.

"For what it's worth. I agree with my sire," Hugie said.

Mom stood and smoothed down her wrinkle-free pants. "Why are you here?"

Hugie turned to Raven again, a sad smile spreading across his face. "I'm here to formally invite Raven to attend the High Court Fae Council in two days." Hugie paused. "Though the summons is framed as an invitation, do not make the mistake of taking it as such. Your presence is demanded and if you refuse to attend, such a choice will have dire, and most likely painful, repercussions."

Raven sighed. She already knew about the meeting and had the dress—or more accurately underwear—to prove it. "Thank you, Huginn Muninn. I have a low pain tolerance and no inclination to test it. I will be in attendance unless something unforeseen and unavoidable prevents me from attending."

Hugie nodded. He bowed first to Raven, then Mom, Dad and Rourke before heading to the entrance.

Dad stepped out of his way, giving side-eye that would've made Juni proud.

Hugie paused and turned back to face the room.

"I'm sorry things ended the way they did with us," he said to Mom. "Although I have grown accustomed to saying goodbye over my immortal existence and the short lifespans of mortals, I was not prepared, nor did I want to part ways with you so soon. I did what I had to in order to protect you and the children." He paused and looked longingly at Mom. "I'm sorry those actions came at the cost of your pain."

Hugie drew himself up, transforming into the dangerous fae warrior he was and contrasting with the thoughtful words he just spoke. "I'm not sorry we created two beautiful souls. Nor am I sorry they had you as their mother. I'm proud of who Branwen and Bjorn have become, but I'm even prouder of you, Elizabeth. The pain I caused you in your life is fleeting and thankfully healed by the love of a good man and your own innate strength. My curse is thought and memory. I will forever be plagued with thoughts and memories of you, long after you have departed from this world. Whatever hatred you hold for me—if in fact you still have any—please let it go. It does you no good and it is unnecessary. I have already received a harsh and unforgiving punishment."

Without waiting for a reply, Hugie strode from the house and closed the door quietly behind him. Seconds later, the sound of heavy wingbeats filled the otherwise silent room.

Raven stood beside her parents and looked at Rourke for some guidance. How in the Underworld did anyone segue from such a speech?

Rourke eyed the door Hugie had just disappeared through, possibly contemplating escape. Oh, no, he didn't. If he made her stick around, he had to stay and suffer, too.

"So, that was your Scandinavian god?" Dad said.

They all turned to Dad and his amused smirk.

Oh no. Now was not the time for a Dad joke. "Dad..."

He widened his eyes at her. "What? I think puns about Norse gods are Loki the best."

Raven smacked her face with her palm.

Rourke groaned.

"Terry," Mom warned.

Dad looked the opposite of innocent. "Thor subject?"

"Please stop." Mom threw her hands on her hips. "This isn't funny."

"Just Odin-ary?" Dad waggled his brows.

A snicker escaped Rourke's mouth. He looked as surprised as the rest of us.

"How long have you been waiting to use those?" she asked Dad.

"How long have I been with your mother?"

Cole chose this moment to walk into the living room along with Marcus—apparently, the rest of them too focused on terrible Dad puns to notice their entrance into the house. Well, most of them.

Rourke nodded at the Lord of Shadows. Though Rourke had looked surprised and somewhat distraught at giggling over one of Dad's jokes, his lack of shock at Cole and Marcus' entrance indicated he'd caught their approach to the house.

She glared at her caomhnóir. They needed to work on their communication.

"What did we miss?" Cole glanced around the room with confusion.

Oh, where to start?

Chapter Twenty-Six

"I don't want to go to heaven. None of my friends are there."

~Oscar Wilde

Raven wrapped her arms around her chest and glared at the rock in Marcus' open palm.

"Are you sure this is going to work?" she asked.

Marcus closed his hand around the smooth rock and snatched his arm back before looking around her basement bedroom, avoiding eye contact with Cole and Rourke. "Yes. Your Raven's Eye and this talisman will shield you from the backlash and prevent you from becoming overwhelmed. You'll still have to act fast though. You can use Cole's power and the dubious amount of magic you have left to untether your spell. Because the spell I cast will temporarily bind you, your guidance will be all that's required to pull Cole's power past your magical knot. Once the magic is released, you will direct the energy back to yourself."

"But?" she said when the silence stretched too long.

Marcus cast a wary glance at Cole before stepping close and gathering her hands in his own. "Do you trust him?"

Cole snarled and the room darkened around them.

Marcus pulled his shoulders back but maintained the intense eye contact and refused to release her hands. "You will be extremely vulnerable during this time. Because Cole's magic is technically what you will use to untether the spell, he will have the opportunity to steal your power."

She smiled at Marcus and squeezed his hands. "I trust everyone in this room."

Marcus sighed. "That's what I was afraid you'd say."

The room darkened more. If Raven wasn't present, she wasn't entirely sure Cole would have let the male witch take another breath.

"How long will the binding spell last?" she asked.

"Only a few minutes. Long enough for you to tap Cole's power and untether your own. I'll activate the ward as soon as the magic fireworks begin."

"Not before?" The idea of possibly experiencing even a small bitch slap of power wasn't appealing to Raven. Low pain tolerance, and all.

He shook his head. "A ward works both ways. This one is a buffer and acts to slow the flow of magic. You don't want to waste what little strength and time you have trying to work through a buffer."

"It's like swimming through molasses," Cole said.

Marcus pursed his lips and glared, but Cole's analogy must've been accurate because he didn't correct him.

"Let's do this," Raven said. She'd spent entirely too much time talking and asking questions and frankly she was no less confused than before. She was a tactile kinesthetic person. She learned by doing.

Marcus nodded and muttered something under his breath. His magic snapped onto her wrists and Marcus' chant grew louder. Ice shimmied along her skin and her Other energy vibrated as if trying to dance away from the witch magic. Cole's power slammed into her.

She gasped.

"Now, Einin," Cole hissed.

She closed her eyes and focused on their power. It bubbled and twisted, bucking against the invisible confines of Marcus' spell. She focused on the vibrations of their magic, slowing hers down until it matched Cole's. The magic hummed with power, oscillating in harmony and straining to escape. It glowed with a shiny blue-purple hue and pulsed with a warm glow.

Ooooo. Shiny.

"Hurry, Wenny," Marcus' voice sounded strained.

She clenched her teeth and pushed her awareness and magic outward, past the barrier for the Mortal Realm and into the murky Realm of Shadows.

There, as if contained in a glowing hot air balloon, her spell loomed. Little pings and dents formed and rebounded off the surface.

"Magical attacks," someone far off murmured. "Trying to break the spell."

She drifted with the magic, moving closer to the tethered area which resembled a hastily tied knot. She reached out with her combined power and touched the thread. The magic coursed through her veins, thick like syrup, heady like vodka. A companionable familiarity danced along her skin. At least her magic knew its owner.

"Hurry, Einin..."

She gripped the thread and pulled.

Nothing happened.

Shit. The spell was supposed to unravel without much effort from her.

She tugged again.

Still nothing.

Her power waned and her vision of the spell faltered. Oh no. She'd run out of time. Power started to drain from her grasp. No! She couldn't let this happen. She reached out again with both hands and gripped a large band of magic caught up in the knot.

"Now," Cole's faint voice slipped into her mind.

"Arrrgggghhhh." Raven gathered her remaining energy and pulled the thread as hard as she could. The knot slipped. Slowly, so painfully slow, the spell unraveled.

Someone yelled in the distance.

Men's voices.

Power slammed into her. Pain shot through her mind and then she drifted. While her mind reeled and her body tingled, power flowed into her body, winding around her core like wool spinning on a loom.

Raven's mind transported to a different time—a simpler time when her only concern was keeping up with her brother and getting home before dark, hearing the cackling laughter of her siblings, feeling the warmth of their mother's love and later their new dad's. The time Bear had double bumped her on the trampoline and she flew off and broke her arm—Mom had been so mad. Squealing along the beach as the tide chased her. Lazy summer afternoons under the Canadian sun. Drinking from the hose. Wiping out on her bike and playing outside until the sun began to set.

The childhood memories drifted away, replaced with more recent ones. Ones filled with a man full of depth and mystery, shrouded in shadows yet open to her, and only her, to read like a favourite book.

Someone held her. Someone with strong arms who smelled of a magical forest when the light had already slipped away and the mystery of darkness took over. He whispered sweet things into her ear and smoothed her hair from her face. He told her he loved her as she continued to drift in a sea of power, detached from the world to recharge and reform as the Queen of Corvids.

Chapter Twenty-Seven

"Come here glorious coffee. Let me sip your sweet nectar while you tell me all the lies about what we're getting done today."

~ Raven, practicing her dark fae seduction routine with her morning coffee

A cool breeze carrying familiar scents of Underworld florals caressed her face. She opened her eyes to a stone ceiling. Immersed in a cloud of over-stuffed comforters and fluffy pillows, she lay in her Corvid Court bed. She turned to the heat source spread out beside her and found Cole awake.

His one hand rested on her pillow and he ran his fingers through her curling hair.

"You're awake." His deep voice rumbled over her skin.

"You're perceptive." She smiled and reached out to place her hand on his chest. She needed to touch him, to confirm this wasn't some dream. "And you brought me here instead of your place."

"Less eyes on this place to see you vulnerable. You did well, Einin. How do you feel?"

She'd say she felt like she ran a marathon, but she'd never done that. She didn't understand the whole running for fun thing. If there wasn't an ogre or bear chasing you, then why bother? Growing up in a family of runners didn't help with getting it. Now, flying...that she understood.

Her Other energy rose within her and the birds stretched at the thought of flight. They begged to be released, to play in the air. The familiar grip of her Underworld power felt like throwing on a favourite sweater or worn-in jeans—comfortable and reassuring.

"I feel great," she said and meant it. The exhaustion initially masked the realization she had her powers back. "How long have I been drifting?"

"A day and a bit. It's Sunday. We spent Saturday recuperating. You drifted in and out. You told me you loved me and called me your favourite book. Do you remember any of it?"

She shook her head. "Did I say anything else embarrassing?"

"Other than professing your undying love for me? No."

She snorted.

"I'm glad you're feeling okay." Cole stretched. "Because I suspect the Underworld council will send someone to 'escort' you to the meeting soon."

"Don't you mean us?"

He smiled again. She liked him like this, when it was just the two of them and he relaxed. Unguarded, Cole was breathtaking. She sighed.

"Are you sure you're okay?" he asked.

"Peachy."

Cole slipped from the bed and walked around to her side. "To answer your question, the escort will be for you. I will attend as your advisor, or guard or lover...whatever you want."

Or as her anam cara. His unspoken words hung in the air.

She wanted the man. That went without question. She also wanted the bond. From the moment Cole explained it to her, the idea felt right. But now wasn't the time. They had council meetings to attend, spite goats to find, and a Lord of War to alienate. From what she gathered about the bond, it meant a lot to Cole and a lot to her continued survival as a queen. If it was important to Cole, it was important to her as well. She just didn't want to rush the process. She wanted to savour it. "As my trusted advisor, what do you advise?"

He didn't hesitate. "Bring me as your bodyguard. To command a powerful—"

"And humble—"

"And humble lord will adjust some of the other Underworld nobility's perceptions." He held his hand out to her.

She sat up, pulled the covers back and swung her legs over the side. "Don't they know the truth?"

He shrugged. "Maybe, but it speaks of power and that's all they know how to respect."

"I have to wear the metal bikini, don't I?" She planted her hand in his and let him haul her to her feet. The stones were cold, the air frigid. The bed was warmer. She ran her hands along the comforter. Maybe they could slip back under the sheets and spend the day keeping each other warm.

Cole leaned in. "Just think what fun I'll have taking it off you later."

"Promise?" The thought helped warm her chilled skin.

Shadows streaked across the room and within seconds, a familiar decorated gift box hovered in front of her. She plucked it from the air and held it with both hands.

"Thank you," she said, dryly. "Do you have the matching banana hammock?"

Cole chuckled and shook his head. "I need to get ready as well. I'll be back in under an hour. If someone arrives before then, do not leave with them no matter what they say or try to threaten you with. You are a queen and in your own domain. They can wait for you. Remember that."

She gulped. "I'm not sure I like the sound of that."

He stepped in and cupped her face in the palm of his hand. "You will be fine. You're Raven fucking Crawford and these Others are not worthy of your time or presence. They should all bow before you."

He kissed her then, hard, and stole her breath away. Her lungs didn't taste air until the shadows carried Cole away. And she was okay with that. Breathing was so overrated.

With the tingles of Cole's kiss still on her lips, she threw the gift box on the bed and scowled. She may as well use the time to get ready, but she didn't have to be happy about it.

Chapter Twenty-Eight

"I may look calm, but in my mind, I have killed you three times."

~ *Unknown, but also Raven in the presence of certain dark fae lords, kings and gods*

Raven stepped into the large courtroom, her boots smacking the tile and sending echoes down the hall. Rourke looked up lazily from where he rested against a pillar and froze. His gaze scanned her body and his brow furrowed.

"I look stupid, don't I?" Though the outfit flattered her curves and had neat little inserts in the bra cups to store all sorts of goodies like lock picking tools and two small, flat daggers, she felt exposed. She'd never identified more with the fish out of water analogy than she did now. Here she was, flopping and flapping awkwardly for everyone to see.

"That outfit speaks to your power better than any flowery speech could." Rourke pushed off the pillar. He gave her a slight bow before straightening. "You look like the queen I swore to serve."

"Speaking of serving, I'm surprised to find you out here instead of closer to where I was getting into this contraption." She zipped up the small satchel she'd strapped to her waist. As neat as the inserts in the bra were, they couldn't hold her cell phone.

"Ah..." He looked away.

"What?"

"You had some unwelcomed, uninvited guests while you dressed."

"Is that so?" She looked around the room and found a suspicious smear marking the granite floor in the far corner.

"They were dealt with. You also have two guests seeking an immediate audience."

"Oh really?"

"Trolls."

She only knew two trolls by name. "Nerthach and Gwawrddur?"

Rourke flashed his jagged teeth at her. "And you almost pronounced their names right."

Ass. She could recite their names every day for the

rest of her life and still never get the complicated sounds correct. But in truth, she hadn't given the two much thought since she saw them last. "What do they want?"

Rourke shrugged.

"Very helpful."

"I'm your caomhnóir, not your secretary."

"What do you think they want?"

He shrugged again. "Also, not a seer."

Raven threw up her arms. "I need you to protect me from my enemies, but I also need you to protect me from my own ignorance. What do you think I should do?"

Rourke went silent, hopefully, contemplating her words carefully. "I think you need to hear them, but it would be best to wait until Camhanaich returns."

She nodded, coming to a similar conclusion. "But waiting for Cole will also make me look weak." And she was consistently told about the fae and their abhorrence for looking weak and disdain for those who were weak. She started to really hate this aspect of fae society, even if it explained why so many dark fae grew to become giant douche canoes. Didn't they realize it took more balls, or lady balls, to own their mistakes and admit their short comings? Humility and honesty were more attractive than false bravado.

"I don't think it's a coincidence that they showed up a few minutes after Cole left. If you stall them until Cole returns, they'll use that information and spread lies that you can't stand on your own."

Gah! Though Raven had a supportive family, she'd always strived for independence. This wasn't a matter of her being afraid of appearing weak, this was a matter of her asserting her own power and position in the Underworld. She needed to establish a reputation that she was not someone to mess with or else everyone would try to mess with her.

Well, wasn't that the rub. She was more dark fae than she'd like to admit.

"Send them in."

Rourke clenched his jaw, nodded and stalked toward the doors.

Raven pulled her shoulders back and willed herself to look regal, calm and collected in front of the trolls. She couldn't let them see her uncertainty or fear. That would be a mistake.

The two trolls shuffled into the room, appearing just as grotesque as before. Raven didn't consider herself a shallow or cruel person. It wasn't their outward appearance that made her cringe so much as what she sensed was on the inside—hate and greed. The two powerful, yet, ugly emotions flashed in their gazes as they surveyed the room and studied her with clear contempt.

She returned the favour. "Nerthach and Gwawrddur. Welcome to my hall."

They grunted in response and Nerthach jerked his head at Rourke.

She considered her caomhnóir and he remained where he stood.

Nerthach snarled. "We wish to have a private audience. Not one filled with the Lord of Shadows' spies."

"Rourke is my caomhnóir, not Camhanaich's."

Nerthach and Gwawrddur stiffened. They exchanged a look.

Yeah, didn't expect that did you, boys?

Rourke pulled back his shoulders and for the first time since Raven acquired Lloth's position, she felt she did something right. Fuck yeah, Rourke was her caomhnóir. Not bad for a relationship that started with one of them throwing a knife at the other's head.

Gwawrddur's lip curled up and his nostrils flared. "We wish to discuss the barrier."

"The barrier has been lifted." Crap. How many people knew she was the one behind the temporary blockade? Did they assume it was her because of her position as the Corvid Queen? Or did they glean the information from the spell? Did her magic carry some sort of marker or signature? Or had spies tipped them off?

Did it matter? None of those answers helped her unfold this situation.

Despite painting another target on her back, and even though she was completely winging it, at least this act would let others know she was capable of something. Maybe they'd think twice before sending assassins. Whatever the case, there was no need to waste everyone's time with fake outrage and denials.

"We would like to enter an arrangement with you,"

Gwawrddur said.

Oh no. Nope. She almost lost her sanity meeting the demands of her last deal. She'd rather read bedtime stories to Mrs. Humphreys for the rest of her life than go into debt with an Other again. Dark fae might deal like they worked at a casino but this was another aspect of Underworld society she was uncomfortable with.

Rourke appeared bored. At least on the outside. She had no doubt he would snap into action if needed.

"What type of arrangement?" she asked.

"We would like you to reinstate the barrier, permanently."

"Seems like everyone wants a barrier in place these days," she mused. Maybe there was a way to permanently install one, but she wouldn't try what she did again. "Why do you want a barrier?"

The trolls exchanged a glance.

"Our reasons are our own," Nerthach said.

Raven bit back a snort. She knew the answer even if they hadn't telegraphed it in that look. Greed. Their answer had to relate to profit. Trolls loved collecting tolls and if they wanted a barrier resurrected, they must have a way around it. Cole had said their domain operated outside the Other Realms and Mortal Realms. Their tunnel-like domain could provide a passageway and the trolls saw an opportunity to make money and boost their position in the Underworld. Another delightful way to extract tolls from the desperate.

"I can guess. Power, gold and perhaps slipping away from Odin's rule?"

The trolls grumbled.

It felt good to get something right on the first swing for once. The trolls were very motivated to install a new barrier. No wonder they had their toes dipped into the Closers business. They must be financing or helping the group somehow with the hopes the Closers would figure out some way to build a barrier.

"What's in it for me?" she asked.

Nerthach narrowed his eyes and Gwawrddur's thin lips curled into a sneer.

"Your family's continued existence relies on it," Nerthach said as if discussing the weather.

Rourke snarled.

Without thinking, Raven reached across the ether and snatched her scythe. The weapon materialized in her hand, the solid wood a comforting presence. She let her dark energy curl around her and flood the room. As if answering a call she never made, corvids flocked to the ceiling free courtroom and perched on the ramparts.

"You dare to threaten my family?" She dropped her voice. "In my court?"

Nerthach and Gwawrddur froze.

"No, my queen," Gwawrddur said hastily, raising both hands and fanning them up and down as if it would somehow calm the rising fury inside her.

She wasn't his queen.

She owed these two nothing.

"We simply meant to point out that they would benefit from this lucrative deal. The free passage of

Others is detrimental to the health of those less powerful." Nerthach licked his lips.

Lies.

All lies.

These two were full of shit.

She pointed her scythe at them. "Give me one good reason why I should let you leave this room alive."

Rourke flashed his jagged teeth and two long daggers appeared in his hand.

"We didn't mean to offend you," Gwawrddur said.

"Yet you have, and dark fae have killed for less," Raven said.

"We will return to our retinue," Gwawrddur said.

And there it was. The reason she couldn't kill him and also another implied threat. These two blatantly threatened her family, letting them leave now might be a mistake, but taking on a retinue of trolls with only Rourke as backup was definitely a misstep, too.

She snarled and let her power coat her skin and pulse. "Leave now before I regret it."

The two scurried out of the courtyard, moving their legs quickly without running.

The doors shut behind the retreating trolls and Rourke turned to her. "That was a mistake."

"Can you take on an entire troll retinue?"

"No, but those two would be dead and not able to lead them. You could've used a portal to take us away."

She nodded. "But can I afford to start a war with the trolls right now?"

Rourke sighed. "No, but I'm issuing an order to kill

any troll who comes near your family."

"Deal." She wouldn't allow her family to take the brunt of her poor decision making. They had to be protected at all costs.

Even if that cost was her life.

Chapter Twenty-Nine

"Lead us not to temptation...Just tell us where it is, we'll find it."

~Sam Levenson

Raven stepped through her portal gripping her scythe for emotional support and thanking Odin's left nut she had the Lord of Shadows guarding her back. Cole wore his court clothes—black matte armour lined with shining silver and a billowing black cape that moved with the shadows he commanded.

Sometimes the imbalance of power between them

worried her, but then she reminded herself of all the times Cole could've used her or abused his power and didn't. Even in situations where he must've wanted to take over, he held himself in check, not manipulating or coercing. He strove to raise her up so she could become his equal. She felt comfortable with him to ask questions and grow.

She couldn't say the same about the other occupants in the hall.

Mingling around tables covered with gilded platters decorated with fruit, meats and cheeses, were the upper echelon of the Underworld aristocracy. Odin scowled at her from the other end of the room and she tried to squash the urge to call out to "grampy" and finger wave.

"Did you just finger wave at the God of War?" Cole asked, his voice light with amusement.

Raven lowered her hand and shrugged. She tried to stop herself from finger waving, but she hadn't been successful. At least she hadn't called him "grampy."

Odin resembled the grittier version of the paintings and sketches portraying his likeness—long white beard, grizzled skin, square jaw, blind eye, scar running down half his face, broad shoulders and chest and prominent expression of disgust. He looked like he always smelled something bad. If this was the Lower Mainland, it would fit, but the air was clean here.

A giant raven perched on Odin's shoulder, indicating at least half her biological father was present, but she couldn't tell if it was Huginn or Muninn.

Another familiar dark foreboding man lurked in the shadows of the room—Erebus. A shiver sped along her spine. She wouldn't forget Cole's father anytime soon. He wore the same outfit as he had during his little visit to her stone balcony—the skeletal crown, the partial face mask and the black matte armour that resembled Cole's a lot more in the light. His white eyes blazed and when their gazes met, he jerked his chin up. He seemed a likely candidate to be the first person to laugh if she tripped and fell to the ground in her bikini armour.

She hadn't met anyone else in the room, but potent fae magic flowed heavy in the air and she had no doubt they were all deadly. The question was who wanted her dead and who merely wanted to use her?

The council members were also considerably more dressed than she was.

"I'm naked," she said.

"Keep your chin up. You don't wield the same power as they do and this outfit, though minimal, will remind them of that," Cole whispered in her ear.

Why did she get the feeling she missed some context? Maybe because she was always missing a few pieces of the puzzle? What did she have to remind them of? That she transformed into a conspiracy of ravens? A flock of birds hardly inspired fear.

Her attention drifted to Odin again. Ah. That's what he meant. She needed to remind them of her connection to the Allfather.

A gust of wind rushed through the room and another portal snapped into place. Bane, the Lord of

War, stepped from a fiery background and dusted off his impeccably cut suit as if the heat of his previous location still clung to him. What was he doing now? Cole had told Raven only kings, queens and gods received "invitations."

An intense dislike rose from within and the condescending scowl Bane directed at her didn't make anything better or change her opinion of him.

Cole's hand pressed into her back and he ushered her forward. The trepidation didn't ease with each step farther into the den of fae.

"Branwen, Queen of Corvids." Odin bellowed from across the room and raised a heavy looking goblet. "Daughter of Huginn and Muninn, Child of Odin."

The room grew silent, but instead of turning to her with derision, the crowd swiveled to an elegant woman with blood red hair cascading down her back. She slowly turned at the introduction.

She was stunning.

With a dark red cloak matching the shade of her long wavy hair, she wore shiny black armour that molded to her curves and reflected the candlelight in the room. With flushed cheeks and rosebud lips, she'd appear innocent or naïve like one of the fair maidens from the fairy tales Mom read to her growing up, except the harshness in her expression and hard gaze gave her away. Nope, not mistaking her for sweet and kind. This goddess would rip Raven apart given the chance.

Why would everyone turn to this woman when

Raven was announced? Did they have some sort of connection?

Someone slipped into the space behind Cole. The timing and direction raised every alarm bell in Raven's brain. She gripped the scythe, its magic and awareness already coursing through her veins and spun. Metal flashed under the light and she brought the weapon down in one swift move before the man could thrust the knife into Cole's back.

The man screamed and blood spurted from his amputated arms. Both of his hands fell to the ground, one still clutching the obsidian black blade.

Cole turned and his shadows lashed out to wrap around his unknown assailant. The shadows hoisted him into the air.

"Who sent you?" Cole growled.

The man jerked and foam frothed from his mouth.

Cole sighed and his shadows released the assassin. The body fell to the hard stone floor with a thump and blood continued to pour from the wounds.

"Nothing like an attempted assassination to start this meeting off right." Bane clapped Cole on the back before offering his arm to the stunning woman. Ah, Pretty Boy was an escort. He appeared jovial, as if he hadn't had a major tantrum in her brother's living room a couple of days ago. She wasn't fooled and the murderous glare he cast her before turning away confirmed his true feelings. He didn't like that she'd outsmarted him.

The other council members stepped around the

severed body parts and pool of blood as if the crime scene was an inconvenient puddle on the road.

"Someone clean that up," Odin barked somewhere behind her. He probably had an army of servants somewhere.

"Why would someone attack you here?" Raven whispered to Cole. "Was it Bane?"

"I doubt he was behind this attack. He prefers to do his own dirty work." Cole leaned down to reply quietly. "The council meeting is a target rich location. There will most likely be additional attacks and they could be on any of us. Some Others consider the potential payout worth taking a gamble with their lives. Keep your chin up and your eyes open."

She swallowed and nodded. Somehow, someway, Raven had to survive this council meeting and she suspected the path to success lay in following Cole's example. She needed to keep her mouth shut and her eyes and ears open.

She'd always excelled at the latter of these things, but she'd never claimed mastery over her own mouth.

Chapter Thirty

"Her skin is pale. Her eyes are red. Her laden voice commands the dead to rise and stand beside their dreadful queen. No mortal power escapes her thrall. Her hunger will consume us all. And even now I hear her call: Jolene."

~ *noot noot riot (@fauxparse, Twitter)*

The dark fae filed out of the large boardroom that wasn't modern in any way. Instead, it was a private dining hall with a heavy live edge wooden table, padded throne-like chairs and flickering candlelight. Raven carefully picked her way through the room, moving with the crowd and tried to contain her annoyance and anger. All that build up, subtle threats and importance hung on the existence of this mysterious council meeting and...wah, wah, wah. Nothing.

They hadn't learned who Cole's attacker was and Raven still didn't know the identity of the mysterious woman or why people looked to her when Raven's name was announced. What Raven did figure out was she didn't need to be here. This was a complete waste of her time. She'd let this approaching meeting ruin her sleep and stress her out for no reason. Why had the council summoned her? Everyone talked over her and she had nothing to contribute. At least nothing she wanted to offer, or anything they'd want to hear. Their subject matter still had her blood boiling.

She leaned into Cole. "I can't believe I missed roast night for this."

The corners of his eyes crinkled, and his hand pressed into the small of her back. "I'll make it—"

"A moment of your time, Branwen," Odin spoke behind her when she'd made it within a couple feet of escape.

She turned slowly with Cole while the remaining Others pranced, stalked and glided past them. No cheery goodbyes or love lost between anyone. They dispersed like robots given an order, except as gods, queens and kings in their own right, no one had issued any orders, which made Raven's surroundings even more disturbing.

Along with her annoyance from the apparent unimportance of the meeting and her anger at the subject matter, Raven's head still reeled from the sheer information intake of the meeting. There had been no orientation for noobs. A lot of the dark fae dropped names like bunnies dropped babies. Cole had given her a rundown on all the heavy hitters and some of the names thrown around sounded familiar, but it was a lot to take in. She filed the information for mentally dissecting later.

No one had asked for her feedback or comments, and she didn't offer anything. She also walked away from the meeting without making any deals or owing anyone anything.

Well, almost. She hadn't escaped yet. Odin and the stunning woman from before stood together and waited. She must've ditched Bane, because the Lord of War was nowhere in sight. Smart woman.

Raven leaned over. "Who's that?"

"The Morrigan. I didn't expect her to attend, she normally doesn't. That's why I didn't brief you on her appearance, beliefs or powers."

Raven's stomach dropped. The Morrigan. Since Cole hadn't provided any cliff notes on the dark fae standing beside her grandsire, Raven had to rely on her shoddy mortal realm knowledge. Like her, the Morrigan was a powerful woman capable of taking the form of a corvid. Raven had researched the goddess to search for possible connections years ago.

She'd found nothing.

What she had found was a vast amount of conflicting information on her appearance, identity and focus. Some claimed she took the form of a crow, others a raven, wolf or eel. Some said she was a single, individual goddess, yet, a number of powerful women from mythology with different names were referred to as the Morrigan by more than one source. What the research all agreed on was the Morrigan's fierceness and connection to warriors and battles, which explained Bane's presence as her escort.

In addition to providing a brief synopsis of the attendees, their powers, weaknesses and known plans and alliances, Cole had also detailed their physical appearances. The cliff notes on the Morrigan would've been appreciated. Raven's previous research on the Morrigan had turned up a variety of descriptions for what the goddess looked like. None of them matched the striking woman who emanated power and death standing in front of Raven. She reminded Raven of a spitting cobra—a beautiful, mesmerizing beast that could transition from an almost statuesque poke to striking out with vicious accuracy or spit venom in a foe's face.

Right now, the Morrigan seemed content to pose.

"Should I bow?" she whispered to Cole.

"Definitely not. You stand on your own and bow to no one."

The last dark fae drifted from the room leaving Cole and Raven at one end and the Morrigan and Odin at the other. Raven and Cole walked together to close the distance, Cole stopping them when they got a sword's length away.

"Branwen. I'd like to formally introduce you to the Morrigan." Odin's expression remained unchanged, giving Raven no indication about how he felt about this introduction—if in fact he felt anything at all.

Raven dropped her chin.

The Morrigan's dark gaze settled on her as if analyzing every flaw in her head with cold, calculating detachment. "Branwen? A bit on the nose, wouldn't you say?" The Morrigan's voice was deep and sultry like one of those women in the late night 1-900 commercials.

"You think that's bad." Odin leaned toward the Morrigan. "She goes by Raven."

The other woman snorted. "Shall I call myself Crow now?"

"Trust me," Raven interjected. "My mother wasn't pleased."

The Morrigan's gaze flashed. "Ah, yes. Your mother." She turned to the Allfather. "You said she'd been taken care of."

An icy shiver ran up Raven's spine. She already knew Odin had ordered Mom's death if she stepped back into the Underworld, just as she knew Hugie warned Mom and cut all ties with her, allowing Mom to live and Raven and Bear to be born.

Odin rolled his eyes upward as if reflecting on his own existence and what life choices led him to this moment. "It is fortunate then that I did not succeed.

We now have a grandchild who holds a position of power."

Hold up. "We?"

The two powerful supernatural beings turned to her with blank looks.

"You're my grandparents?" She waved her finger back and forth between the two of them before focusing on Odin. "I thought you said Huginn and Muninn were your creations."

Odin let out an exaggerated sigh. "Silly child. Has no one explained the birds and the bees to you? Yes, I created Huginn and Muninn with magic, but you can't create something from nothing. Matter is neither created nor destroyed."

Raven's mouth dropped open.

"I grow weary of this mundane conversation." Intense corvid energy rose up, snapping in place instantly and transforming the woman into a single giant crow. With a flap of her wings, the Morrigan launched from the floor and flew from the room. That cold entity inspired none of the warm fuzzy feelings she associated with her charismatic, and slight psychotic, Grandma Lu.

"Glad she's gone," Odin said. "She's not much of a conversationalist."

Wow. Pot meet kettle.

"She's much better at the doing than the talking." The mighty Allfather, her grandsire, the would-be murderer of Mom almost thirty years ago, waggled his eyebrows.

Ew. No.

"I wanted to talk with you in private." Odin changed the topic abruptly. "How much did you understand of today's proceedings? Now be candid, girl. Give me the truth."

Raven straightened her shoulders. "The Others despise mortals and want to obliterate the bulk of them and enslave any survivors."

The anger still rolled inside her, but it came in waves and had been fading until now. Speaking about the arrogance and prejudice demonstrated at the table, though, brought everything surging back.

"Yes, and we can't allow that to happen," Odin said.

"Because it will break the order you laid down and ruin your reputation?" A total guess, but dark fae seemed obsessed about appearing strong. She barely managed to suppress an eye roll.

Odin shook his head. "Because we can't create or destroy energy."

Raven frowned and her brain stuttered to dredge up the memory pinging from those words. He'd said something earlier about matter, but this time he was talking about energy. "You're quoting one of Newton's Laws to me?"

"You're thinking of every action has a reaction and that fits here, too," Odin said.

Cole leaned in, a constant reassuring presence at her side. "It's the Law of Conservation of Energy, which was first coined by William Rankine, but Sir Isaac Newton has been given credit for the origin of the principle in his work."

Raven blinked at him. Apparently, everyone was a fucking scientist but her. She didn't want to know how he knew more about physics from the Mortal Realm than she did.

"Some believe if we destroy mortals, their energy and therefore power will flow to us since it can't be destroyed."

"But not you?"

He shook his head. "It will not transfer. Death causes energy to transform. And it will create a vacuum, sucking power from the Underworld until—"

"It reaches an equilibrium," she said. She might not be a scientist, but she didn't skip classes, either.

"The process already started when the barrier first fell. That is why I enacted a truce. I saw how things were playing out, but they were not in our favour."

"Why won't anyone listen to you?"

"Arrogance," Cole said.

Odin glared but didn't contradict the Lord of Shadows.

Cole's words made sense and that sent all kinds of wrong shivering down her spine.

"No one wants to believe they are subject to anything, let alone the confines of physics," she summarized, not needing or expecting a response.

Odin set his mouth into a grim line. "You must stop this from occurring."

"Me?" She jabbed her forefinger into her breastbone. Why her?

Odin nodded. "You must reconstruct a barrier and exert your power over the crossing."

Everyone wanted a barrier. Geez. Message received.

"It's not just the power of the Other realms that's at stake," Odin warned.

Odin didn't need to elaborate because her mind had already rushed to that conclusion. The room grew chilly, not from the weather outside or her barely-there outfit. Instead, the reality of the situation sunk in and raised the hair follicles on her skin.

If she failed, her family, everyone she loved, would be at risk.

And that was unacceptable.

Chapter Thirty-One

"*My mind is like my internet browser: nineteen tabs open, three of them are frozen, and I have no idea where the music is coming from.*"

~ *Unknown, but obviously someone else who struggles with multitasking*

Raven stepped into her basement room surrounded by the familiar smells of home and comforting warmth. She'd stayed the rest of Sunday night and the majority of Monday letting Cole work away the tension knotting her muscles until she became languid and reassured.

She hadn't bothered finding a replacement outfit for her she-warrior armour. Instead, after showering at Cole's, she'd donned the battle bra once again, lock picking set and daggers included, and travelled home to put on some real pajamas.

Her bond with Rourke let her know her personal guard lingered somewhere outside the house. Most likely walking the perimeter of the block. Warm and safe, she could now relax and decompress everything that had happened recently. But the sleepwear would have to wait a few minutes. Now at home, she needed to prioritize her tasks first.

Complete promise to Bane. Check.

Pay off debt and set up contingency funds. Check.

Confront Megan. Check.

Survive Underworld Council meeting without making deals or owing anyone anything. Check.

Sort of.

Odin's warning replayed in her head.

Still to do:

Wear pajamas.

Resolve blackmail situation.

Find Pepe.

Prevent an all-out war between the Underworld and the Mortal Realm. No big deal. As long as no one else flounced by and dumped something else on her plate, she might actually have a shot of coming out of this alive.

She flopped down into one of the armchairs and sighed. Okay, more like moaned. Loudly.

"Raven?" Mom shrieked from upstairs. "Is that you?"

Raven cringed. Mom sounded more shrill than usual. Maybe she'd sensed Raven's ambitious plans to relax.

"Yeah, Mom," Raven called out and dropped her head back into the worn cushion. "What's up?"

"We need you."

Those three words had Raven springing from the chair and racing up the steps. The words and the tone mom used sent ice down Raven's body and flushed away her earlier exhaustion and longing for pajamas. Without knowing what would meet her at the top of the stairs, Raven bound into the kitchen and slid to a stop where everyone turned to face her with grim expressions.

Everyone except one.

"Juni's missing, Rayray," Dad said, tone solemn.

And those words sent Raven's world crashing down.

Chapter Thirty-Two

"Me: I'm finally happy
Life: LOL, wait a sec."

~ *Unknown*

Dad's words hung in the air like a death knell. In a house full of private investigators, "going missing" as a teenager or as an adult wasn't a case of rebellious behaviour or adolescent angst.

Raven shook the ice clinging to the back of her neck. Now wasn't the time to freak out.

"Cell phone?" she asked.

"Disabled. Found in her bag in her locker. We got a

call from school—the automated one to notify us she missed at least one class. When we called in, they said she missed her third and fourth period." Mom's hysterical tone had drained away, replaced with steely resolve.

"Someone nabbed her at lunch, then," Raven said. Secondary schools in Burnaby only had four classes in one day—two before lunch and two after.

Dad, Mom, Mike and Bear nodded.

Raven glanced at the clock. "She's been gone a max of four hours, a minimum of three." Juni had never gone silent for that long. Ever. Something was very wrong.

Raven gathered her magic and cast her awareness out, holding onto her love for her sister—attitude and all—and pushed. She came up against a wall.

Huh? That wasn't right.

She tried again.

Another wall, with a hint of her sister's essence on the other side. She couldn't locate to her sister. It wasn't as if she didn't exist anymore. It was almost as if... "They've blocked me somehow," she growled.

The shoulders of her family dropped in unison. They'd been hoping she could travel to Juni and that quick resolution fell through in less than a minute. The disappointment on their faces mirrored what Raven felt inside, and was devastating to see.

Raven swallowed the lump in her throat and pulled her shoulders back. She couldn't fail Juni. "Witnesses?" Her voice cracked.

"She wasn't with Dani or Donna. They both said she went out with some schmoe called Lincoln." Mike's lips curled down.

"What happened to Robbie Featherhead?"

"Feathermore, and she lost interest in that dropkick after he became obsessed with that stupid bottle flipping game. Anyway, Juni's friends used that weird app to ask Lincoln what happened, and he replied. He said he took her for coffee, and they came back to school. He didn't know she was missing."

"Believable?" she asked.

Mike shrugged. "Hard to pick up tone on text-based communication. We already have his number and home address. We should follow up."

Raven waited. Just his number and address? Mike would've gotten more.

"She didn't use her debit card and neither did he. If he took her anywhere, he must've paid cash. Juni never has cash on her."

Raven nodded. "I'll pay him a visit. We need to put a timeline together." She pulled on her power and the scythe snapped into her hand. Its now familiar magic danced in her veins waiting for her command.

Dad and Mike nodded.

Mom hesitated. "Wearing that, dear?"

Raven looked down. She still wore her warrior bikini from the Underworld Council meeting.

The men also scanned her outfit, their gazes widening as if only now registering her very un-Raven-like outfit.

251

"Yes, wearing this." Raven squeezed the shaft of the scythe. "Juni is missing. Fuck changing and fuck worrying what other people think. I'm the motherfucking Queen of Corvids and I'm done hiding."

Chapter Thirty-Three

"The women whom I love and admire for their strength and grace did not get that way because shit worked out. They got that way because shit went wrong, and they handled it. They handled it in a thousand different ways on a thousand different days, but they handled it. Those women are my superheroes."

~ Elizabeth Gilbert

Mike nodded at Raven's proclamation as if she announced going off carbs. "Word."

She turned to her brother. "I need the address."

He rattled off a number and street.

"I don't know where that is. Give me something nearby that's familiar. I'll locate to that and walk the remaining distance."

"It's right behind that cheap movie theatre you used to take us to as kids."

"The Dolphin?"

Mike nodded.

"On it." Without any more words, Raven gathered her power once again, pulled up memories of popcorn, butter, pop and that old movie theatre smell and reformed on the Burnaby sidewalk in a swirl of dark energy.

A woman shrieked and clutched the baby strapped to her chest.

"Really?"

The woman bowed her head and scurried away in the opposite direction, looking over her shoulder every few steps to ensure Raven hadn't decided to give chase and snatch away her crotch fruit.

Raven caught her reflection in the large display window for the theatre. She barely recognized herself. Her hair still wavy from the dark energy clinging to her, the fetish fae undergarments and the gleaming weapon in her hand were not things she typically associated with herself. But she gave zero fucks about any of it. Things changed. Her world had changed. Her role within it had changed and she needed to change. To adapt.

What Raven would not accept or tolerate was any

change, risk or threat to Juni's life and well-being. With rage powering each step, she stomped to the boy's house, ignoring the stares and shrieks of mortals as she passed them. The cold air sliced her exposed skin. Anger fueled her. The sense of impending vengeance heated her. The power pulsing in her veins provided strength.

Raven stalked up the steps and knocked on the door, gently rapping her knuckles on the smooth wood.

Soft footsteps padded against a hard surface on the other side. Someone gasped.

No one answered the door.

"Open up," she said. "I know you're there."

A neighbour popped her head out their front door and looked over. The woman's eyes widened. "Eep!" She ducked back in her house, slammed the door and turned the deadbolt.

Raven waited, her patience quickly draining away.

"We don't want any trouble." A young man's voice cracked.

Raven turned to the street. The house didn't have a garage and there were no cars parked out front. It was later in the afternoon, not even five o'clock. His parent or parents were probably still at work.

"We." Raven snorted.

There was probably a tactful way to handle this situation. A delicate coddling of a young impressionable adult who possibly witnessed her sister's abduction and might hold valuable information in a fragile mind.

And kept it to himself.

"Arrrgh!" Raven shot out with her magic and scythe and blasted the door open. Wood splintered and fragments and chips flew by her.

A young man stumbled and fell backward onto the stairs leading to the second floor.

"Who...who are you?" His face still held the smoothness of youth, but even now he had good looks that would only get better as he matured.

Totally Juni's type.

Raven could see her sister near-swooning when this guy, Lincoln, asked her out as if she stood right beside them.

"I'm Juni's sister."

Lincoln's eyes widened.

"And you're going to tell me where my sister is."

Chapter Thirty-Four

"My life feels like a test I didn't study for."

~ Unknown

Lincoln's lip trembled as Raven hovered over him, murder flowing in her veins.

"I...I don't know where Juni is. I already told her friends I don't know anything."

His gaze told a different story. When people lied, their eyes tended to dart back and forth because they felt uncomfortable. Given Lincoln had a dark fae, scythe-wielding queen in an armoured bra looming over him, she might overlook this tell, but he also looked up to his right before he answered her question. When someone right-handed lied about something they saw, they often looked in that direction to access their imagination. He had to think up a response instead of recalling the truth.

In addition to the long blinking, pursed lips, excessive sweating, head shaking and blushing, Raven had found a liar.

"Ah..." She pointed her scythe at his face. The weapon didn't care if he was a minor. It hummed with anticipation and begged for her command. "But you're not telling the truth, are you?"

"I honestly don't know where she is," he repeated.

"Maybe not anymore." She leaned in. "But you know something, don't you?"

He shook his head and looked down to the right this time. Lying about sensations.

She lifted his chin with the flat edge of the scythe. "You never made it to coffee. She never made it back to school. She would've gushed or complained about her hot date with her friends the second you left her, but they didn't get any messages."

His guilty expression confirmed her suspicions.

"Cut the act, kid. Your pouting and feigned innocence don't work on me. You saw who took her."

He gulped and nodded. "But I don't know who he is."

"Why don't you tell me everything?"

Lincoln glanced down at the scythe at his neck before squeezing his eyes shut. "I don't want to die."

"If you don't start talking, you're going to wish you did."

Lincoln's shoulders slumped. "I don't know who the guy was. He offered me one thousand dollars to take Juni out for coffee today at lunch. When we arrived, a black car pulled up, men hopped out, grabbed Juni and drove off."

The anger inside Raven surged up again. She squeezed the weapon in her hand and clenched her teeth. Using every ounce of will power and self-control, she held back and didn't chop the guy's head off. "You set my sister up for one thousand dollars? That's what her life is worth to you?" Juni was priceless, asshole.

He gulped again. "My mom's had a hard time making rent. It was supposed to be a birthday present to her."

Raven closed her eyes, took a deep breath and lowered her weapon.

"Are...are you going to kill me?"

"Not right now." She straightened and stretched her neck.

"Um?" Lincoln looked back and forth. He still sprawled on the stairs with the remains of the front door scattered around him. "Can I get up?"

"No."

He froze.

"You're going to answer all my questions and if you try to lie to me again, I will kill you. Do you understand?"

He nodded vigorously and Raven started grilling

him, squeezing out every ounce of information and detail until Lincoln sagged into the steps, and Raven was satisfied he didn't know anything more.

She left him like that—alive and scared—and stomped down the front steps of the house to get some fresh air.

Raven wasn't a natural born killer. She couldn't and wouldn't take this boy's life. Yet, he'd set up her sister and placed the value of her life at a thousand dollars, and on top of that he'd misled Juni into thinking he liked her. Raven's heart ached for her sister.

Lincoln also had no idea who the man was. He couldn't provide any details about his appearance, clothing or accessories besides being "kind of white" and in a fancy suit. His details of the men involved in the actual kidnapping weren't much better. He couldn't tell her the exact number of men, but thought it was three. They had covered their faces and wore gloves and matching black tracksuits. Lincoln didn't get the make of the vehicle or the licence plate and he'd already banked the money so she couldn't confiscate the bills for Mike to sniff.

Lincoln did explain how Juni's phone and backpack made it back to school. She hadn't taken her bag with her at lunch and she'd dropped her phone during the abduction. He'd "thoughtfully" returned the device to Juni's locker like a good little accomplice. Raven made a mental note to lecture Juni about keeping her locker combination private, along with some other stuff.

She breathed in the cool air and waited for an idea

to come to her. Lincoln was an opportunist lacking morals and the man who approached the boy, whomever he was, was probably just some patsy, but the lack of details still gave her something. Though the trolls had low-key threatened her family, they didn't normally deal with humans, aside from charging ridiculous toll rates. She couldn't remove them completely off the list because they *had* threatened her family and were connected with the Closers, but she mentally moved them down the list of suspects.

Raven also gleaned the location of the abduction. Before she could travel there, she needed to decide what to do with Lincoln. He was useless for providing tips and he needed to pay for his crimes against Juni. Raven knew just who to call for advice.

Running her index finger along the blade of her scythe, she let the small amount of blood trickle down her finger. "Beul na h-Oidhche gu Camhanaich."

A flurry of shadows swirled around her forming a vortex of darkness, and from the depths, Cole stepped onto the sidewalk.

"My love." His deep voice curled around her as he took in their surroundings. "An interesting choice of location."

"Someone took Juni."

Cole's relaxed posture disappeared, replaced with predatory anticipation and a snarl. Just like that, he flipped the switch to lethal assassin and he did it for her sister.

"Who?" Anger flashed in his gaze. A chill ran up

her spine and this time it wasn't the cold air. Cole didn't get his ruthless reputation for nothing.

"We don't know yet." She jerked her thumb to point at the busted door on the house behind her. "One of Juni's classmates set her up for a thousand bucks from a stranger."

Cole's expression turned glacial and a long dagger appeared in his hand. "I'll kill him for you."

"He's just a boy."

Cole scowled. "I was just a boy when Nyx started sending assassins after me because she hated seeing evidence of her lover's past affections and infidelity. This boy had to have known what he was doing was wrong. His moral compass is fucked. He might not have known what the stranger planned to do with Juni, but anyone with two brain cells could've figured out it wasn't to have a nice chat. Did he even pause to think what would happen to her? Did he ask what the stranger's intentions were?"

"No."

"Then he didn't care. She could be beaten. Raped. Killed. Or merely held as a bargaining chip. He had no way of knowing and it didn't matter to him." Cole snarled. "Let me kill him. I'll make it quick if you prefer."

"I can't kill him, and I don't want you to either, but he needs to be punished. And if something bad does happen to Juni, then I'll let you end his life."

"Punished?"

"Severely."

"Torture?" Cole seemed entirely too pleased with the idea.

"No. Not yet. Not until we know what happened to Juni." Raven's moral compass was a giant pain in the ass, but at the root of the problem was her reluctance to kill and killing someone not directly threatening her life or those she loved seemed too cold of an action.

"Servitude?" Cole asked.

"Yes." That sounded right. "Servitude and made an example. I want others to know there's a cost for crossing me."

Cole smiled a savage, proud smile. "I'll take care of it and return to you." He glanced around again, and a new scowl scrunched his mouth. "Where's Rourke?"

Oops. That poor fae was probably sick of her leaving him places.

Cole glowered.

"Take care of Lincoln. I'll go home and pick up Rourke."

"Next plan?"

"I'm going to where they took her and see if I can get any more information."

Cole nodded, grabbed her by the plated bra strap and pulled her in for a quick, fierce kiss. "Take Rourke this time."

"Aye, aye, Captain."

"You say the oddest things." He walked past her, and his armoured boots hit the paved walkway through the dead lawn with the finality of a death knell.

Lincoln's cry of terror should've upset her. Maybe it

would've a few weeks or months ago. His fear didn't make her happy, either. Not with her sister still missing and enduring whatever sinister plot her abductor planned.

No, his shrieks didn't scare or delight her. They provided grim satisfaction. At least one person was already paying a price for hurting her baby sister.

Hopefully, more would follow.

Chapter Thirty-Five

"Not to brag, but I don't even need alcohol to make really bad decisions."

~ *Unknown, but also Raven*

Raven stepped from her portal onto a sidewalk at the western edge of Burnaby with Rourke in hand and Mike curled up in fox form in the crook of her arm. She stood outside a café a little too far from the school to be attended by students on their lunch break unless supremely motivated by caffeine and not by the three closer cafés.

A well-thought out location that provided minimal

witnesses.

Raven scowled.

Mike yipped and squirmed in her grip.

Oops. She'd squeezed him a little too hard.

Raven still hadn't changed from her gladiator undies and from the gasps and looks of fear and disgust, her unusual attire hadn't gone unnoticed. The café had already closed by the time they arrived, but with Mike and some PI skills, the location could still provide after-hours information.

"You're up." She patted Mike's head and set him down.

Rourke had released her hand on arrival and positioned himself at a good vantage point to watch over them. He still wasn't speaking to her for leaving him behind. Again.

Mike trotted around the corner, scratching the cold pavement and sniffing the ground. He whined and kept moving. His ears perked up and his pace quickened. He'd caught Juni's scent and followed the trail. After running down the sidewalk, Mike reached an area right before the corner of an intersection, circled around, whined and sat down.

"Hey! You can't have your dog unleashed here!" A man yelled out at her.

Raven turned to face him, reaching through the ether to grab her scythe.

The middle-aged man with wide shoulders and square jaw skidded to a halt. His eyes widened. The golden retriever who stood beside him on a thick red leash panted at her.

Raven gathered her power around her body like a cloak. "Funny you would notice an animal without a collar or leash, but you failed to notice this is not a dog and I'm not someone to piss off with bylaws."

The man gulped and took a step back.

She stepped toward him. "Nor did you, or anyone else in this neighbourhood notice a teenaged girl getting abducted from this very street. This spot. Right here. No one called the police, which means either no one saw or heard a thing or if they did, they decided to ignore it." Her anger had returned full force, it still came in waves and the surge of rage continued to rise.

The man straightened. "I just came home from work. When did this happen?"

"Lunchtime."

He nodded and pulled out his phone. He looked like a Chad or a Sean. Maybe Steve. "Most people on this street work during the day, but I'm on the block watch. I'll send a text to see if anyone was home and saw something." He hesitated. "If I find something, how do I get a hold of you?"

"Call Crawford Investigations. They're also on this case."

He finger stabbed the phone and nodded.

Raven turned away from him and his smiling dog to analyze the location where Mike sat with his head down.

The large hedge behind him would've blocked the view of anyone sitting in the café or visiting the other shops in the small complex from witnessing the abduction.

In fact, until Juni walked past the hedge into the parking lot, they wouldn't see her approach at all. But Juni never made it past the hedge.

No one saw.

A pit sank in her stomach. They'd still canvass the now-closed businesses, but they'd likely lead to a dead end.

"Mike?"

Her brother looked up at her with his sad brown gaze.

Her heart wrenched. She needed to stay focused. Juni needed her. She needed all of her family.

Raven pointed at the nearby streetlights. Everything had cameras these days and everything was digitalized. If it was controlled by a computer, Mike could hack it.

Mike followed the path of her finger-pointing and must've followed her train of thought as well. He leapt up and sprinted toward her, jumping into her arms.

She turned to Rourke and held out her hand. "Time to go."

Chapter Thirty-Six

"Dear Life, could you at least start using lubricant?"
~ Unknown, also Raven Crawford

When they reformed in Raven's basement room, Mike leapt from her arms and raced up the stairs. Rourke released her hand and looked around the bedroom, pausing to taking in the Christmas lights strung along the wall.

He raised an eyebrow. "Interesting decorating choice."

"I'll add some skulls, old broadswords and cracked shields to make it more fae-like for you."

He shook his head. "What's the plan?"

Raven sighed and rested the scythe against the nearby wall. "Juni is fifteen years old. Her daily life consists of how to copy the latest makeup trend, whether Lincoln McDoucheNozzle likes her and the outrage at being forced to learn how to factor trinomials when she can't foresee any possible use for them."

Rourke frowned.

"She has no real enemies aside from Closers who hate anything supernatural, including cute fox shifters. There's no one who would specifically go to this much trouble to target her for something she did."

"You suspect her abduction is linked to you," Rourke concluded.

"Don't you?"

"From the start."

"Me, too. While we wait for Mike to hack Transport Canada to access the traffic cameras, my mom and dad to track down the business owners and their employees, and the shops to re-open, I plan to pay the usual suspects unannounced visits."

"Which ones?"

"All of them." The crazy bat next door, the Closers, Tony the Tooth, Bane, and the trolls. Heck, even Tarzan and her asshole ex-boss were suspects. "Could Frey escape the dungeons?"

Rourke shook his head. "We stripped all his belongings from him, and the cells are shielded from portalling out. Not his style anyway. He just wants to kill you."

She nodded, already coming to the same conclusion. Frey smashed things.

Rourke hesitated. "Are you going to change?"

"Fuck, no. I'm digging the power suit."

A genuine smile flashed across her caomhnóir's face before his solemn and serious expression returned. "Camhanaich?"

"He'll join us after he's finished doing something else for me." She hesitated. "Unless you think we should wait for him?"

Rourke shook his head and stepped close. He held her hand again and squeezed. "I think you're doing just fine on your own."

A pep talk from a dark fae assassin guardian was surprisingly just what she needed.

"Who's first?"

Raven knocked lightly on Tarzan's front door, the hard surface cold to the touch.

"What's this guy's name?" Rourke turned to her on the landing.

She shrugged. "He introduced himself when he first moved in, but we started calling him Tarzan when he began strutting around his property shirtless. He progressed to full nudity in the evening fairly early on."

"So, you don't know?"

"Of course, we know. Dad ran a full background check on the guy and has a file on him. I just don't remember because it's never been important. It's something incredibly normal."

She knocked again and when no one answered, she glanced up and down the street. No pedestrians. The road and sidewalks were a barren wasteland, covered with the quiet darkness that came with the early winter sunsets.

She pulled out her picks from inside her warrior princess bra and worked the lock. Thank sweet baby Odin she remembered to load up her "armour" with all the nifty gadgets like her lock picking set before they left for the council meeting. Within a minute, the lock clicked. She pushed open the door and nodded for Rourke to come with her.

The air from inside the two-story house was cool but refreshing. Tarzan paid top dollar for an air freshener spell. Rourke closed the door behind them, and Raven rifled through a small stack of unopened mail sitting on the dining room table.

"Chad Berkley." She dumped the letters back on the table after reading the labels.

Rourke walked around the room, his frown deepening with each step. "He hasn't been here for a while."

Raven nodded. "No lingering smells of food or soap. There's also no hint of Juni, so either he never brought her here or he's not involved."

"I don't understand why he was a suspect to begin with."

She walked through the kitchen and cleared the

bathroom and nearby office. "Two weeks ago, someone stole my Dad's spite goat and used a scent blocker to cover their trail, but it only extended to the end of our short block, meaning either my bigot neighbour, Tarzan, or someone who parked right outside the house took the goat. Mrs. Humphreys suggested I look into Tarzan when I questioned her about Pepe. If he was involved with stealing one thing from us…"

"Maybe he stole another…" Rourke finished.

"Exactly. He's one of the more far-fetched suspects, but he's also the closest. I need something to do. I can't wait around the house or my mind will start going down the 'what if' paths and I can't do that. Juni needs me. I thought we'd start with him. Incidentally, I don't pick up any traces of goat, either, so we can probably cross Tarzan off our list of suspects for that crime, too."

"Probably?"

"Let's search the whole house first. I need to be thorough and if he has access to scent blockers, he could've used them inside the house as well as outside."

They methodically moved through the house, checking each room until they made it to the basement.

"Something's not right." Rourke confirmed the odd feeling creeping along her neck.

She nodded and pushed open the door at the bottom of the stairs. The hairs on her arms stood up the moment she walked through what felt like a magical film.

Rourke cursed.

"What is this?" She stepped into the dark room

illuminated by a vertical swath of blue swirling light and turned to Rourke.

"A permanent personal portal, usually referred to as a three-P, but this one is not for the Underworld." He tensed and his daggers appeared in his hands, reflecting the bright blue light at her back.

A shadow passed over them.

"You're trespassing." A male voice spoke behind her.

Raven spun around and, in the same moment, Rourke positioned himself between her and the naked man stepping out of the blue portal to bask in its ethereal glow.

"Tarzan?" She shielded her eyes from the glare.

Tarzan stepped away from the glowing blue portal and the light finally illuminated his face instead of blanketing his features in shadow. Tall and tanned with golden hair and eyes, Tarzan looked like gold personified.

"Is that what your family calls me?"

From his expression, he wasn't pissed, but he wasn't happy to find them trespassing in his basement, either.

"My sister is missing," Raven said. "Did you take her?"

She had a feeling he wasn't the abductor the moment she saw his face, but she had to ask anyway.

"Juniper Crawford? Why would I take your loud-mouthed sister who tries to take selfies with me in the background?"

"A scent blocking spell was used to cover this block

when someone stole Pepe. We thought to eliminate you from our list of suspects since you're literally next door." She glanced around the basement and studied the portal.

Rourke remained tense with a snarl twisting his lips. Her caomhnóir said this wasn't a portal to the Underworld, which meant...

"You're a Roller, aren't you?" Raven had never knowingly met a supernatural being from the Realm of Light before, and this entire time she'd lived next door to one.

Tarzan dipped his chin and his lip curled up. He didn't have the angelic wings she'd read about. Nothing unfurled from his back or glowed above his head.

Raven relaxed a little and straightened. "Why are you here?"

"The God of War and the Morrigan created a child of power infused with both their magic and lineages—a child and a creation all in one. And that child grew up and remarkably, despite the odds and the improbability, managed to successfully impregnate a fox shifter. But not any fox shifter. Oh no. The direct descendent of Inari."

Inari? She'd heard that name before... "The Japanese god?"

"Goddess. At least at that particular time."

"But...Inari is Japanese and the kitsune messengers are pure white." All her family's fox forms were orange, and aside from Raven and Bear, her mom and siblings

275

had red curly hair of various shades. Nothing about their outward appearances or family traditions hinted at Japanese ancestry. Then again, that didn't mean it wasn't true.

"Your particular line had a thing for ginger fox shifters and that trait persisted over the generations." Tarzan smiled, his impossibly white teeth glowing in the blue portal light. "You're an absolute genetic mashup of three realms and a descendent of gods from both sides of your family tree. I was sent to watch you."

"And?" What else was he sent to do?

He cocked his head again. "And nothing. I have no orders to intervene or initiate anything. My only task has been to report."

What did he report on? Dad's uniform? Mom's impressive ability to scare the crap out of people without raising her voice? How much screen time Mike got or how long Juni spent trying to tame her hair? How much of his reports detailed the craziness of her family? She cringed. "Have you noticed anything unusual lately?"

He raised both eyebrows.

"More than normal? Any dark vehicles parked out front or driving by ominously."

Tarzan frowned. "Actually, yes. There's been a black sedan in the afternoons. I noticed it because it's a nice vehicle for this area—a Lexus LS."

"LS?"

"Luxury Sedan."

"Didn't happen to catch the licence plate?"

He shook his head. "Not the full plate. Started with a G and ended with an eight, I think."

A partial plate. They could work with a partial plate. Silence descended on the room. Tarzan had a large clock on the main floor, not a grandfather one, something smaller, but the ticking echoed down the stairs.

"I'm sorry for breaking into your house."

Something flashed in his gaze. "Over the time I've watched your family, one thing has been abundantly clear. You all love each other very much. It's one of the first things I reported. I don't need you to tell me that you would do anything for your sister, including breaking and entering."

She froze. "Did Rollers take Juni?" If they sent someone to spy on her, would they take a beloved family member to control her?

"No, child. The Realm of Light doesn't make a habit of abducting children and quite frankly, you don't have anything we want."

Rourke growled, but they both ignored him.

"And while I understand your motives for breaking into my sanctuary, you owe me for this trespass."

She groaned on the inside. She did owe him. She'd greatly insulted him, and the only alternative was to fight and kill him, which was not happening. Frankly, she'd take another truckload of debt if it meant she could get Juni back.

"Agreed." She nodded. "I owe you."

Chapter Thirty-Seven

"You can't be sad when you're holding a cupcake."
~ Unknown, fellow lover of cupcakes

Back at the kitchen counter in the Crawford residence, Raven went through the list of suspects while Mike ran possible matches for the partial plate Tarzan provided in between trying to hack into the city's transportation cameras. Apparently, they'd upgraded their systems and security, so it was taking a little more time to get in.

Neither Mom nor Dad attempted to lecture them on their illegal activities. Instead, Mom kept busy by calling the residents near the abduction site to see if they saw anything while Dad tracked down the owners of the nearby businesses and their employees who'd been on shift.

Cole had also joined them and hovered over her shoulder. Other than Cole confirming he took Lincoln to the Underworld to start serving his sentence, they hadn't spoken in detail of Lincoln's fate. Instead, she filled him in on the visit to next door.

"Tarzan's a Roller?" Cole said.

She nodded.

"And you're a child of Inari?"

Mom snorted. "Going back about one hundred generations or so."

"Is that why you never told us?" Raven looked up from her list.

"I honestly didn't believe half the tales my mom, your grandma Lu, told me, and I had enough trouble keeping you and your brother from revealing your dark fae nature. I didn't need or want to add this descendent stuff to your list of secrets. Do you honestly think Bear would've contained the whole descendent of a god thing? He was barely tolerable as a teenager as it was. And really, it doesn't change a thing."

"Tell that to the Rollers." Raven and Bear's ancestry meant enough for someone to send a Roller to spy on them.

Mom jabbed her finger on her phone screen to dial the next number.

"Who's next?" Cole asked.

"The Closers, but I don't know where the leader is located and he's not a relative I can locate to."

"Didn't you follow your friend to another Closer house?" Cole asked.

"Yes, but Rourke and I went there after visiting Tarzan and it's been abandoned already."

"So, what's your plan?"

Her heart warmed that he knew and had confidence that she would have one. "I'm going to call Megan and see if she can get an address or set something up. We can cross Mrs. Humphreys off the list. She doesn't drive and this doesn't fit her style at all. After the Closers, we'll look into Bane. Then Tony. Then the trolls. They might still be pissed I said no to them. Heck, even my boss from the diner could be a possibility."

"Doubt that," Cole said. "He doesn't seem like the type to spend time plotting and bribing."

Rourke nodded. "More of a baseball bat to the headlights kind of guy."

Nailed it. That's exactly what Dan would do.

"Why aren't the hyenas higher up on the list?" Dad asked. "They tried to blackmail you."

"They're not as easy to roll up to and interrogate. Not unless I want to start a fight, slaughter them, risk my life and others, only to find out they weren't involved. I'll need to be sure it's them before I stop by for a visit." She nodded. "I'm not sure this fits them, though. As far as they're concerned, they've successfully blackmailed me into doing their bidding.

Why would they nab Juni now? I also feel like Tony's the type of guy to send a finger in the mail or call or something."

The room grew silent.

No one wanted to think about the reason for the silence. Raven tried really hard not to think about why they hadn't received a call asking for something yet.

"This is my own fault," Raven said.

The whole room said "No" in unison.

"This is the abductors' fault," Dad said. "You can't control the actions of others."

She sniffed and pulled out her phone to dial her friend. Megan picked up on the fourth ring.

"Hey, Rayray."

"Megan. I need a favour."

Chapter Thirty-Eight

"The trouble with being punctual is that nobody's there to appreciate it."

~*Franklin P. Jones*

Hoping no one shot her from the surrounding forest, Raven stepped from the shadows and into the cascade of light from the overhead lamp. A man stood by the lone park bench facing the opposite direction.

Jaime Bartlett, the Mystery Man in a cheap suit who regularly met with Closers at a popular downtown café on Richards, turned at her arrival and flinched.

"Megan promised no harm would come to me if I agreed to meet."

His voice was just as thin and whiny as she remembered it.

Raven nodded. "And I'd like to think the armed men you have stationed around our meeting location pointing their guns at me are merely here to enforce the safety of our meeting, and not to attack me unprovoked."

The man shut his mouth, took a deep breath and spoke again. "Are they still alive?"

"Of course, I'm not a monster."

The man's lip curled up. Clearly, he didn't agree, but Raven didn't ask to meet this hateful douchebag to argue.

"My sister is missing. Did you take her?"

Jaime somehow succeeded in narrowing his eyes any farther without closing them. "Why would I do that?"

"One of your Closers took my brother."

"That was—" He looked away. "Regrettable."

"Regrettable? My brother's nineteen and did nothing wrong. He was beaten and chained to a wall and left to think he was going to die in a filthy basement alone." He still had nightmares about it, waking up screaming or crying and soaked in sweat. He refused to talk to anyone about his torture or the dreams, but he never had problems sleeping before, so they all drew the same conclusion. If Robert was still alive, Raven would kill him all over again. Just slower.

"And Robert paid for his error in judgement, wouldn't you agree?"

Not enough. She crossed her arms and grumbled.

"We know you killed him."

She unfolded her arms and reached for her scythe. It snapped into her hand. She had no patience for more blackmailing attempts. She'd do more than show her teeth. She'd annihilate the man cowering in front of her. So what if it made him a martyr? He wouldn't be alive to enjoy it.

Jaime's eyes widened and he stepped back. "We don't have any proof, but we know. Haven't you wondered where his body went and why there was no news about its discovery? Haven't you wondered why we didn't tell anyone? We could've gone to the hyenas or the police. Tony wouldn't require evidence, he'd act on our word alone, and the police would've pulled enough forensic evidence to link you to the crime scene. A dark fae suspect with motive is as good as a guaranteed conviction these days, wouldn't you agree?" He paused for her to say something, but she waited. "Instead, we disposed of the body and kept our mouths shut. Haven't you wondered why?"

All the time, but her life was in a chaotic mess right now and finding out what was in the leader of the Closers heart of hearts didn't rank high on her list of priorities.

"We're not so different, you and I."

She recoiled. "I disagree with that statement."

Jaime shook his head. "We both care about our

families, our loved ones, and our people. We would do anything to keep them safe."

"Do not compare me to a group of hateful people."

"I needed and still need those who are truly passionate to get things done. Hatred is powerful fuel. Yes, I have incited rage and violence, Yes, I have pushed people to embrace their prejudice and bigotry. I have given their anger the acceptance they yearned for and the comradery they desperately needed to bolster their confidence. I need an army. A passionate army. But I'm not a hateful person. I want to protect the Mortal Realm and I've seen a way to accomplish that task. We're running out of time."

"What do you mean? You're talking as though we're already at war. There hasn't been a war since Odin's Proclamation."

"The war never stopped, it just went underground. Are you trying to tell me there aren't those who would take over the Mortal Realm if given the opportunity? Those who despise Odin's rule and would see the proclamation ripped apart to lay waste to what is left of our world? To slaughter and enslave us?"

Wow. Nailed it. She looked away, knowing her silence or her words would give away the answer.

Jaime nodded. "I thought so. We knew Bane used us, too, letting us grow in strength and power. Allowing us to gain entry to his realm to poke and prod the Underworld with our inexperience. He must've known all along the instructions in the Murdoch Manual wouldn't work in the Realm of War, just as we knew all along he couldn't be trusted. But we had to take the chance, don't you see? We had to try. And we worked on borrowed time."

Jaime took a deep breath. "Part of our agreement with Bane specified he couldn't attack us as long as free travel existed between the realms. Bane gathered enough supporters to rally against us and wage war despite Odin's ruling, but he couldn't touch us. Not until a barrier was erected."

Uh-oh. Raven knew where this was going.

"When a temporary barrier was erected, he was blocked as well. That's when I knew you could be an ally to the Closers. You saved us from destruction."

Raven wanted to throw the truth in this guy's face—that she didn't set-up a blockade to save the Closers, but it wouldn't hurt to have the Closers feel indebted to her, and she wanted to keep him talking. He'd already answered why Bane had to have a barrier set up to attack the Closers in the first place, which had always bothered her. "Why would Bane agree to that protection clause?"

"He needed to incite more hatred among his own people, but he also needed one of our manuals."

"The Murdoch Manual?" Raven asked

Jaime shook his head. "That's what most people believed. Only a few of us knew the truth. He wanted to view a lesser known scientific paper by one of Murdoch's colleagues called the Lindt Law. Lindt's research focused on magical tunnels created by opposing forces and black holes. We couldn't make any sense of her research and the findings don't match anything we know about the Force of Magic."

Bane's motivations crystallized but something was still off about the arrangement and she couldn't quite put her finger on what she was missing, nor did she have any time or patience to sit around and dwell on it.

"So, you didn't take my sister?" she asked.

He shook his head and as much as she disliked the man standing across from her, she believed him. "Did you order anyone else to or know who did?"

He shook his head again.

"Did you steal my father's goat?"

Jaime tugged at his coat pockets. "Oddly specific, but no."

"Thank you for your time. I'd wish you well, but I don't agree with your methods."

"We'll have to agree to disagree." Jaime held up his hands like the mob mentality rising within the ranks of his organization was beyond his control.

She really wanted to punch him in the face. "The hatred you inspired got my brother hurt. If you or any of your Closers come near me or my family, I will consider it an attack and react accordingly."

Jaime's narrowed his eyes. "The same goes for you, Queen of Corvids. I will do whatever it takes to protect the Mortal Realm from the dark fae scourge."

Chapter Thirty-Nine

"When something goes wrong in your life, just say 'plot twist' and move on."

~Unknown

Raven, Cole and Rourke stood outside Marcus' apartment building. Going to each suspect might work at keeping her busy and giving her the satisfaction of doing something, but in terms of efficiency, it took too long. With her witch friend living close, she changed the course of action. Marcus hadn't picked up her call, again, so another impromptu visit was in order. Normally, she'd take the hint, but Juni was missing.

Cole froze on the sidewalk and grimaced.

"What's wrong?" she asked.

"I'm being summoned."

"Can you ignore it?"

"It's my father." Which was Cole's way of saying, "No."

She rose on her tiptoes and gave him a peck on the lips.

Cole grunted, gripped the back of her neck and pulled her in for a longer, harder, head-dizzying kiss before disappearing in a swirl of shadows.

"Are we going to stand here and stare into the night wistfully until morning, or..." Rourke broke the spell of Cole's touch.

"Let's go."

They turned to the building. A woman walked out the front entrance while texting and didn't look up. Rourke caught the door and waved Raven into the building. They moved through the complex without speaking and arrived in front of Marcus' apartment door without incident.

Raven knocked on the door and they waited. Footsteps stomped down the hallway on the other side of the door and stopped. The door remained closed.

Raven was getting a bit tired of this reaction.

Why wasn't Marcus opening the door?

"Open up, Marcus."

"I have company."

"You have a terrible ability to lie." If he had a lady

friend over, he wouldn't have come to the door at all and he certainly wouldn't be walking around in his boots.

"It's not a good time, Wenny."

"Wenny?" Rourke scowled. "Still? Why haven't you corrected him?"

"Shh." Yeah, she got it. It was a terrible nickname. She waved Rourke away and turned back to the door. "Juni's missing."

Marcus sighed loud enough for them to hear, flipped the deadbolt and opened the door. Dark bags lined the underside of his eyes and his expression was drawn. "I know," he said.

He stepped back and let her in, but kept his gaze trained on Rourke. "Can you...wait outside?"

Rourke snarled.

Raven turned to her guardian. "It's okay, Rourke."

He grumbled but stepped back into the hallway and crossed his arms.

Marcus closed the door after Raven walked past him, but didn't lock it, leaving Rourke access if he needed it. Hopefully, that would make her caomhnóir a little less pissed.

"What are you wearing?" Marcus asked.

She glanced down at her armoured bra. "Long story."

Marcus shrugged. He'd been an honorary member of their family for, well, almost forever, so he was used to crazy.

"Did Bear call you?" Why would he answer Bear's

call and not hers?

Marcus returned his attention to her face and nodded. "I've been going through every tracking and tracing spell I know, and they've all been blocked. The person or people who took her are either well versed in spell craft or they paid top dollar for someone else to do the work."

Fuck. There went that option.

"Bear's been tracking down every contact he has, and nobody knows anything," Marcus continued.

"Why didn't you want to let me in?"

"Not for the reason you think." Marcus cast a worried glance over her shoulder. "Because—"

A familiar bleat sounded behind her. She spun around and familiar eyes stared back.

"Pepe?"

Chapter Forty

"Learning to ignore things is one of the great paths to inner peace."

~ *Robert J. Sawyer*

Raven scratched Pepe's head and stared at Marcus. "I don't understand."

He sighed and flopped down on the couch beside her. "I didn't mean to take him. It kind of just happened."

"Happened? How does stealing my dad's spite goat just happen? Do you have any idea how upset my dad is? Up until Juni's disappearance, he's been moping around the house holding Pepe's collar and involuntarily sobbing."

Marcus cringed. "No Wiccan plans to find or bond to their familiar. It just happens when they first meet. If your dad hadn't removed Pepe from the property when I came over to ward the house, this would've happened even sooner."

She stopped scratching Pepe's head. "Familiar?"

Marcus nodded. "I'd always imagined something badass like a mountain lion or wolf."

"Or a raven."

He smiled, but it was a sad one.

"So, you came over, met Pepe for the first time, accidentally bonded to my family's pet goat, panicked and ran away with him?"

"Pretty much. I've been trying to figure out how to tell Terry."

"Use words, you coward."

Marcus ducked his head. "I deserve that."

Pepe leaned forward and butted her shoulder. Ouch. She lifted her hand and resumed scratching his forehead and behind the ears.

"It's just that I've been a part of your family for so long. But lately, especially with Bear acting like a butt, I haven't been. I wanted..." He looked away and took a deep breath. "I didn't want to burn a bridge that already felt like it was falling apart."

"My dad would've understood. He still will."

Marcus' frown said he didn't quite believe her.

"Is that why you were coming over? To reconnect?

293

Or was it to check on the wards?"

Marcus tensed and for the first time in a long time looked genuinely unsure. "I came to talk to you."

"I'm just a phone call away, Marcus."

"Not for this." He shook his head. "The conversation I wanted to have with you would've been better done in person."

That didn't sound good. She pulled her shoulders back and lifted her chin. "Here I am. Why don't you talk to me now?" She didn't bother pointing out the other opportunities Marcus had to speak with her face to face.

"It's a little pointless now."

"Try." The one word came out a little harder than she intended, but her patience was wearing out, even for Marcus.

He hung his head. "I've loved you since we were kids. But you've known that, haven't you? No? I thought it was so obvious. I stayed away at first out of respect for Bear, then because you were with that idiot and seemed happy, and then you were getting over him. And now? Now when I finally decide I'm done waiting, it appears I'm too late. The only thing good to come of finding my familiar is he saved me from making an ass out of myself. I hadn't realized things with that shadow guy had intensified so much." He looked up then, gaze sad. "But I'm making an ass out of myself, now, aren't I?"

"Not at all," she whispered.

"Ahhh no. Please don't pity me. I don't want that.

But I'm right, aren't I? I'm too late?"

She bit her lip and nodded. She would've loved those words years ago, maybe even months ago, but a lot of things had changed since Cole walked into that diner. "And you ended up with a rabid goat as your familiar instead of confessing your feelings?"

"Shitty deal, right?"

"Totally." She would always have a place in her heart for Marcus, just not filled with the kind of love he wanted or thought he wanted from her.

He chuckled and shook his head. "I can't figure out how to tell your father and not get murdered. I need your help."

"No, you don't. You know how to tell him. Take Pepe back to the house, walk up to the door, knock and then explain everything."

He blinked at her.

"Maybe leave out the whole planning to confess your undying, unparalleled love for his exquisite daug—"

"You're pushing it."

She winked. "But yeah, leave that part out. You'll be fine. You've always been an unofficial Crawford."

"I know you're right. After we find Juni, I'll do as you suggest." Marcus sighed. "I have something for you. I found a spell that might work for building a new barrier." He pushed off the couch, walked over to his desk and pulled out a scroll from the top drawer. Someone had tied a dark red ribbon around the browning paper.

"A Wiccan spell?" She stood and walked around the couch to join him. Pepe bleated at her.

"Yes and no. It's a spell, but it's based on some scientific theories instead of Wiccan. I adapted it for you because the original called for energy from Hecate. You probably don't want to invoke her. Not when you have magic of your own."

She took the scroll from his hand. "Do all witches have access to this spell?" And if so, why hadn't anyone tried it before? Or maybe they had and failed. Would this spell even work?

Marcus shrugged. "Maybe. It's been copied from another source, but I don't know anyone who could use it." He nodded at the scroll in her hand.

"Why's that?"

"It requires a connection with something called the void. I believe this refers to the Realm of Shadows."

He was leaving out something else.

"It also requires a vast amount of power. I'm not sure you'll be able to complete it on your own."

"How much power?"

"Like your temporary barrier, but at least double."

Damn. She waved the scroll in the air. "Thank you, Marcus. At least it's a starting point."

And they needed all the help they could get.

Chapter Forty-One

"I always wanted to be somebody, but now I realize I should have been more specific."

~ *Lily Tomlin*

The cold air hit Raven's face when she stepped from Marcus' building with Rourke trailing behind her. Her phone vibrated and she pulled it from the small armoured satchel still strapped to her waist.

"Hey." She answered Mike's call.

"I got in, but there's no clear shot of the licence plate of the vehicle. Make and model confirm Tarzan's information."

She nodded even though Mike couldn't see her.

"There's more. A man matching Lincoln's vague description exited the café before Juni arrived with Lincoln."

Raven squeezed her eyes shut. Either Lincoln tipped them off, which meant he had a phone number and withheld that information during her interrogation, or the kidnappers assumed his compliance. Maybe she should've killed him.

"Café employees?" she asked. "I can go over and interview them."

"Already on it. Dad tracked down the owner of the café and Mom's already heading over to the home of the barista working at that time."

"She got the address of an employee from a business owner?"

"No, just the name, but that's all we needed. Mom's on a rampage. The owner never stood a chance."

And now, Mom headed over to the barista's home. Why not just phone?

"The barista doesn't have a phone," Mike answered her unspoken question.

How could anyone exist in today's world without a phone number?

"Thanks."

Mike hung up without a goodbye.

Rourke waited while she ran through scenarios and suspects. She still needed to question Bane, Tony, the trolls and Dan, and she should probably wait for backup from Cole before confronting the first three and the last wasn't a very probable suspect.

Her phone rang again from an unidentified number. "Hello?"

"Is this Crawford Investigations?" a familiar voice asked. Where had she heard this man before? "I called the main business line, but the answering machine said to give this number a call if it was an emergency."

"Yes, this is Crawford Investigations."

"My name is Sean and I head a block watch. I ran into a pretty intimidating woman earlier looking for an abducted teenager. She said to call if I found anything."

Ah! Block watch dude with the golden retriever.

"Yes, we're looking into the disappearance. Did you find out anything?" She held her breath.

"Mrs. Feldman saw two men in black usher a young woman into the car."

"Was she struggling?"

"No, which is why she didn't call the police. There was another teenager with her, and he appeared unconcerned. Mrs. Feldman figured they were just collecting a wayward daughter."

They must've had guns or threatened either Juni's or Lincoln's life. Or both. But Mrs. Felderman needed glasses. The men wore masks. No one sent goons to collect their daughter. "Any description of the men?"

"I'm afraid not. They were big, dressed the same and scary looking, according to Ruth. She also said she thought there was another man in the car because she saw movement in the backseat when the door opened, but she didn't see a face and the windows were tinted."

Raven's mind was already running through the possibilities. While a completely new enemy could be behind this abduction, or someone completely unrelated to Raven's life, only one of her remaining suspects had goons at his disposal to do his work. Dan wouldn't want to pay anyone anything he could do himself, the trolls tended to stick with working with other trolls and would've been easily identified even with the masks, and the entire time she'd known Bane, she'd never seen him work with others.

That left one suspect.

"Tony," she said. He'd threatened her family once already to get her to meet with him and he'd tried to blackmail her, so his name had always been on the list of suspects, but this move didn't make sense. Why kidnap Juni when as far as Tony knew, Raven was being a good little worker bee?

"Excuse me?" Sean spoke over the phone.

"Oh sorry. Thinking out loud. Thank you for the tip."

Sean tried to say something else, but she hung up on him, already turning to Rourke.

"You need to be sure before you storm the stronghold of one of the strongest gangs in your area," he said.

She nodded, dialing Mike as Rourke spoke.

"Yeah?" Mike picked up after the first ring.

"Have you run that partial plate for Tony the

Tooth's vehicles?"

Mike grunted. Of course, he had.

"Can you run make and model instead? Lexus LS. And expand the search to all known associates and his daughter."

"You think Tony took her?"

"Yes, but I want confirmation."

"On it." Mike hung up.

Her phone started vibrating again before she had a chance to put it away. She glanced at the screen and accepted the call. "Hey, Mom."

"Did Mike already call you?"

"Yes."

"I'm with the barista who saw the man. She said he was a shorter guy with hazel eyes. Wore an expensive suit but gave her a scary vibe. She thinks he may have had a scar on his face, but the lighting made it hard to tell."

Sounded like Tony, but the description was vague enough it wasn't a guarantee. "Are you with them now?"

Mom paused. "Yes?"

Raven pulled her power letting it curl around her.

Rourke cleared his throat.

Right.

She reached out, grabbed her assassin guardian's hand and portalled to her mom. They formed in a small dorm room with cement walls.

"This is cozy," Rourke muttered, sandwiched between Raven and a closet.

Mom and a young woman turned at their arrival.

"Eep." A young woman scrambled back and bumped into a built-in bookshelf. She had black hair with dark purple streaks and a stud piercing through her bottom lip.

Raven flicked through the pictures on the phone she still clutched, found one of Tony and turned it to the barista. "Is this him?"

Mom threw her hands on her hips. "Branwen Lulu Crawford. I taught you better manners than that."

Raven glanced at Mom. "Juni."

Mom's expression darkened. She nodded and stuffed her trembling hands in her pockets.

"Yeah, that's him." The barista interrupted them.

"Thank you." Raven stuffed her phone away in the satchel, grabbed Mom's hand, held her other out for Rourke, who took it, and portalled home.

Raven returned the group to the alley behind their home.

Rourke let go of her hand and frowned. "Why here?"

Mom lurched away from them and threw up on the side of the road.

Raven jerked her chin in Mom's direction. "That's why."

Mom staggered a few more steps, dodging the mess she'd made and straightened, only to double over again and dry heave. She closed her eyes briefly before wiping her face with her sleeve. "You're never allowed to portal me from this moment onward."

"No promises."

Mom pulled herself upright for the second time and walked back to them. She almost managed a straight line. "You could've left me there. Now, we'll have to go back to get my car."

"I'm not leaving you anywhere while Tony the Tooth is plucking family members off the street. You need to get inside where it's safe and warded. Let me deal with Tony before you go gallivanting around town to get your car."

Mom smirked and crossed her arms over her chest. "You know who you sound like right now?"

"Don't say it."

A small smile cracked Mom's serious expression. "Grandma Lu. I wish she could've seen you like this. Seen what a strong formidable woman you've become. She would've been so proud. Like I am."

Ravens eyes stung. She swiped at her face. "Fuck, Mom. Don't make me cry. I can't go after bad guys acting like a cry baby."

Rourke hissed in warning.

She turned in his direction and found three grotesque men standing on the other side of Rourke. Gray-skinned, short, twisted creatures with two ribbed horns protruding from their temples, gangly limbs, oversized ears, thin upper lips, uneven teeth and black gums. They focused intently on Raven and Rourke with their black-eyed glares. Trolls.

"You're not going to have to worry about going after the bad guys, bhanrigh." Nerthach stepped out of the shadows. "Not when we come to you."

"This isn't a good time," she warned, grabbing for her scythe. The weapon popped out of the ether and into her hand. Its violent energy reassuring her wound up nerves. *It will be okay*, it said. *We'll slaughter them and then go get your sister. Just give into the magic.*

The power and knowledge of the weapon ripped through her veins. She could handle this. She was the Queen of Corvids. She had to handle this.

"We don't care if this is an *inconvenience*," Nerthach said. "You need to come with us."

"I'm not going anywhere with you."

"We know you have the spell of Lindt."

Raven froze.

"Who do you think made it possible for your witch friend to stumble upon it?"

She swallowed the lump in her throat. She knew Marcus. He hadn't set her up.

"And now you'll come with us and we'll help you resurrect the barrier at the chosen time. It's what everyone wants, including you. We're merely providing support."

Support her ass. They intended to benefit from the barrier, and it all centered on their unique magic and tunnel-like kingdom. If they orchestrated for her to get the spell, why try to coerce her now? Why not wait for her to use it on her own. Unless...Unless they wanted to ensure certain features of the new barrier were included with installation. Features that benefitted them.

"If I place a barrier in between the realms, and that's a hard if, it will be on my terms, not yours." She swung the scythe. It responded beautifully, catching the moonlight on its sharp blade.

The trolls exchanged a worried glance. Had they expected her to come easily? To cower before them and shuffle her feet behind them like a good little girl as they led the way? Probably not, but they hadn't expected her to wield the scythe so well. Nerthach and Gwawrddur hadn't warned their fighters.

"Take her." Nerthach snarled and his expression told her what his words didn't. He wished he could just kill her, but if he did that, the mantle would pass to Cole and then they'd never get their way. "Take her alive."

Rourke growled and became a whirl of blades. The original trolls didn't reach her, but more and more spilled from the shadows and unfolded from what had appeared to be large rocks.

"Raven!" Mom screeched.

"Get in the house!" Raven swung around, the scythe taking over her reflexes and instincts. "Get behind the wards."

More trolls poured out from whatever crevices they hid in. Raven became a flurry of movement, the weapon's shaft twirling and sliding in her hands, the scythe's blade slicing and slashing anyone in her path. She was a tornado of death.

None of these trolls would stand in her way of getting her sister back. Anger from their interference and delay boiled up along with the battle rage. They wasted her time and every second spent cutting them down meant a second more Juni spent in captivity. Juni counted on her.

Mom screamed something else, but the blood rage had taken over. Raven cut down her enemies with Rourke at her back until no one else attacked. The last of the troll retinue slid from her scythe and she looked up to find Nerthach staring at her wide-eyed about twenty feet away.

"Come closer," she demanded, sweat and blood dripping from her face.

Nerthach shook his head, drew an intricate design in the air and stepped into a shimmering portal.

Rourke threw a dagger at the glimmering air, but the portal disappeared, and the weapon clattered to the ground. He snarled something vicious in dark fae.

"Mom!" Raven spun around to find Hugie helping Mom to her feet with one hand while his other clutched a long sword dripping with blood. Blood spatter decorated his armour and drenched the hem of his cloak.

Mom's hair was a hot mess and her pants were muddy, but she appeared fine.

Why had the trolls attacked? Well, she knew why—they wanted her to reinstate a barrier—but why now? Why here? Just...Why?

She whispered Cole's name. There was enough blood dripping, so she didn't need to draw her own to summon him.

Nothing.

She whispered his name again.

Nothing.

She exchanged a worried glance with Rourke. Cole had never ignored a summons from her before, but he was also with his dad.

She sliced her finger open and tried again.

Still nothing.

"Daughter." Hugie bowed to her. He'd cleaned and sheathed his sword. "You fought well."

She didn't know what to say to that, so she dipped her chin in a gesture a lot of fae favoured. "Thank you and thank you for protecting my mom."

Huginn Muninn cast Mom a long look. "Always."

Without another word, he broke into two ravens and launched into the night. He'd probably head to Odin next and report everything he saw here.

Good. The Allfather needed to know what the trolls were up to and that saved Raven one trip.

Her phone vibrated in the satchel. She flicked blood from her hand and fished it out. Mike had sent a text: *Confirmed. Vehicle registered under Sarah's name. Last digit a three not an eight.*

Raven took a deep breath and calmly returned the phone to its storage place. "Mike confirmed Tony."

"We'll need to locate them." Rourke cleaned his daggers on a nearby shirt of a fallen troll.

"I can portal to them."

"How? That only works for blood relatives or if you've been summoned."

"Or if I've been there before."

Rourke straightened and a vicious smile spread across his face.

"Well, I'll leave you to your murder and mayhem, then." Mom rubbed her arms vigorously. Her whole body shook. "I'll just go inside the wards."

"Mom." Raven walked over to Mom, but the other woman halted her with a raised hand.

"No! You're covered in blood." Instead of a hug, Mom placed her hand on Raven's cheek, her palm soft and warm against the cold air. "Please be careful. You have my heart."

"I will." Raven dipped her head and waited until Mom had safely made it into the house behind the wards. Hopefully, she'd know what to do with all the dead troll bodies in the alley because Raven had no idea who to call or how to report it, or whether they should rent a van and haul the bodies somewhere remote and drop them in a ravine.

Raven sliced her finger and tried to summon Cole again. Still nothing.

Rourke walked up to stand beside her. "That can't be good. We should find out what happened to him."

"I'm not waiting for him. My sister is my priority and he'll understand that."

Rourke hesitated.

"Do you think the two of us can take on a gangster and his goons without Cole?" Police were out of the question. They'd just arrest her and her family for being suspicious and leave the hyenas alone. She didn't want to bring in more family for this. What was the point of saving one sibling if it came at the cost of losing another?

Rourke's mouth split into another serrated smile in answer. "We just defeated a troll retinue for the prince of trolls. Yes, we can take them."

Finally, some good news.

Chapter Forty-Two

"The same boiling water that softens the potato hardens the egg. It's about what you're made of, not the circumstances."

~ Unknown

The shadows cleared around Raven and Rourke as they stepped from the ether and into the foyer of Tony the Tooth's mansion and pandemonium broke out.

Men shouted, guns were drawn and a woman, somewhere, screamed.

Raven ignored all of it and focused on her sister,

bound and gagged, sitting on the bottom step of the grand entrance staircase that curled up to the second floor. Juni's eyes widened and her shoulders slumped with visible relief. They must've been preparing to move her somewhere else. Probably a remote, secure location that Raven couldn't access.

"Last time I checked, Ms. Crawford, dark fae and Others are just as susceptible to bullets. It was a mistake to come here." Tony stepped from the adjoining room.

"It was a mistake to take my sister," she growled.

"You seemed to need some additional incentive to look into my case, and when I found out you were so much more than we thought, we knew we had to take something important as collateral. I expected you to be angry. What I didn't expect was you to find us so quickly. It's only been a few hours."

"PI," she said.

"Yet, you haven't located Robert."

"I know where Robert is." She gripped the staff and let the power of the scythe ripple through her veins. "Well, more precisely, I know what happened to him. I don't know his exact location anymore."

"He's dead?"

"Yes."

"Why didn't you just—" His eyes narrowed. "You killed him." A slow, sly smile spread across his face, he leaned against the bannister of the staircase, dangling his gun toward Juni's head. "And you didn't want me to blackmail you with the information."

Raven snorted. He never intended for Raven to live past her usefulness to him, at least not until he found out who she was. That's when he must've planned to take Juni. He would've squirrelled her away somewhere as an insurance policy so he could control the Queen of Corvids. She'd do anything to keep her sister safe from harm, even becoming a gang leader's dark fae to command, and he knew it.

"Let's stop pretending this was going to end with something as tame and simple as blackmail," she said instead of the long string of curse words flowing through her brain.

Tony's grin was anything but kind. In the moment it took him to move and nod his head at his goons, Raven was already in motion. She severed the nearest guy's hands before he pulled the trigger.

Raven let the rage fuel her—rage for her sister being abducted, rage at the bruises on her arms and face, rage that her fifteen-year-old sister had to witness this massacre that would likely traumatize her, rage that they hadn't bothered to blindfold Juni which meant they never intended to return her safely to her family, rage that they deemed both Raven's and Juni's life as disposal when they were also human fucking beings, thank you very much, but most of all, rage that Juni's pain and planned murder were because of Raven.

She became a whirlwind of blood, slashing, slicing, and hacking with her scythe. She lost track of Rourke, but she knew her caomhnóir protected her back.

The spinning stopped when she had the sharp edge

of her blade pressed against the soft flesh of Tony's neck. He lay semi-sprawled on the steps in a similar position to Lincoln. His men lay dead and bleeding around him. No help was coming, and no mercy would be given. Her family would never be safe if she let him walk away.

Tony lifted his chin, gaze hard. "Who are you?"

Raven snarled. "I'm the Queen of Corvids. I'm the guardian of the void between realms and today, I'm your death."

She ran the scythe along his neck. She didn't stand over him, sadistically watching the light fade from his eyes. She was already turning to where Juni had taken cover during the fight. Rourke knelt beside her sister and finished cutting the rope from her hands and ankles. Juni ripped the gag from her mouth, stumbled to her feet and ran to Raven.

Raven dropped the scythe and opened her arms.

"Rayray!" Juni flung herself into Raven's waiting arms.

She clutched her sister as hard as she could, burying her face in her neck and fuzzy red hair. Juni was okay. She was safe.

Raven held her sister and let all the pent-up worry and stress out. She'd held it in and held the emotions back to focus on finding Juni, but now that she'd found her, everything tumbled out.

Juni sobbed into her shoulder.

"You're both horrifically ugly criers," Rourke noted, tone dry.

313

She waved him away. "You're ruining the moment."

"We need to leave, mo bhanrigh."

Juni pulled back and swiped at the tears and snot to glance at the room. "That was so badass."

"That was death, Juni, and not something I enjoy."

Her sister nodded, her hands curling into shaking fists. "He tricked me. I thought he liked me, and he tricked me. I even got in the car because they said they'd shoot him. If I'd known he was a two-faced piece of shit, I would've let them." She sniffed, and in a quieter voice, repeated. "I thought he liked me."

Raven rested her hand on Juni's shoulder. "He will pay for that."

Her sister's bottom lip trembled. "Don't. Don't kill him."

"I won't, but Cole took him to the Underworld to carry out his punishment as a servant to the Lord of Shadows."

Juni sniffed and wiped her face with her sleeve again. She turned back to Raven and the pain eased from her gaze as she studied her. "What in the Underworld are you wearing?"

Raven grabbed her sister and Rourke and pulled on her magic to take them home. Sisters.

Chapter Forty-Three

"I survived because the fire inside me burned brighter than the fire around me."

~Unknown

Raven watched from the side of the room as her family enveloped Juni in a giant, sobbing embrace. Her limbs ached and emptiness gnawed the inside of her stomach. When had she last eaten? Maybe she should take Rourke through a drive-thru and see his reaction.

Rourke leaned against a nearby dining chair. Blood dripped from his clothes to the floor. He grimaced. She leaned closer. Not all the blood running down his armour and staining Mom's rug was from their opponents. Rourke's face was pale and drawn.

"You're bleeding."

Rourke flinched.

"How much of it is yours?"

He pulled his hand away from where he'd held his side. A wound gushed blood. It didn't look good.

Raven's head swam and her stomach churned. That definitely didn't look good. He must've caught one of the bullets from Tony's henchman. "Why didn't you say anything? We need to take you to the hospital."

Rourke turned to her fully, then, the pain creasing the corners of his eyes. "Mortals often paint dark fae as vicious conniving seducers who take advantage of them whenever and wherever possible with no feelings of remorse."

"Okay...not sure where you're going with this." Or what it had to do with him talking and bleeding out instead of letting her take him to the hospital.

"Part of that is true, but mostly, we are the way we are because of a self-perpetuating negative cycle."

She still didn't see how this had to do with how he gripped his side and scowled. She needed to take him to a medical professional.

He batted away her hands. "Most of us would give all our worldly possessions to experience what you have."

She looked at her hugging, sobbing family.

"The love of your family. I might not get to

experience it, but I do get to see it. There's no wound in the realms that would make me interrupt the moment you had with your sister." He jerked his chin toward her family, his smile melancholy. "Or this moment with your family."

"Can I take you to the hospital now?"

Rourke shook his head. "Not yet. Despite your nagging, I'm enjoying this." He took a deep breath and kept talking while watching Mom cradle Juni's face in her hands, telling her to never scare them like that again, telling her how much she loved her, telling her how scared they all were.

"I never quite got Camhanaich's obsession with you," Rourke continued. "Until I witnessed your capacity to love and be loved. Then I got it."

She handed him a nearby dish towel, a clean one, to press against his wound. Thankfully, the stubborn mule didn't bat that away, too. "Is this when you pledged to be my caomhnóir?"

He nodded.

"We need to get you to the hospital." She glanced over her shoulder at her still-hugging family. "You'll have plenty of future opportunities to witness my family in a sobbing mess, trust me." Hopefully, not for such serious reasons.

"There's a faster way."

She watched him pull his bloody hand back to apply the towel.

"I'm waiting."

"You could accept my oath. The process will heal

317

me. As your caomhnóir, my life will be linked to yours. As long as you live and breathe, so will I."

Her brain misfired. "You're my caomhnóir. I already accepted—"

He shook his head. "It takes blood, remember? You need to agree to the terms and accept me."

Cole hadn't warned her against any negative repercussions of accepting Rourke as her caomhnóir. In fact, he'd seemed downright pleased. Rourke had also fought for her and guarded her back. He helped save Juni. She didn't need to know the terms to know she'd already agreed to them in her heart. "What do I need to do?"

Rourke straightened and blanched. That movement cost him. He swallowed a couple of times before answering. "You need to cut both our palms, hold my hand so our blood meets and claim me as your caomhnóir."

She grabbed his dagger and sliced her palm open. She grimaced. She may have cut a little too aggressively. Rourke snorted and held out his hand. She made sure not to cut his palm as deep, he didn't have much more blood to give. She placed the dagger on the nearby counter, held Rourke's hand so their bloody palms mushed together and placed her other hand on the side of his stubbly face. She stared into his dark Other eyes, eyes of the Underworld like hers. "Rourke of the Underworld and Assassins guild, I claim you as my caomhnóir, to be at my back always. To be an honorary Crawford."

Power ripped from inside her and spread through her hands and into Rourke's body. He glowed from within, his eyes becoming incandescent. His body tensed and he closed his eyes, shutting off the light, and sighed. The pinched expression eased into something more relaxed. She couldn't tell if his wounds had healed, but no more blood soaked through the towel and his colouring returned to his cheeks. Raven let Rourke go and stepped back. Despite releasing her hold, an awareness of her guardian tingled in her mind.

"Looks like you're truly stuck with us now." She tapped the side of her head. "I can sense you."

He nodded and smiled. "Same. Now, tracking you down after you forget to bring me along will be easier."

"Um..." Juni's voice interrupted them. "What are you two doing?"

Raven laughed and turned to her family. "We have a new member of the family."

"Not another one." Mike groaned. "Rayray, you have to stop adopting stray dark fae. They're not cats."

"I'm not a stray." Rourke beamed. "I'm an honorary Crawford."

Mike scowled and Juni appeared confused, but Mom and Dad looked relieved, as if without telling them, they already knew this meant they had someone else looking after their daughter. What they probably didn't realize was Rourke would protect them as well.

Her caomhnóir placed his hand on her shoulder. "We need to find Cole."

And with that proclamation all her good spirits

came crashing down.

Chapter Forty-Four

"I love you as one loves certain obscure things, secretly, between the shadow and the soul."

~ *Excerpt from* Sonnet XVII, *Pablo Neruda*

Raven was an idiot. She didn't have a blood connection to Cole. He'd travelled to her countless of times, but he'd either been summoned or he knew the location. Or...as she just found out, Rourke had lurked in the shadows and summoned Cole instead. At least her guardian had the decency to look sheepish.

According to Rourke, if she'd completed the anam

cara ritual with Cole, she could've popped into his presence with a snap of her fingers. If she knew where he was, she could portal to the location. But Raven had never been to Erebus' Night Court, and apparently, arriving unannounced and uninvited by the God of Darkness or Goddess of Night wasn't just frowned upon, it was a death sentence.

"What in the Underworld am I going to do?" she asked Rourke who stood beside her in the grand courtyard of the Corvid Court. Neither had cleaned up or changed, silently agreeing taking time to freshen up was out of the question. If Cole wasn't answering her summons after this much time had passed, he needed help and he needed it now.

The dried blood started to itch on her skin and crusted flakes fell from her metal armour. She finished her snack bar and looked around for a garbage can. Not finding one, she slipped the wrapper in her satchel with her phone. Her stomach stopped complaining, but she needed real food soon or she'd fade away into nothing.

"We can use a lodestone for entry into his realm. He has a designated location for entering where they won't automatically sever our heads. Then we need to either request his return or find and extract him." Rourke chomped down on the mint chocolate chip keto bar and grimaced. "Since when is chalk food?"

He held the bar out, presumably for her to take and finish. Raven shook her head and pushed the bar back to him. She pointed at his chest. He needed food, too, and Mom's diet bars were the fastest and easiest thing to grab as they left the house.

"Return him? On what grounds? Please give me my boyfriend back?"

Rourke grunted. "He might be fine. If we arrive at an untimely moment, we might ruin whatever he's up to."

"Do you honestly believe that?"

"At first, it was a realistic possibility, but now, too much time has passed, and I find it unlikely. If only..." He bit off the words.

"Say it."

"If only you two completed the anam cara ritual instead of dancing around each other."

If only he didn't keep bringing this up. He'd made his point already. She folded her arms across her chest. "It's not a decision to take lightly."

"Yet, you both want it. What are your objections?"

"I'm not sure I have any. Everything is happening so fast and I thought we had time to go through the ritual later. It's important to pause and think before I leap. I haven't known Cole for long. There are many things I don't know or understand. He's more powerful than me. There's an imbalance of power that I'm not quite comfortable with. And..."

Rourke waved impatiently at her to continue.

"And my feelings for Cole have always been so intense. Right from the start. We grew up with the stories of dark fae seducing stupid mortal girls with their looks and power. I didn't want to become another cautionary tale."

Rourke chuckled.

"What's so funny?"

"That you think this infatuation is one-sided. When the fae fall, they fall hard. Most of the Underworld is watching the mighty Beul na h-Oidhche gu Camhanaich falling over himself with his obsession for you with great amusement."

"Lovely. We're the laughingstock of Others."

"And yet, a source of great envy," Rourke said. "Most dark fae struggle to feel anything. They use and sometimes abuse. That stiffness and distance is often what gives us away as Other-kind in the Mortal Realm."

"Should you be telling me this?"

"If I still served Cole, probably not. But I serve you, now. Not him."

"So, if I asked you to shank Bane, you would?"

Rourke's expression grew grim. "I would try, but I would hope you'd value my life and my role to protect you as more than something to throw away. I would serve you better carrying out tasks that have at least a small chance of success."

Her comment didn't seem so witty anymore. Guess joking about someone's life wasn't funny. Great. She was an asshole. "I do and will continue to value you and your life, Rourke. I freely make that promise to you. I'm sorry for making that comment in jest."

Rourke dipped his chin to acknowledge her apology. "All your reasons for hesitating to complete the anam cara bond are valid but let me ask you this. Has Cole ever used this imbalance of power or knowledge to control you?"

"No."

"Do you trust Cole?"

"Yes."

"Do you love him?"

"Yes."

"Then the rest will sort itself out. My life is now tied to yours, remember. I wouldn't exactly be pleased if you planned to bond with just anyone. You need to trust your gut. The anam cara isn't even about lovers. It's about trust and mutual aid. Even if your romantic relationship turns sour, Cole will be your anam cara for life and that's backup I don't think you should reject or deny. Frankly, I don't think you can afford to."

"You're speaking too much logic right now."

"And you're not dumb enough to ignore it."

"Challenge accepted."

Rourke's smirk grew into a pointy-toothed smile. "Let's go get your man."

"How?" The light-hearted joking only succeeded from temporarily relieving some of the dread twisting her stomach into knots, but now that they refocused on the task at hand, she almost doubled over from the overwhelming nausea stabbing her midsection with what ifs.

Please be okay, Cole. You have to be okay.

"I have a lodestone for the Night Court. Try not to break anything once we get there or start a fight."

325

She punched him in the arm. Her fist connected with hard muscle, which meant he let her get the shot in. "Why didn't you say anything?"

"It still would've been easier to locate directly to him. The Night Court is huge. It will take time to find him and if we're not going to grovel at Erebus' feet and beg for Cole's safe return, we will risk detection sneaking around."

"Can't we start at the dungeons?"

"Which ones?"

Her stomach sunk. She stepped toward Rourke while he fished out a disk-shaped rock. Her skin tingled and a cool breeze drifted over her skin, whispering her name. She froze and shot out her hand to grip Rourke's forearm.

"What is it?" he asked.

She'd know that deep voice anywhere, even faint and on the wind like it currently was.

"I'm being summoned."

She gathered her magic and embraced the call, pulling her caomhnóir with her.

"Wait!" Rourke barked. He stiffened under her hand as her magic wound around him and dragged them both through the ether.

The energy faded away from them to reveal a cold, dark room. Cole knelt on the ground with a weird collar around his neck and shackles binding his wrists in front of him. Though obviously intended as a prison of sorts, the room lacked the grit and despair clinging to the walls that she'd expect from a dark fae dungeon.

Instead, the floors shone from recent cleaning and the air smelled lilac fresh.

Anger rose up hot and potent. "Who did this to you?"

Cole lifted his bruised face, a thin line of blood trickled down his chin. He must've bitten his own tongue to draw blood for summoning. "Juni?"

"Safe."

His shoulders relaxed and he let out a long breath. "Some good news, then."

She called her scythe to her and the weapon materialized in her hand at the same time the door to the dark room flew open.

The wooden door crashed against the stone wall and lit torches from the hallway outside spilled light into the room.

"Ah, Beul, you brought guests." A woman dressed entirely in black strode into the room alone. Normally, Raven would feel confident in a three against one situation which included Rourke and Cole at her side, but the fae magic radiating off the woman's skin in waves made her think twice about the odds.

Dark hair, dark eyes, the tall woman with a lithe build and haughty expression standing in front of Raven raised an eyebrow and smirked, giving "dangerous" a whole new look.

"Nyx," Raven guessed.

The woman bowed her head. "I've heard a lot about you Branwen, Queen of Corvids, Daughter of Huginn and Muninn, Child of Odin. I have no quarrel with you."

"Yet, I have one with you."

Rourke groaned somewhere behind her and Cole sucked in a breath. She didn't need to look at him or Cole to know they stared daggers at her. So much for her promise to Rourke not to start a fight.

"Oh?" Nyx sauntered closer. "He's merely your advisor and perhaps a lover. You have no claim on him."

"He's my anam cara," she said. The moment the words left her lips, they wound around her with comfort and a feeling of rightness.

Cole froze beside her and the magic also curled around him and intensified. His heated gaze bored into the side of her face and she wanted nothing more than to drop her weapon and throw herself on him to hold him close. But the shackles would get in the way of what she wanted and Nyx standing three feet away with death magic put a damper on the moment.

Nyx frowned. "I felt no bond."

Crap. She hadn't considered the anam cara bond was something others could sense. She shrugged and didn't elaborate. Sometimes silence was the best option. People often revealed a lot in their efforts to fill the silence.

Nyx just stared at her.

Double crap.

This wasn't working. She couldn't look at Rourke for direction and give away her ignorance and uncertainty.

"Why have you taken Cole?" she asked. Especially when Erebus summoned him. Was Cole's dad a part of this, too?

"Cole? Is that what you call him? He has a perfectly acceptable fae name. Why wouldn't he use that?"

"Maybe because Beul na h-Oidhche gu Camhanaich is a bit of a mouthful?"

Nyx just stared at her again.

"Erebus summoned him, why are you guarding him?"

"Because I took him." She jabbed her chest with a finger. "Me."

Apparently, kidnapping the Lord of Shadows was an accomplishment. Cole had mentioned Nyx's attempts to assassinate him since a young age.

"But why?" Raven ran her finger along her scythe, hoping Nyx wouldn't notice the move or the blood trickling down her hand. "Surely, his father would object."

"His father?"

Raven nodded. "Erebus, God of Darkness." She spoke his name and sent her magic along with the words, hoping her silent intent to summon Cole's father would be felt, while also hoping the addition of another player to the small, dark room wouldn't make things worse.

Nyx snorted. "His father notices Beul as much as one notices the dried blood crusted near the hilt of a blade. He's an unwanted nuisance."

"If he felt that way, why has he thwarted your

attempts to kill Cole before?"

Nyx scrunched up her pretty face. "Who said anything about killing Cole? Does this look like a room to hold chattel before the slaughterhouse? I'm merely holding him here. Against his will."

"Holding him?" Raven looked down at the man she loved, who still, despite being chained and beaten, held himself upright with the promise of murder in his gaze. His glare could've withered daisies on a spring day. "Holding him for what?"

"Yes, my love," a deep voice spoke from the darkest corner of the room.

Everyone jumped and turned in time to see Erebus step from the shadows, his gaze still blazing. His wings unfurled to reveal his black plated armour. "Why have you captured and held my son when he came here freely on my summons?"

Nyx ignored her lover, whirled to Raven and jabbed the space between them with her forefinger. "You've ruined everything."

Nyx spun on her heel and stalked out of the room.

Erebus watched her leave. Whether he was amused or indifferent was hard to tell with the glowing eyes and face mask. He followed Nyx but stopped at the doorway to turn and address the room. "Take him and go, but next time you enter my domain without permission, there will be a price to pay."

Raven nodded and waited a full ten seconds after Erebus left before flinging herself to the ground to hold Cole. He rested his forehead against her shoulder and took long breaths.

"Your family scares the shit out of me," she whispered into his ink black hair. "Why didn't you summon me earlier?"

"Too dangerous," he said. "I had to wait for her to leave."

"Why not summon your father?"

Cole laughed, the sound bitter and pained. "I couldn't be sure he wasn't involved. And even if he wasn't, if I summoned him to help me, he'd be just as likely to kill me for showing such weakness."

Raven sent out a silent thank you for her crazy, loving family. She never had to wonder whether they'd smite her or love her if she came to them for help.

Raven leaned back and cupped Cole's face. "What did Nyx want with you?"

"She wanted to stop me from helping you."

"But she said she had no quarrel with me."

"She doesn't view you as powerful enough to be threatening. Don't scowl. She's one of the first goddesses in existence who's still relatively sane. Arrogance should be her middle name, and it's not necessarily misplaced. Apparently, my father agrees with Odin and has no wish to lose his power. It's what he summoned me to discuss. Nyx is thirsty for war and more slaves. She decided I was somehow the lynch pin to your success."

Rourke tapped her on the shoulder and jingled a ring of keys near her face. She looked up, mouthed a thank you, and took the keys from his hand. "She's not wrong."

Cole shook his head. "You'd find a way without me. You're resourceful like that." Cole looked between the two of them. "And you've finally come to your senses and claimed your caomhnóir."

"Meet the newest Crawford."

Rourke's chest puffed out a bit from where he stood to the side.

Raven unlocked the shackles and collar. They hit the stone floor with a clank. She dropped the keys next to the discarded restraints and held Cole's stubbled face in her hands. "I've come to my senses about a lot of things."

His shadows curled out of the corners of the room as if only now awakening. The shackles and collar must've restrained his power somehow.

Cole wrapped her with his magic and slid his arm around her waist. "The anam cara?"

She nodded, the intensity of his gaze rendered her speechless. She leaned forward, lost in the pools of his eyes and seduction of his power.

Rourke cleared his throat theatrically behind them. "Maybe it's best to continue this conversation somewhere else? Before your fickle father changes his mind or Nyx tricks him again?"

Raven smiled and dropped her hands from Cole's face. She didn't take her gaze off him to speak to Rourke. "You're such a mood killer."

"Yes, well, excuse me for not wanting to be the audience for this love fest."

She reached up and after an irritated pause, Rourke grabbed her hand. She held onto Cole's shoulder, called her power and transported them home.

Rourke took one look at her Corvid Court bedroom, snatched his hand back and stomped to the door. "Later."

Cole reached forward, slipping his hand along her cheek. "That's three times you've saved me now. We're almost even."

She frowned. "I count once."

"Today with Nyx and the other day in Odin's court."

"And?" Raven didn't have Mike's sense of numbers, but she could count to three.

Cole smiled, a tender smile he didn't often show. "And when we met. I've already told you I was in a dark, lonely place."

"You're the Lord of Shadows," she said, dryly.

He ran his hand down the side of her face and used his other hand to tug her closer. "Literally and figuratively, and you were and are the light that drew me out." He leaned forward and kissed her, a sweet, slow kiss that made her yearn for more.

She pulled back and met his dark gaze, swirling with shadows and love. "Will you be my anam cara?" she asked.

"I already am." He ran his hand over her hair and then wrinkled his nose. "Maybe showers first."

Chapter Forty-Five

"Her bruised heart covered in scars is far from pretty, but it would offend any warrior to be described by such a tepid word. Her heart is stunning, courageous, and it beats too strong to be called anything less than what it deserves after everything it has endured."

~ *Daniel Mercury*

Raven stepped into her cold Corvid Court bedroom and shivered while Cole softly closed the door behind them. The scalding hot shower water had cooled on her skin and though she'd toweled off, some remaining water ran down her body to hit the floor. She gripped the towel for added warmth, but of course, being an ordinary towel, the action didn't make a difference.

"We don't have to do this." Cole had "run" back home to also clean up, now looking every ounce a dark fae lord in jeans and a sweater. He'd refused her offer to shower together, for efficiency, of course, saying he wanted to do the anam cara ritual "right" and he'd be too tempted to take her in the shower.

She still didn't see what was wrong with that.

"I'm no longer in danger from Nyx," Cole continued. "You've already fulfilled your promise to Bane, and you have your power back."

"That's precisely why I want to do this," she said.

"Hmm." His frown deepened.

"Don't you get it? Our hands aren't forced for once and I still want you. Had I come to my senses sooner, I would've been able to find you right away." She'd been her most vulnerable with this man and relished every second of it, yet, now nervousness spread through her. A weird insecurity that didn't match any of his actions.

Cole stood by the door and waited. What for? Why did he seem so distant all of a sudden? Or was it all in her head?

She gave into that niggling voice of insecurity. "Have you changed your mind?"

"Have you?"

"No."

"Same. You seem nervous."

"I am." And cold.

The hardness around Cole's eyes softened. "Why?"

"Because even now when I know my heart and yours, I still hear my Grandma Lu screaming at me to protect myself."

"To plan for the worst?"

She nodded. "My brain and heart are at war again."

His gaze flashed and the shadows spread through the room to slide up her body and cocoon her in a blanket of power.

"That's an easy fix," he said. "First and foremost, my goal has always been to protect you." A rope as thick as her thumb and as long as one arm materialized out of nowhere to hang suspended between them, the shadows propping up the fae binding chord. "I promise never to use the anam cara bond against you. I promise never to compel you against your will. I promise this bond will not be used to force or seduce you to pursue any romantic relationship, whether with me, or someone else." His face twisted at that last part. "This bond will be a partnership of power. I will not draw on your magic without your knowledge or consent unless under attack or to protect you or your loved ones." He paused and looked up at her. "Did I miss anything?"

She shook her head, not trusting her ability to speak.

The rope flashed with power. His magic curled around as he repeated the words in dark fae and tied a knot in the rope. The lilt of his speech danced along the cord before it drifted closer to her.

"The fae language is so beautiful. It's almost as if it's meant to go with your magic."

A slight smile cracked Cole's serious expression. "The language of the dark fae, or Underworlder, as some call it, is the language of magic."

Huh. Not sure how to tackle that hurdle mentally, the chicken and egg debate started pecking at her neurons.

The rope drifted closer. She gripped both ends and met Cole's gaze. Her towel miraculously held in place. "No kiss to seal the deal this time?"

His smile grew. "That comes later." He nodded at the rope. "This is a business agreement and will remain as such no matter how much you try to seduce me."

Raven snorted and repeated Cole's promise. A tendril of her magic wove around the rope as she tied the knot beside Cole's.

The shadows carried the rope away, engulfing it in darkness.

"Do you have some sort of mortal side safe house?"

Cole winked.

Of course, he did.

"Is that where you sent the rope?"

"Yes, Einin. And before you ask, yes, that's where I went while Rourke took you to see Marcus. I will show it to you sometime. It's not that I wish to keep it hidden from you, it's that we've been rather busy."

Raven crossed her arms over her supersized towel. "We're not under a strict deadline to resurrect this barrier. We have time now."

Cole sighed. "And risk someone attacking us? News will spread that we have the Lindt Law."

She'd filled him in on the events he missed while he was held captive by his father's psychotic wife. "Are we behind schedule, General?"

"I'm happy to report we're ahead of schedule."

Warmth spread through her body. She didn't need Cole to tell her the barrier spell carried serious risks. She didn't need him to tell her the possible outcomes, but if she faced the possibility of death, again, she wanted to lose herself in Cole's heat and the taste of his skin.

Her smile grew. "Then we have some time to spare?"

Cole's gaze flashed with a predatory gleam and his soft smile disappeared altogether. "What do you have in mind? We still need to complete the anam cara and you will require some *coaching*."

Raven dropped the towel and stepped forward to close the distance between them. "Is that what they call it these days?"

He grinned and his shadows swept up her body, running feather light tendrils of touch along her skin, and smoothing down the goosebumps from the cold air.

"Can we not kill two birds with one stone?" she asked.

"If I'm the one killing it."

Raven pinched the bridge of her nose.

"Actually, I think it may help with the ritual if you were more...relaxed."

"You're just mentioning this now?"

He shrugged. "I was going to suggest a massage."

"Sure you were."

"With my penis," he admitted.

Shadows surrounded her and suddenly Cole was right there, his hand sliding up her neck to cup her face, his delicious mouth on hers, his strong body pressed against her.

Mmmm. Yes.

"So, what's the plan?" she managed to ask.

Cole trailed kisses along her neck and ran his hands down her sides. "I thought that was obvious." He pressed his erection into her thigh.

She laughed and pushed him back a little. "With the anam cara."

Cole's shadows continued to caress her body as he also took a step back. "We open ourselves to allow our souls to flow together."

"That's it? Didn't we already do that?" She waved her finger back and forth between them. "You know...that last time..."

Cole grinned and without words, she knew he recalled the exact moment she referred to. "Pushing and pulling magic during sex is similar and highly rewarding in its own right, but its main purpose is stimulation. The anam cara goes beyond lust and sexual gratification."

"But it's similar," she said, pressing. "At least in the process?"

"Yes. Instead of our energy brushing against each other, it will be our souls. It's not as easy as it sounds. You have to be completely open." He reached forward and took her hand in his. "We can always try again if this doesn't work for us today. Or we can find another way to create this barrier or maybe we squirrel your family away to a safe place and let the fae and regs have their war. They're not our responsibility. You can change your mind."

She reached forward, grabbed his hand and brought her mouth up to his, pressing her naked body against the softness of his clothes. The kiss quickly turned from sweet and a little demanding to naughty and full of orders—kiss me, touch me, taste me, love me.

Fabric stretched and ripped as she tugged and pulled at Cole's clothing.

"I was so scared," she said, running her teeth along his neck. "When you didn't answer my summons, I knew something was wrong."

Cole's belt hit the ground with a clank. Fabric fell to the floor, armchair and nearby lamp.

"I'll never leave you." Cole's mouth on hers was hot, wet and full of his devious tongue. He picked her up, stalked across the room with her legs wrapped around his waist and splayed her over the bed. He didn't give the cold air long enough to cool her skin again before he was on top of her and in her, thrusting and grinding while his mouth continued to taste her skin.

Raven gripped her dark fae energy and spread it out, bathing Cole in her essence.

He paused and shuddered, dropping his head against her shoulder to take in a deep, ragged breath.

She liked that she held the power to undo him—to

rattle and rock his world like he did hers.

"Minx," he whispered into her ear.

"I'm a bird, not a rodent." She nipped his neck and arched against him, asking for more.

"Behave," he growled.

"Never."

His chuckle rumbled against the sensitive skin of her neck. "I don't want this to end prematurely. If you keep doing that, it will."

She let her magic fall away a little and he thrust into her hard and deep. At the same time, his magic cascaded over her in delightful waves.

Her orgasm hit her quick and unexpected. She cried out and arched against Cole's hard body.

Cole rocked inside her, his magic still curled around her and caressing her skin. "Open your mind, Einin."

Mmmm. "Yeah. Okay."

She wrapped her legs around his torso and moved with him, swaying up and down as he continued to rock.

Cole chuckled against her neck again. "Let me show you." He reached out with his magic, wound it around hers and pulled her power to him, all the while rocking inside her and stoking the flames.

Geez. Raven barely managed patting her head and rubbing her belly at the same time.

"Focus, Einin."

"Your coordination is hot."

He grinned, his lips curling against her cheek, his breath warm on her face. He brought her magic into his mind and suddenly she was *in* his mind.

Raven sucked in a breath. So unexpectedly in his head, she felt what he felt saw what he saw, all while retaining her own senses. The duality, especially in such an intimate position, was overwhelming.

Pulsing within his mind, more than anything else, though, was a glowing red ember. As she mentally drew near, the heat basked her mind and then when she realized what the ember was, his heart. But not his anatomical heart, something else.

Cole nodded and kissed her forehead. "What you sense is my heart of hearts and what's inside."

"Your love for me," she whispered.

"Now do you see? Now do you understand why there has only ever been one option for me?"

She nodded. The sight of the pulsing red ember imprinted on her mind. It was beautiful.

And shiny.

Cole chuckled. "Such a raven."

"Can you read my thoughts?"

"No, but when we're entwined like this, I get images or impressions of strong feelings."

She smiled. Her birds really did love shiny things.

"Now watch," Cole said. "A lot of people believe the soul is housed within the physical body but look outside my mind. What do you see?"

Raven turned her mind's eye outward. At first, all she saw was her own face, which was odd at best and downright disturbing at worst, but then like a thickening fog, the air between them grew denser and more colourful.

"Our souls shine all around us," Cole said.

"Like an aura?"

"There is no such thing as an aura, only whispers of your soul for those gifted with the sight to glimpse. There is only your soul and it surrounds you like a plume of luminous air."

"Yours is blue and silver. What colour is mine?"

"Open your mind like I did and see for yourself."

She withdrew her power from Cole and brought it back to unlock and open the doorways in her own mind as Cole had done. Like searching an empty unfamiliar school after hours, it took her a few tries to find the correct doorways and go down the appropriate halls, but when she turned the right corner, in front of her mind's eye, a red ember hung suspended in the air.

Cole sighed and his hold on her tightened. He'd stopped moving inside her when she'd vacationed in his own mind and had gone a little soft, but the moment she opened the door to her own heart of hearts, he was rock hard again. He clutched her waist and drove into her.

"Like what you see?" All she could do was hold on.

"You love me, too." His smile was so smug.

"Of course, I do."

Cole grunted and thrust into her again. "Look out from your mind this time."

She did as he said while relishing the rhythm and pace he set with his hips and a shimmering wall of blue and purple surrounded them.

Cole pushed his blue soul outward, sending warm tingling sensations through her mind. She mirrored his actions, pushing her soul toward him. Their souls flowed together, mixing and merging and moving together. A sense of completeness, of wholeness, filled Raven. She was one with Cole. She had finally arrived home, and she hadn't realized she'd been lost.

Cole groaned and dropped his head to her shoulder again.

They continued to push and pull their souls, letting them flow past each other and lace together until the air between them shimmered with purple and blue.

The sensations built on each other, layer by exquisite layer. The physical pressure intensified. Tension wound tighter and tighter until it broke and rippled through her. Raven cried out.

Cole growled at the same time and sagged on top of her, breathing ragged, body hot and shuddering. She ran her fingertips up and down his body, enjoying the new closeness they shared.

"Cole?"

"Mmrmph?" He mumbled into her neck.

"Can we do that again?"

"Right now?" His tone was incredulous.

"No, not right now, but again, later, after you're recuperated."

"You want to see the shiny wall of blue and purple again, don't you?"

She nodded eagerly. "And the feels. I loved the feels, too."

Cole swore. "You might be the death of me."

"Nope." She shook her head, hair plastered to her face. "I'm your anam cara."

He kissed her temple. "Yes, you are."

Chapter Forty-Six

"My goal is not to be better than anyone else, but to be better than I used to be."

~ *Wayne Dyer*

Raven and Cole walked into the empty courtyard holding hands like high school sweethearts and Raven wouldn't change it for anything in the world. They'd slept the rest of Tuesday and a healthy portion of Wednesday morning. "Sleep" was a misleading word, but Cole helped her see the blue and purple wall of shimmering light multiple times before fatigue took over and they had to search for food.

"What's the plan?" Rourke leaned against a pillar, arms crossed, one leg bent to rest his foot on the concrete.

"Plan?" Raven asked.

He shrugged. "You've paid off your loan, financially secured your family, found Pepe, resolved your debt to Bane, mended your friendship with Megan, squashed the blackmailing attempt, scared the Closers, and gave the trolls a very strong 'fuck off' message. What's next?"

She held up the scroll Marcus had given her. "We're going to establish a new barrier."

Rourke pushed off the pillar, expression grim. "Why?"

"It's what everyone wants. Well, everyone except the blood-thirsty fae gods who want to demolish the Mortal Realm, which will inadvertently render dark fae powerless. I don't really care as much about that as I do about my family and friends being placed in mortal danger again. I can't let that happen."

"And I can't let you install a barrier." Bane stepped into the room. A magical film fell off him and washed away.

How in the Underworld had he portalled here without anyone sensing it?

Bane shook his cape. Dressed in gold and red armour, he looked every inch the Lord of War.

Cole leaned over and whispered, "Cloaking spell."

That answered one question, but Raven had a lot

more than one. "Why?"

Bane tilted his head. "I'm the Lord of War. I thrive on conflict and anguish and I've been feeding too long on the scraps of this truce. I'm starving." He clenched his hand in a fist. "I want to feast."

"Even if it will destroy you all?" Raven asked.

"It will destroy most. Not me. Those Closers were so arrogant, thinking they tricked me, when it was the other way around. The Lindt Law showed me a way to avoid any magical fluctuations."

Interesting that Bane would comment on the arrogance of others when he never seemed to have a shortage of it. "I'm going to install a barrier, Bane. It will act like a border with controlled points of access."

"How human of you."

"I'm half-human." Well, half-mortal shifter really.

"It's a human solution to a dark fae problem." Bane sneered. "And who will guard these controlled points of access? You can't possibly watch over them all."

Cole stepped forward, his cape flowing with him and whispering against the floor and his matte black armour. "My assassins will act as sentries."

Bane roared. Without any further warning, his rage lashed out and slammed into them.

Shadows struck out from every corner, forming into sharp, pointed spears to strike Bane. He dodged and ducked and swerved out of the way of Cole's shadow spears, drawing his sword to deflect the daggers Rourke threw at him.

Cole also unsheathed his sword and they met in the

center of the courtyard in a clash of metal. The scythe popped into her hand and filled her with battle rage. She ducked in and swiped, narrowly missing Bane's midsection. He twisted out of reach and thrust savagely with his sword. The scythe's power moved her out of the way in time, but Bane was already blocking another vicious attack from Cole. Where Bane depended on power and technique, Cole excelled in quick, efficient attacks that drew on a variety of fighting styles.

The power flowed in her veins and she fought alongside Cole and Rourke. Their connection strengthened and they moved in coordinated attacks. Yet, Bane held his own. Rage and anger broiled in his magic and slashed at them. A wall of hate plowed into Raven and knocked her back. She fell on her butt and slid along the black slab tiles.

Cole, Rourke and Bane continued to dance, two against one. They lunged, thrust and slashed with their weapons. The moonlight glinted off the flurry of sword movement. They gave no openings.

Bane kicked Rourke out of the way, caught Cole's blade under his arm between his protective armour, twisted and slammed his dagger into Cole.

"No!" Raven screamed. Without asking, without thinking, she reached for her magic. She opened the gates and let her power travel through the bond, but instead of flowing out, Cole's power rushed in. Cold, shadowy and full of lethal malice. The room thundered with their combined power. The floor shook. Her body trembled as she held it all in her grasp.

Bane pushed away from Cole and staggered back, eyes wide, yet furious. Blood dropped from a slash running down his cheek. One cut had narrowly missed his eye.

"Anam cara?" he spat. His furious gaze cut between the two of them. "Anam cara?"

She let the power build, forming a wave of shadows.

Bane snarled and the air around him ripped open. Sweltering heat blasted the courtroom. "You've won this round, bastard son of Erebus and puppet queen, but I will win the war."

She released the power letting it slam down on Bane, but he was too quick. He stepped through the spliced realities and the portal snapped shut behind him. The magic crashed against the tiles and flowed back to her like the tide.

Cole turned to her, blood running down his breastplate from where the dagger protruded. He'd twisted at the last second, to catch the dagger there instead of in the heart.

He was alive. He was safe. The threat of Bane had diminished, at least for now. She released her hold on his seductive power and shadows. The magic fell away from her in a whoosh of glittering air and left her weak and lightheaded.

"You're breathtaking," Cole said. He clutched the area around the dagger. "Also, I had that."

"Of course, dear."

Epilogue

"The great pleasure in life is doing what people say you cannot do."

~ Walter Bagehot

Bane's hissy fit did little to derail Raven's plans. If anything, his tantrum made Raven more motivated to follow the adapted portion of the Lindt Law outlined on Marcus' scroll to establish a barrier between realms. With Cole's power combined with her own, full control of the Shadow Realms and full bellies, accomplishing a self-sustaining barrier proved rather easy. Almost too easy.

The Others had known how to construct a new barrier all this time, but the one person with the right power and position had no inclination to follow through with one until now.

Raven would do anything to protect her family, including move the very nature of reality and the realms to build a magical wall with assassins as sentries.

Not all Others had been happy, of course. There had been a few assassination attempts and a number of infuriated dark fae had visited the Corvid Court demanding Raven reverse her decision. Once they saw her on the dais wielding the Scythe of Corvids, wearing the Raven's eye and sitting on the throne with her anam cara on one side and her caomhnóir on the other, their tone quickly changed.

She hadn't heard from Bane, but she knew him well enough now to know silence didn't mean acceptance. That whole, "No news is good news," saying didn't apply to the Lord of War. He sat in some room, probably by a fire, stewing and planning his next move. They'd implemented safety measures, but they'd only find out how well they prepared when Bane stopped sulking long enough for a counterattack. Apparently, he could sulk for years, if not decades, and Raven was okay with that.

Today, she discarded her warrior bra and panty set for regular mortal clothes and sat around the dining table with her family for Sunday dinner. Mom had purchased more chairs to fit Rourke, Cole, Chloe and Marcus at the table.

"So, we're just going to sit around the roast and pretend everything is normal?" Juni asked, dishing out a heaping portion of mashed potatoes.

Pepe bleated in the yard outside and Marcus flinched. The beast was probably complaining non-stop about his ravenous appetite from outside and his witch had to listen to all of it.

Dad had been more pissed at Marcus for thinking he wouldn't forgive him or understand than he was from Marcus taking Pepe without telling them or losing Pepe as a family pet. "Well, dear," Dad had said to Mom after Marcus sheepishly came over to admit his guilt. "I have to forgive him. He's like a son to us and how else am I going to see Pepe again?" Dad had also said having to listen to Pepe's whining was probably punishment enough.

Mom reached across Juni to grab the potatoes. "Honey, dear. I don't think this family has ever been normal."

Juni rolled her eyes and went back to admiring Rourke who now sat beside her. She'd decided that the former assassin was her saviour and behaved as anyone would expect a fifteen-year-old to behave when infatuated.

Rourke's expression flip-flopped between amused and pained, and he probably regretted becoming a part of the Crawford family.

Cole, sitting beside Raven, reached over and squeezed her hand. His presence warmed her heart in ways she never thought possible. The anam cara fulfilled its promise letting them share power without restrictions and, so far, had only made their relationship stronger.

Juni rested her cutlery on her plate and stared at her food. "What happened to Lincoln?"

Everyone froze. Juni had said very little about her time with the hyenas aside from saying she was glad they were all dead. She still had nightmares according to Mom. Mike's had lessened, but now her baby sister dealt with the aftermath of being caught up in Raven's dark fae world.

Raven swallowed the lump in her throat. Her fault. Mike and Juni's pain and invisible scars were her fault and no matter how she atoned for it, she would have to live with that knowledge.

Bear leaned down and whispered into her ear, "Not your fault."

She wished she could believe that. They all had a little healing to do.

Cole turned to Juni and smiled. "He cleans the dungeons in the Corvid Court."

"Is he miserable?"

"Very much so."

"Good," she whispered. "Good."

"Would you like to see him?"

"Cole!" Raven hissed and dug her fingers into his hand. He squeezed back but didn't retract his offer.

Juni straightened in her chair and lifted her chin. "Yes. Yes, I would."

Cole nodded and his power pinged against Raven's,

reached across the ether, bypassed their barrier to the Shadow Realms and grabbed Lincoln from her compound. He hauled the young adult to the dinner table to stand awkwardly and frightened beside Juni. Lincoln still wore the same clothes, but now dirt creased the hemlines and smudged his face. Maybe his punishment should end soon.

No one gasped or jumped in surprise when Lincoln appeared. They were foxes and dark fae. They adapted to change.

"Juni!" Lincoln stepped forward but Cole's bands of shadow stopped him.

Juni calmly pushed back from the table and stood to face her former classmate.

"You need to get me out of the dungeons, Juni. There's a humongous fae who keeps spouting poetry about his lost axe and talking about smashing some bitch's head in."

Oops. Forgot about Frey. Hopefully, someone fed him. Raven had staff, apparently, but with everything going on, she'd forgotten to follow up and make sure Frey's basic needs were taken care of.

Cole shook his head at her as if he read her entire thought process. "Frey is fine."

"Who's Frey?" Mike asked.

"Some guy who kept trying to kill me," she answered. "Kind of like that Chihuahua down the road with a spiked collar who always tries to gnaw our ankles off when it gets out."

"That's a fucking big Chihuahua," Rourke

muttered.

Lincoln's eyes widened and he turned to plead to Juni. "Please get me away from these psychos."

On second thought, maybe his punishment should continue a little longer.

Juni tossed her red curls from her shoulders. "These psychos are my family."

Bear sat straighter in his chair, chest puffed out and chin high. Chloe giggled, her laughter tinkling like fairy bells. Mike muttered something under his breath, probably taking offence with being lumped in with the other psychos. Tough. He was theirs, too.

Lincoln snapped his mouth shut.

"Maybe you should have thought about that before you pretended to like me and lured me into a trap." Juni struck out with her fist, punching him hard in the gut. "Tell me how you like me now, asshole!"

The smack of the impact echoed in the otherwise silent room.

Lincoln groaned and doubled over in pain.

Juni turned away from him and straightened her clothes. "I'm done."

Cole smiled and Lincoln disappeared. Juni rejoined them at the table as if she'd gone to fetch more butter, not punched her crush for his betrayal.

Grandma Lu would've been so proud.

~The End~

"You may shoot me with your words
You may cut me with your eyes
You may kill me with your hatefulness
But still, like air, I'll Rise."

~ Excerpt from *Still I Rise* (Stanza 6), Maya Angelou

Did you enjoy reading Queen of Corvids? Please help me out and tell someone or leave a review. Your support is much appreciated.

RAVEN'S LIST OF SERVER PET PEEVES

Psssht! Raven no longer cares about such menial things like tooth-pickers, butt pinchers, tip stiffers or customers who wave her down with flailing arms for the cheque. She only despises former bosses who try to screw over vulnerable employees instead of encouraging them to reach for their dreams.

GLOSSARY OF TERMS

Anam cara: Roughly translated from dark fae to English, Anam Cara means "soul friend." It is a deeply felt, eternal fae bond that allows two souls to flow together in a way that transcends time, place and definition. The anam cara bond allows souls to access each other's strength, power and magic. According to John O'Donohue, "when you are blessed with an anam cara...you have arrived at the most sacred place: home." (Anam Cara: A book of Celtic Wisdom, 998).

Bhanrigh: dark fae for "queen."

Caomhnóir: guardian who is blood sworn to protect fae nobility.

Jotun: trolls.

Mo bhanrigh: dark fae for "my queen."

Mortal: any inhabitant of the Mortal Realm. Note: All entities of all the realms can be killed, but this term is reserved for anyone who is not an Other. Used as a derogatory slur by Others.

Other: Any inhabitant NOT from the Mortal Realm. Any inhabitant from the Realm of Light, the Underworld or the Shadow Realm. Mortal, but not a mortal.

Reg: A "regular" human being from the Mortal Realm without any supernatural powers or skills.

Regulators: An organized group of regs who despise Others and hold meetings to bitch about the unfairness of life.

ROL: Realm of Light. An Other realm full of Rollers who look down on everyone else.

Rollers: supernatural beings from the Realm of Light.

Seomra Cumhachta: Roughly translated from dark fae to

English, this refers to the "Room of Power." These rooms are used in castles and fortresses to maximize a magic wielder's power by taking advantage of the natural environment and the infrastructure around them.

Three-P (3P): permanent personal portal.

Toonie: A Canadian two dollar coin.

Travellers: group of Closers who travelled to the Realm of War to test hypotheses found in the Murdoch Manual to re-establish a barrier. Ultimately unsuccessful.

Underworld: An Other realm, often in direct conflict with the Realm of Light. Contains multiple, smaller realms, such as the realms of War and Lust.

ACKNOWLEDGEMENTS

Any errors contained in this book are my own, despite my best efforts to research and consult experts, and everyone's best efforts to steer me in the correct direction.

I'd like to thank my beta readers Karilyn Bentley, Wendy P., and Nicole Flockton. Thank you for reading the rougher versions of this story to help me smooth everything out.

Thank you to my super fab editor, Lara Parker, and my lovely proofreader, T.P. from Book Nook Nuts.

Another huge thank you to Anna L. Spies from Eerilyfair Design for yet another stunning cover.

Thank you to my friends and family for their continued love and support.

Most of all, thank you to you, the reader, for trusting me with your precious reading time. I hope you enjoyed this story as much as I enjoyed writing it.

About the Author

J. C. McKenzie is a book-loving, gumboot-wearing, unapologetic science geek. She's the author of the Carus Series, the Obsidian Flame Series and the Raven Crawford Series. Born and raised on the West Coast, J. C. sets the majority of her books in the Lower Mainland of British Columbia, Canada. She writes urban fantasy and paranormal romance with sassy heroines and brutish, alpha-type men.

Visit her at www.jcmckenzie.ca

Amazon: www.amazon.com/author/jcmckenzie
Blog: jcmckenzie.blogspot.ca
Goodreads: www.goodreads.com/JCMcKenzie
Twitter: twitter.com/JC_McKenzie
Facebook: www.facebook.com/j.c.mckenzie.author
Instagram: www.instagram.com/j.c.mckenzie